STEPHEN
SAYERS

BY ANY MEANS
NECESSARY

Britain's Next
BESTSELLER

First published in 2016 by:
Britain's Next Bestseller
An imprint of Live It Publishing
27 Old Gloucester Road
London.
United Kingdom
WC1N 3AX

ISBN-13: 978-1-910565-91-9 (pbk)
www.britainsnextbestseller.co.uk
@BNBSbooks

Dedications

I'd like to dedicate this book to two very special people who my brothers and I look upon as family.

Ellen Havelock; a pillar of strength who supported our Mam though thick and thin. She was the daughter she always wanted but never had.

Thank you and God bless. We love you like a sister.

John Brooks; A true friend in every sense of the word who has been up and down the country and visited me and my brothers in every jail we have been in.

God bless you Big John. We love you brother.

Stephen, John and Michael

For Kelly . . .
>   who endures,
>   survives
>   and never falters

David

'Condemn the fault, and not the actor of it.'

Measure for Measure (Act 2, Scene 2)

'Grab yourself a seat, get comfortable and let the bad boys into your life.'

Stephen Sayers

'Be afraid... be very afraid.'
The Fly

Prologue

1986
Newcastle Upon Tyne
Tyne and Wear

"You're a dozy cunt, you know that?"

Jack Hudson's voice sounds muffled like a bad telephone connection, most likely due to the punches that connected with the side of my head. All the training, all of those fights, but when it came down to it, I couldn't remember a fuckin' thing. Not when it mattered. Dave would be ashamed.

I shake my head, somehow thinking it'll stop the ringing in my brain. Hudson is waving his fuckin' shotgun around in my face. I want to laugh and say, "If you're not careful with that thing it'll go off," but I don't. Even I know when I'm in the shit. On a good day, I would have knocked him the fuck out. He'd be lying on the floor missing some teeth with snot and blood pouring from his broken nose. He'd be begging me to stop pounding on him, telling me how sorry he is. But instead, the sneaky bastard jumped me from behind. No fuckin' honour that man, none whatsoever.

"You Myers', you're all the same. Always whining about the hand you've been dealt. Karen, Alan... moaning all the time

about having been pissed on from a great height. You need to learn to get over things, move on. None of you are too bright either. All this time and you still haven't figured it out," Hudson drones on. "Don't you know who Campbell was workin' for? He may have fired the gun that killed your brother, metaphorically speaking, but who'd ya think loaded it in the first place?"

I feel the anger rising up from my bruised gut, my face flushing. I'll fuckin' kill him. I'll kill them all. They just have to give me a minute and I'll rip them each a new arsehole.

"You've no right to be up here with the big boys. Who the fuck do you think you are? Michael Corleone? Just because you did some time, you think that makes you somebody? You're a fuckin' nobody and you know the thing about nobodies? Nobody misses them."

And that's when the gun goes off. Weird, like it's in slow motion. The flash from the barrel seems to be minutes before I feel anything in my chest. When I say anything, I mean excruciating, blistering, explosive pain that radiates outwards from my sternum, to my ribs and around my back.

It's funny how you feel when you're looking down the barrel of a gun. I realise that no matter how helpless I might have been before, nothing actually compares to the utter fear and hopelessness coursing through my body at this very moment, knowing I'm about to die. All the things I was going to do. All the places I was planning to go. They're erased from existence, one by one.

I want Hudson to believe I don't give a shit. That in my final moments, I'm still the hard lad... the big fella. But my eyes'll be betraying that fact that I'm scared.

Scared and utterly defeated...

Act One

1960s

"We have a contract of depravity; all we have to do is pull a blind down."

The Hustler

Chapter One

Mary Myers could hear Chubby Checker belting out *Let's Twist Again* from the jukebox downstairs, its rhythmic vibrations like bursts of muted energy flowing through the framework of the building. The shrill sound of drunken laughter from The Horse & Hammer's patrons was a cacophony of screams and shouts, rising and falling in time with the swell of the music as though competing for attention.

She gently caressed her eyelashes with mascara, considering them the finishing touches to her make-up. Thomas had already commented on the fact he thought she'd overdone it, stating with laughter and a smile that she looked like Marcel Marceau. He had immediately taken a few steps back and looked her in the eyes, following up his statement with a truth – she didn't need any of it, she was beautiful as she was. He kissed her forehead and carried on laying the table with the small buffet prepared for the New Year's Eve celebration.

With her long, thick black hair and wide-spaced blue eyes, Mary had always considered herself reasonably attractive. Makeup was just something she wore to hide the imperfections in her skin and, by extension, part of herself. A walking contradiction in terms, she had always known that men paid attention to her because of her looks yet hated her own appearance. Granted, that hadn't stopped her flirting and dallying her way around a dance floor whilst embracing life to the full. But she had only ever had eyes for Thomas.

She'd been 17 when she'd first met her husband. Working on her Gran's bookstall in the flea market outside Tynemouth Station, he had wandered up to her – full of swagger – and asked if she knew a good place to eat. His departing wink made her blush, his return later to ask her to a dance an unexpected but pleasant surprise.

Once they were courting, she learned of his renown for being a bit of a hard lad, and yet she'd only ever seen him as a gentle soul. He made her feel safe and boy, did he still have that swagger. He only had to look at her now and she got butterflies.

More than that, Thomas Myers had given her the greatest gift she could have ever asked for, and because of it would probably forgive him anything. After a few setbacks and necessary medical tests, life had found a way to give them children – three miracles in succession. She would have taken up religion there and then to thank God if she had believed.

Spiritual providence or the persistence of nature, someone or something had seen fit to bless her with the lives she now cherished. Alan had been first, followed by Faye and then Thomas Jr, or Tommy as she preferred him be called. The children had only served to bring them closer as a couple, nourishing a maternal side of him she hadn't expected. Nowadays he was looking a little battered around the edges, was going grey and could be a bastard sometimes, but she loved the very bones of him. And anyway, on tonight of all nights she could afford to overdo it with makeup and food. She wanted this New Year's Eve to be memorable.

4

The Horse & Hammer was doing great business and had been for the past year. Pubs like The Forge Hammer or The City did the big money, but for a small boozer just off the Tyne it did okay. Even though their clientele consisted mostly of draughtsman, prostitutes, steelworkers and dockers, Mary had noticed they were getting their fair share of seamen and the odd foreign individual. She guessed it had something to do with the speculated re-urbanisation of South Tyneside. Newcastle City Corporation had taken the decision to redevelop Byker, there was talk of Newcastle gaining its own university, and she'd even heard of plans for a new transport system that would link the Tyneside area.

You would still see children playing amongst the crumbing ruins and hear mothers talking about their unemployed husbands who sat and daydreamed about times gone by, but post-war austerity was giving way to an energy and freedom. It felt like a new start was coming and that there were better days ahead. Seeing this New Year out on a positive note would only engender the next to start the right way. She was happy to be a Sandancer, born and raised in South Shields. She never got tired of reading about its detailed history. In another life, Mary had always imagined herself a history teacher. Tommy called her his 'lush librarian'.

"Every time I turn round you've gotta book in your hands," he would often say.

"Well, one of us has to have all the smarts," she'd reply.

From the Romans building Arbeia fort in South Shields to provide supplies to the soldiers along Hadrian's Wall to King Oswald uniting the kingdoms north of the Humber and South of the Deria to create Northumbria, everything about her small part of the country was steeped in history.

The pub was her dream and their livelihood. As much as it

pained Thomas to admit, it made them more money than he did and was a huge contributing factor to the life they had. When it came to the business, Mary ruled it with precision and Thomas helped where he could when not working as a scaffolder.

Tonight was going to be special, because of who they were, what they had accomplished, and the future they had to look forward to. Nothing short of a force of nature would ruin it. And she would wear as much eyeliner as she fucking well liked.

At that moment, their youngest entered the kitchen. Six years of age, with his brown hair and blue eyes, Thomas Jr. was the light of his father's life. They called him Tommy Tittle Mouse, due to his small size and proclivities to get everywhere. Though he would never have admitted it, Thomas was always telling her, "Mary, that bairn'll go on to be proper special. You mark my words. This town'll know his name one day."

Dressed up in his cowboy outfit for New Year's Eve, she couldn't get over how Tommy was able to look so handsome and cute simultaneously. Her and Thomas had promised him he could stay up late and watch the fireworks to see in the New Year, though she doubted he would make it past ten o'clock.

She gave him a gentle clip around the head as he walked up to her with a sausage roll in his hand.

"Oi, you little tinker. They're for the party tonight. No picking."

He smiled a big, goofy smile, crumbs of pastry falling from his mouth that forced her to smile back. Ruffling his hair, she directed him towards his father who was laying out the plates and took a moment to glance around the kitchen, savouring the feeling of satisfaction that washed over her. The table was laden with food, more than enough for them. Turkey, sandwiches, sausage rolls and crisps – all of it for tonight's celebration. They were expecting a few friends upstairs later on as part of the New Year party, and after spending all day preparing the food she wanted it to be perfect.

"Right, we all set?" she asked.

"Aye," Thomas replied. "I think we're pretty much done, sweetheart. The kids are downstairs, the table looks canny and you're beautiful. What do you think, little man?"

Tommy looked around the table, at his Mam and then back at his Dad. "Uh-huh," he acknowledged with a nod.

"Good lad," Thomas replied with a smile. He walked towards Mary with his right hand on his hip. "Shall we?"

Mary smiled and linked through his arm, holding her hand out for Tommy. He skipped towards her and grabbed it, humming what she could just make out as his rendition of *The Lion Sleeps Tonight* by The Tokens.

They walked in unison towards the passage leading downstairs into the bar, the fusion of music and chatter becoming louder with every step. Thomas unlinked himself from his wife and moved down the stairs first.

The violent coughing started as she was halfway down. She'd had a cough for a few months now and thought nothing of it, chalking it up to her 20-a-day habit and working in an environment where nearly every customer smoked. She couldn't be hypocritical about inhaling other people's smoke when she indulged herself.

What started as a slight tickle in the back of her throat seemed to develop into something more aggressive within a matter of seconds. She had to steady herself, the simple act of breathing becoming more difficult with every passing second. Everything began to fade as though lights were being dimmed. She could hear her husband calling her name and shouting for Alan and Faye, but he sounded far away. His calls for her resonated inside her skull until she felt nauseated.

She noticed blood on the palm of her hand after muffling another cough, which came as a surprise as it wasn't something she expected to see coming out of her lungs.

Tommy began crying out behind her but she couldn't find the strength to turn around.

The only thing she could do was become weightless and drift towards the bottom of the stairs into a welcoming pool of darkness. Her last thought was how she hoped the food wouldn't go to waste.

* * *

And that was how it happened, as quickly as that. One minute Mam was taking me to the New Years Eve party, the next she was lying on the floor coughing up blood.

Dad was freaking out, shouting for help, screaming for my brother and sister. I was crying not knowing what the fuck was going on. People were crowding around her, all trying to help. It was madness.

The funny thing is she'd been fine, or at least we thought she was. Yeah, she'd had that cough, but she smoked so much that the general consensus was – there you go, the obvious answer. She'd never complained about it to Dad or the punters and had been proud of the weight loss as a sign she was showing real will power with her diet. Not that she'd been overweight, but as she'd been getting older she had wanted to stay healthy for Dad. Isn't that fucking ironic. Wanting to lose weight to stay healthy and yet really losing it because you're dying. But that's the funny thing about cancer. You don't always know your spirit and soul are being drained away until it's too late.

It's like one huge interruption in your life, a life being slowly taken away from you, never to be given back. Mam became sick really quickly, was in and out of hospital week after week until she couldn't leave at all and then Dad and I were the ones in and out all the time.

Mam fought it of course, that's who she was; a fighter. Always had been. She couldn't have run a pub in South Shields in the 60s if fighting hadn't been in her personality. The bat

8

wasn't behind the bar for show. But there was no bat she or anyone could take to this. It changed her forever, and no matter how much she battled against it, the person that she had been was gone.

Her clarity of mind seemed to disappear, bit by bit. I guess it was because of the treatment, though ultimately it did her no good. We had entered the 'twilight zone' of the cancer world, where she could see us and knew we were there for her but still looked as though she was alone. This faceless, incorporeal monster was taking my Mam away from me and I couldn't do anything about it because I was a kid and didn't understand. It was a vile, ugly, evil creature, intent on destroying everything mentally and physically in her until there was nothing left. It ate and prodded, caused pain with a smile and brought grief with outstretched arms. It was a fucking thief; a robber that was taking away aspects of her without permission. How fucking dare it.

Between us realising she was ill to her actually dying took three months – three fuckin' months. That's how quick it was, how insidious and motivated cancer is. The nurses who primarily cared for her in Conrad House were fantastic. Nikki and Janice were two of the most caring people I've ever met in my life. Nothing was too much of a bother and Mam loved them. Wherever she went, one of them was walking by her side both figuratively and literally. I think they were just as upset as we were when she died, they had formed such a close bond with her in a short space of time. They both came to the funeral and I think Dad really appreciated it.

And of course, you get all the usual, "I'm sorry you've lost your mother" rhetoric. Lost her? I didn't misplace her in the fucking supermarket. I didn't leave her in my other pair of trousers. Sorry, as well-meaning as it is, never softens the wrenching severance you feel when the woman who brought you into the world dies. I honestly felt like one of my limbs had been amputated. Like my heart had been surgically removed.

Violent and raw. Ripped out. Dad became a widower and we became un-mothered. Yes, that's the term for it.

And the world just carried on around us all as though nothing had happened. Everything looked the same. People went about their business as though all was right in the world. I wanted to scream, "Fucking stop! Don't you get it? Can you not see what I've lost... what we've lost?"

You know of course that they don't. Why would they? And nor should they. But for us... for me, every movement and breath I took was painful and heavy, weighted down by a suffocating feeling of overwhelming sadness. I would never get to hug her again, never smell her hair, never talk to her. It never went away... the pain. It diminished, sure. But time is not the healer everyone says it is. Time doesn't heal. Time accommodates. Time shows you that the pain you feel is directly proportional to how much you loved and were loved back. Time gives you memories. Time gave me her voice in my head that could take me back at any moment in my childhood. Unfortunately, time also showed me something else... fear.

Up until the moment she died, I'd never realised that grief felt so much like fear. I'd always believed that anyone who said they were never afraid was either dead or stupid. Everyone felt fear. You could keep it in check, certainly. You could hide it, absolutely. But it would always be there, hiding, goading, compelling you to move faster, fight harder, be stronger. That was how it felt losing Mam.

Butterflies in your stomach, the urge to vomit, the restless feeling that begins stirring in your legs and works its way up your body. Fear – the one common denominator for all human beings. The most natural and yet unpleasant feeling in the world. But it's not that we feel it that's important, but how we control it.

From then on, I was never going to let fear rule my life ever again. I was going to fight for those I cared about, and never stop unless someone killed me. Knock me down, I was going to get back up. At six years-old, I realised that life was fragile and that it wasn't the big things that mattered but the small things, like holding someone's hand or keeping a promise.

On that day I swore I was going to be strong in memory of my Mam because that's what she would have wanted me to be – strong for myself and strong for my family and friends. Strong against those who might try to take what I had.

It wasn't easy. We all suffered, especially Kaz and Alan.

But whereas his suffering was intended, deliberate... insidious, hers took her down a path parallel yet different to mine. Her pain was deeper... irreparable. It made her cold, carving out someone who believed the means justified the ends. I certainly never saw it until it was too late.

The point I'm trying to make is that the world succeeded in breaking me as a child. But those broken places acted like a forge, tempering me with each blow to grow up with the belief that Tommy Myers was not a man with whom to fuck.

"Boy, I got vision and the rest of the world wears bifocals."

Butch Cassidy and the Sundance Kid

Chapter Two

1969
South Shields,
South Tyneside

The East End Boxing Gym was one of those places that you only found out about because someone you knew trained there. You only got to know where it was if you were deemed worthy enough to be told… or shown.

Located in what had originally been the function room of The Horse & Hammer, Thomas had turned it into an illegal boxing gym a few months after Mary had died. One of the barmen, Dave Harris, who had long been a friend of Tom's and a former middleweight himself, had persuaded him that it could be a nice little earner for the both of them. His other leverage had been that it would help take his mind off everything that was going on. Tom had initially been unconvinced but a few weeks later he'd asked Dave to explain his plans in more detail. It wasn't so much that Tom had wanted to be part of anything illegal, but more that he agreed with his friend. He desperately needed something in his life that wouldn't make him think of Mary. His children… even the customers – all reminded him of that which he wanted so desperately to forget. The aim wasn't to *forget* her, just the pain her memory brought with it.

He'd tried to be supportive for his children but had found it difficult, especially in the first few weeks. More than a year later and most nights had still ended with him drunk to the point of being catatonic and carried upstairs by Dave or one of the customers. Donna, one of Mary's friends and barmaids, ended up becoming the children's proxy carer and full-time babysitter. That sense of dependency had blossomed into something more. Starting slowly at first; the odd laugh here, a stolen glance there. But the more time Donna spent with his children, the more she had started to form a real bond with them. Maybe it was because she had a child of her own. A year later she and Thomas were married.

She'd struggled initially with Alan, the memory of his mother so strong that all he could see was another woman trying to take her place. Faye was more accommodating, appreciating the support her dad got from Donna being around. She seemed to understand that Donna wasn't trying to replace their mam, just make certain they were looked after.

Faye had become the unofficial matriarch of the family, forced to grow up quicker than she would have liked. Thomas couldn't have done it, given that he was spending his free time at the bottom of a whisky bottle. So it had fallen to Faye to fill her Mam's role of cook, negotiator and coordinator. Donna's arrival on the scene, however unexpected and initially unwelcome, had given Faye the chance to be a kid again.

Tommy, however, had seemed to gravitate towards Donna and her daughter Karen almost immediately. It was as though he needed her to fill a void that existed in his soul... a hole his mother's death had left.

He and Karen became inseparable, developing an almost symbiotic relationship. Whether the fact they shared the same birthday one year apart was a subconscious cursor for their bond, Donna wasn't sure. The fact was that Tommy saw someone he was compelled to protect, even from a young age.

They became the epitome of a brother and sister relationship, despite their lineage.

Dave took Tommy under his wing. Out of loyalty to his best friend and a fondness for the boy, he sat on evenings telling him boxing stories and child-friendly tales of the criminal underworld. Tommy would often wander into the gym after school to watch Dave training young wannabe fighters and pestering him to let him have a go.

"Your Dad would kill me, sunshine," he would tell Tommy. "Maybe when you're older."

Eight years later and aged 14, his hectoring to be shown boxing tricks had gotten worse. Not only had he grown up to be a handsome teenager who still retained the endearing qualities his mother had so admired, he'd also become a pretty good fighter in his own right. Undisciplined, definitely, but with the potential to be exceptional. Dave had spotted it years ago but avoided encouraging him. He'd wanted Tommy to remain a child for as long as possible. Now he was a teenager, it was becoming harder to dissuade him.

Tommy strolled in as he always did, satchel slung over his shoulders and his white shirt un-tucked and hanging out beneath his jumper. He was eating a chocolate bar and humming a tune that Dave recognised as Chubby Checker.

"Alreet young Tommy lad," he shouted over from the ring.

Tommy waved acknowledgement and walked over to the series of punch bags in the corner. Their leather was cracked, with tape securing the areas that absorbed the most punishment. They looked old, but Tommy had always thought that added to their charm. To endure all they had and to still be hanging there, battered and weathered but ready to go. It was a quality he admired.

Always be the last one standing.

It wasn't that he sought out trouble at school, but more that it seemed to find him. Children can be cruel and relentless at times, their lack of social awareness often goading them to make inappropriate comments. At first it was primary school jokes, mostly about his mam having passed away. The jibe that brought about the end to that round of insults and the beginning of his reputation had been when he was seven. Sitting in English class on a table of four pupils, Stephen Bennett had thought it would be amusing to point out the engraving carved into the wooden lid with a compass:

Mother Fucker.

Bennett had followed this observation up with, "Tommy doesn't have one of those anymore".

Tommy responded with an uppercut to his jaw and a right cross to his face. After that, he and Bennett had become tentative friends and jokes about his mam were never again uttered.

Even as a seven year-old, Tommy secured a reputation as someone who would be problematic if you fucked with him. His height played a part certainly, but it was also his potential callousness which set him apart from the other hard lads at school. It wasn't there all the time – on the contrary – Tommy was known for random acts of kindness and generosity. But, push him too far and that coldness would slowly reveal itself, like a snake once coiled and suddenly awake. Even the older children showed respect for his tenaciousness. Tommy Myers had an edge that was rare.

A second round of comments that had brought this darker side to the fore had been concerning Karen while at Mortimer Road Secondary School.

"Bet that step-sister of yours makes you wanna touch yourself, eh Myers?"

"What's she like in bed, Tommy? It's not illegal to shag your step-sister, you know."

John McNeil would soon realise his mistake. Tommy followed him into the toilets one day.

"You've upset me," Tommy had said, blowing cigarette smoke in John's face. He knew he would probably be given detention again for smoking in school but he didn't care. He loved it, the girls loved it and he thought it made him look cool. At this very moment, it also added a desired edge of intimidation. It was a great prop in a situation like this.

John's face had become animated, his flushed cheeks and rapid blinking indicating his demeanor.

"Go fuck yourself, Myers," he'd replied in a shaky voice. "What you gonna do?"

"I'm going to put this cigarette out in your face."

John stepped backwards a few steps until the wall of urinals stopped him. "You wouldn't dare. You'd be expelled."

Tommy moved towards him slowly removing the cigarette from his mouth and rolling it between his thumb and forefinger by the filter.

"Of course I won't, 'cause they'll never know 'cause you won't say anything, will you?"

He had grabbed John by the hair and pulled his head down towards him, placing the glowing end of the cigarette onto his cheek. John had begun screaming for him to stop, tears streaming down his face. The smell of his skin searing had made Tommy gag a little, causing him to release John and push him backwards. He brought his right fist around and up from his side and punched him in the stomach with considerable force. Tommy had let him drop to the floor and watched as he curled up into a ball, groaning.

"So, as I said," Tommy continued, his voice bereft of emotion. "You'll say... *what* to *who*?"

John was blubbering, his face awash with tears but Tommy could just make out his comments.

"Nothing… I'll say nothing to no one. I swear."

Tommy had nodded approvingly. "And you're…?"

"I'm sorry, I'm *fuckin' sorry*, alreet?"

And that was the last of the jokes about his family. He had sorted it out the way his dad and Dave had taught him a Geordie should – you have a straightener and that's it. One individual presides over the other, you shake hands and walk away, hopefully with respect for each other. John McNeil never showed Tommy any respect after that, but he didn't disrespect him either and that was enough.

He had felt guilty for months afterwards, constantly reassuring himself that he wasn't a bully despite knowing that John McNeil would forever walk around with a scar on his face because of Tommy. Bullying was a systematic wearing down of an individual; his actions had simply been instinctive. Yet he promised himself he would always remember that power, though an important attribute to wield, had to be tempered with wisdom and compassion. Tommy wanted to be known as someone who acted when required, not because he was feeling cruel.

And that was partly why he wanted Dave to help train him as a fighter. Not to necessarily hurt people, but to protect himself and others.

He left the heavy bag swinging after a gentle punch and glanced around the room. The interior walls that had once been institutional white were now grey. The air was thick with sweat, body odour and intensity. He took note of the dozen or so men in the room. Some were skipping, others were shadow boxing in front of a mirror. One of them was in the ring with Dave, striking the pads on his hands as though they were his worst enemy. They all had a weary look about them, their faces hard and passive. He found it fascinating that once they were in this place, they unleashed an ability that transformed them into angry men in an instant, savagely raging against punch bags or sparring opponents. It was as if all of their accumulated frustrations and heartaches were released through their fists. Tommy recognised the majority of them; the same old faces who frequented the pub on a weekend, drinking away their sorrows and fucking away their lives with the prostitutes who propped up the bar with them. But in here, they were warriors whose training was one day going to release them from their mundane lives. Boxing would make them somebody.

Dave signalled to the lad in the ring to take a break and climbed between the ropes, throwing the pads onto the canvas as he walked towards Tommy.

"So, how was school?" he asked, taking a seat against the back wall and gesturing for Tommy to do the same.

"Not bad, I suppose," Tommy replied casually, placing his satchel on the floor beside him. "Same old shit."

"Language, young man," Dave chastised him playfully. "You're not too old to put over me knee."

"I'd like to see you try," he fired back.

"Oi!" Dave shouted. "Behave yourself."

Tommy nodded acquiescently. "Sorry, Uncle Dave."

"So," he said after a short pause. "When are you going to start training me?"

"Not yet, sunshine. Enjoy what you've got going on while you're still a kid, Tommy. You don't want to piss your life away getting the shite beaten out of you and ending up with ears like mine." He gestured to his left ear that resembled a rolled-up cauliflower.

Tommy smiled. "That's a good point."

"Anyway, where's your sister?"

"Which one? The miserable, angry one or Karen?"

Dave looked at him knowingly.

"I haven't seen her. Didn't see her on the way home, actually. I did see that fat bastard though. Greasy pervert… I can't fuckin' stand him."

"*Language*… and listen, Eric Doyle might be needing to lose a few pounds but he's good behind the bar and on the doors."

"Maybe. I just don't like the way he looks at Karen," Tommy replied. "With his little beady eyes and sweaty hands… I wish she wouldn't speak to him."

Dave nodded. "Don't you worry about Eric. You just make certain you're all washed up for tea. You know how Donna gets about things being 'reet for your dad coming home. And don't speak like that about Faye. She kept the family together after your mam… a lot for a young girl to take on when she was still just a bairn."

"Aye," Tommy said with a sigh. He stood and picked up his satchel. "I miss her, you know."

"I know you do, son," Dave replied quietly. "And she would be very proud of you. Her and your dad always said you would go on to do great things, Tommy. And you will. Trust me, *you will*."

Tommy smiled a sad smile and headed towards the bar. He found himself feeling like a small boy again, full of hopeless thoughts about his future. He would have never admitted it, but he wanted to shout and cry. He wanted Mam to tell him everything would be okay.

Yet all the while he couldn't stop the voices screaming in his head, banging so hard he felt like his mind would explode from their deafening roar.

Where would it all end and what was yet to come?

"What I like and what I need are two different things."

The Wild Bunch

Chapter Three

Tommy climbed up the stairs leading from the back of the pub to the flat. He threw his satchel onto the sofa and collapsed beside it. The sound of Alan and Faye laughing with Donna in the kitchen percolated through the air and filtered around the house. Moments of happiness had increased since Donna and Karen's arrival into their lives, but they were infrequent compared to how they'd once been and tended to come across as forced, like it was a necessary requirement to fill a home with positivity.

Standing with a sigh, Tommy made his way into the kitchen and pulled out the chair next to his sister.

"Alreet, our Tommy?" she asked. "Where ya been?"

"Just downstairs chatting to Dave," he replied. "He still won't teach me to box."

"And bloody right too," Donna chimed in as she sliced mushrooms at the workbench and flicked them into a frying pan. "You've got a big brain in that head of yours, our Tommy. Ya don't want to be pissin' it away in a boxing ring."

"Why can't I be both, eh? Why can't I be handy in a ring and some sort of intellectual? Who says?"

"Your dad does," she fired back. "He doesn't want ya getting hurt, son. Why don't you look into working with your brother?

Good money being a scaffolder. Or ask Faye if she can get you a job in the factory"

Tommy's siblings lifted their heads and pulled faces at the mention of their names while Donna continued.

"There's plenty you can do instead of boxing. It's not what ya mam would want for you."

Tommy glared at her. "But she's not here, is she?"

"No, son," came the sad reply. "She's not. But she's still *here*." Donna tapped her breastbone. She looked around the room at the children and smiled. "Reet, the lot of ya go and get washed up for tea before your dad gets in."

Alan and Faye started talking about the weekend as they made their way towards the bathroom. Tommy moved more slowly towards his bedroom instead.

He stood in front of the window and threw it open, looking down at the dockers and prostitutes making their way into the pub as per usual. One of the girls looked up at him and smiled, giving him a wave as she disappeared through the door.

The sounds of children playing and the cold wind from the Tyne helped him shake the thoughts away. He took one last look into the horizon and sighed before pulling the window shut and sitting down on the bed. He'd just lain back when Karen strode into the room, pulling her blonde hair back from her face as she moved and sat on the edge of his bed. At five foot, Tommy already towered over Karen, her petite frame and stature belying a fiery temperament. Despite her being a year older he always felt he needed to shield her from the bad things in life, though would never dare mention her size contributed to his sense of protectiveness towards her. Not unless he wanted a slap.

"Now then," she said in an over exaggerated tone.

"Where've you been? I was getting worried. I waited for you after school… get a better offer, did you?"

"Nah, I met up with some of the girls. You know Wilf and Brenda? They were going down the high street to look at dresses so I said I'd go with 'em. And since I got back I've just been downstairs talking to Eric."

Tommy sat up quickly, his face suddenly becoming stern. "I wish you wouldn't talk to that fat nonce. I don't trust him. He's a creepy shite. He's an old man and shouldn't look at you the way he does."

"Eric? He's harmless. And besides, he's nice to me. He treats me like a grown up, not like Mam whose always acting like I'm still a little girl."

"Hmmm…" Tommy intonated suspiciously. "Just be careful, Kaz."

"I will," she replied bringing her legs up onto the bed and lying down, her head on Tommy's chest. "Anyway. I've got you to look after me, Tommy Myers. You'll keep me safe, won't you?"

Tommy gently stroked her head. "Always, sis. *Always.* Though I sometimes wonder if you'll end up being the one looking after me."

"Quite right too," she replied with a dig to his ribs. "One day, I'll be the one who people look up to and are scared of. Me and you'll be like the Bonnie and Clyde of Tyneside."

"More like Julie and Jock," Tommy laughed.

The sounds from the pub drifted up towards them. Alongside the smell of tea cooking, Tommy felt a surge of happiness. His mam leaving them had been beyond devastating, his dad trying to rebuild their lives with the addition of another woman had been analogous. And for so long he'd felt Donna was just a cheap understudy, trying to recreate his mam with a second-hand performance. But she'd brought Karen into his life who had allowed him to believe that life could go on.

23

Karen had shown him that he could do more than just exist. He could be responsible for someone else. Alan and Faye were older than him and could look after themselves. Karen looked up to him and made him feel as though he was the most important person in her world. There was nothing he wouldn't do to protect his family. *Nothing.*

* * *

Kaz and I were the best of friends.

I loved all my other brothers and my sisters, sure. But Karen was special.

Me and Alan had a great relationship, always getting into scraps with other kids and more often than not with each other. We'd bunk off school together, though I ended up reining that in as I wanted an education whereas he wasn't so bothered. I wasn't stupid; I knew education was important, irrespective of my desires to be a boxer. What if it didn't work out? What if something happened that meant I couldn't fight? You need to plan for these eventualities and mine was attempting to at least have part of a brain. That said, it was one aspiration that never really worked out.

Alan was one of those people who got in with 'the wrong crowd' as Mam would have called it, always in trouble with the police, always looking for an angle. Ironically, when I got out he ended up being the one with the information and the inside details about jobs: the one I ended up relying on the most. That reliance was exploited with the most tragic of costs.

He'd always been introvert, but after Mam he suffered from depression. I know, how can you tell a teenager is suffering from depression? They're moody motherfuckers at the best of times. And it was only years later he was diagnosed with depression. Dad always felt guilty at not having spotted it sooner, though it wasn't his fault. None of us saw it. We were all suffering in our own ways. Alan's poor school performance and lack of interest in pretty much anything made sense now. He masked his pain with jokes. He became reckless, taking risks he'd never have considered before. Looking back, he was using it all to hide his true suffering. Smiling depression... who'd have thought there was such a thing.

Alan got on with Karen, but not to the extent I did. She knew me like the back of her hand and would parade her potential boyfriends in front of me, seeking my approval. But as protective as I was of her, it was none of my business. I guess she just wanted me to like whoever made her happy. And that's all I wanted for her... to be happy. After all, it became more and more unlikely she ever would be after that night.

I think Mam would have liked her... Donna too. No one could ever replace her of course but credit where credit's due, Donna had done a good job of getting my dad out of the bottom of a whisky bottle and back into a functional state. She'd taken on someone else's children and loved them like her own. I respected her for that. Equal and fair, as it should be in all things.

Me and Kaz went everywhere together; the cinema, the town on a Saturday, into pubs in Newcastle we were too young to be in. She could tell what I was thinking and know what I was going to do before I did. I called her my agent of socialisation.

I should have had that kind of relationship with Faye, but I could never relate to her in the same way. I found there was a discord between loving her like a sister and understanding her like a friend. Maybe it was just because she never got the chance to be a kid after Mam passed.

Underneath there was always an undercurrent of turbulence – instability on the constant verge of eruption. Everyone rallied around me, the baby of the family whilst Faye had to cook, clean and essentially become Mam. I honestly believe she thought they loved me more than her. I was the angelic, cute one whilst she was the chubby, mature tomboy who got treated like the grown-up whilst still a child. Ultimately, as we got older we drifted apart.

I still loved her though. I loved them all. I have to confess, if it hadn't have been for them I wouldn't have had a reason to fight. Then again, if it hadn't have been for Karen, I wouldn't have had to in the first place.

Act Two

1970s

"Hokey religions and ancient weapons are no match for a good blaster at your side, kid."

Star Wars

Chapter Four

1977

Newcastle upon Tyne,

Tyne and Wear

Tommy scanned the audience of a few hundred people for his girlfriend and brother.

He could have spotted Alan a mile away, sitting in the front row and dressed in a turquoise suit and white tie. Tommy would have to tell him later that he looked like a pimp.

His girlfriend, however, was nowhere to be seen.

Susan had promised she'd be here to cheer him on for what was probably the most important fight of his career so far. Tommy had seen it as their last chance to make a go of things. Their arguments had become more frequent and her drinking more obvious. The whole relationship had been going to hell for a while, but he didn't want to give up on it until there was no alternative. Karen had no love for his girlfriend, his dad was ambivalent about her and they rarely got to see each other between him working and fighting. But Susan got on well with everyone else and had been supportive of his attempts at a boxing career – something Tommy knew other fighter's partners struggled with.

As the bell sounded out round three, Tommy pushed all of those thoughts to the back of his mind and got ready for the storm.

His opponent, Frank 'The Machine' Gunn, was a well-established amateur middleweight boxer. Six foot one, a long reach and nine fights, all wins by KO, he was someone Tommy had no intention of underestimating.

Walking to the middle of the ring he was immediately tagged by Gunn with a straight and a right hook. Tommy shook his head in an almost apologetic gesture, trying to retain the focus he'd just had battered out of him.

He moved out, waiting for Gunn to chase him. He was tagged again, this time with three quick jabs. Tommy bobbed and weaved, moving from side to side like a metronome, trying to make himself difficult to hit.

Almost immediately double hooks connected before Gunn backpedalled off, returning to hit him with six or seven jabs that felt as though they were traveling through to the other side of Tommy's face.

Dave screamed from the corner, "Lean right, break his jab Tommy!"

He tried to cut him off but Gunn was moving like he was on ice, gliding gracefully, controlled. Tommy was the opposite, trying to make himself small and stay mobile. Gunn's expression was one of pure fire, his intended destruction of Tommy clearly written in his eyes.

He found himself slammed back into his own corner as jab after jab continued to connect with Tommy's face. Left hooks landed, cuts opened… blood flowed. He saw Gunn's guard drop briefly and responded with hooks to the body that drove him across the ring and onto the ropes.

Gunn sprung back to the centre with a stiff right-hander that jarred Tommy down to his feet. Three hooks and a right were followed by a stiff uppercut.

Tommy retaliated with blows to Gunn's body before the bell sounded. Gunn shoulder-barged him as he made his way back to his corner, casting a glance back in his direction of utter contempt.

Tommy sat down on the stool, relishing the sensation of cold water being splashed on his face. Dave pulled the gumshield out, allowing Tommy to swill his mouth.

"You're doing good, son. Let him wear himself out and then go to the body. You can do this, Tommy. It's yours to lose."

Tommy indicated his understanding and spat into the bucket before leaning round Dave's body to stare over at Gunn. He took note of his swollen right eye for future reference. Tommy turned to the crowd and gave his brother a confident nod. Alan came to all his fights to support his little brother. It was one of the few things they'd always done together and Tommy loved it, though would never admit it to his brother's face. It made him believe Alan was proud of him and sometimes that was all he needed to dig deep and find the reserve he needed to win a fight. Tonight would be no different.

Dave quickly rubbed oil across his protégés face and was massaging his shoulders when the bell rang out.

Tommy secured his gumshield in place and stepped out only to be greeted by a few rapid jabs to his face. More punches came as Gunn proceeded to work him over, blow after blow to the body to tire him out. Combinations were thrown, forcing Tommy to grab Gunn's arms in order to postpone the relentless abuse.

Pulled apart by the referee, Gunn was intent on a quick end to the fight. Three jabs quickly found their mark followed by a left-right-jab combination. Punch after punch ruthlessly collided with Tommy's jaw before Gunn retreated and began showboating around the ring in an intimidating fashion.

Circling, jabbing and changing directions, Gunn was doing everything he could to keep Tommy off balance. Jab, slide, jab, Tommy absorbed numerous blows as he tried to work out where his opponent was going and what he was thinking.

Tommy decided he was tired of being Gunn's punching bag and quickly closed the distance between them. He hit him with a left to the mid-section followed by a right to the head.

He chopped a right and continued with a flurry of combinations. Gunn, flailing, tried to sidestep the increasing momentum of Tommy's blows but this ended up carrying him into the ropes. Tommy capitalised and landed double hooks to the body. He dropped bombs powered by an anger rising from an unknown location deep within his body and proceeded to rain a tattoo of blows to Gunn's head and mid-section. Tommy delivered a booming right to Gunn's face, causing him to wobble and reach for the ropes behind him for support.

The bell closed the end of round four, much to Tommy's frustration. He'd almost had him for a few moments there. But this break would be good for him to get his mind straight. He was going down in the fifth. Tommy would make certain of it.

A few aggressive words from Dave, some water and more grease to his face and both fighters were straight out to the centre of the ring when the bell rang. Tommy immediately received three blinding jabs to his face. Gunn was moving around the ring confidently, more confidently than Tommy would have liked this late on in the fight. Gunn didn't seem to be as tired as he was, or at least it didn't show.

Tommy moved in, unleashing jabs and hooks as he took the fight to Gunn. He slipped a few of Gunn's jabs and moved away, changing direction and landing two more swift jabs as he did.

"Right hand over the jab!" Dave shouted.

Gunn moved in and went over Tommy's guard with an express-train jab that rocked his entire body. This was followed up with bombs to his body, hooks and rights. Tommy bobbed and weaved but the blows kept coming through.

A solid right hand shook Tommy down to his toes but he managed to get his hands up successfully enough to defend the savage punches that were raining down on his head, rocking him back and forth.

"*Hold him down, tie him up!*" Dave screamed above the roar of the crowd.

Tommy made a grab for Gunn to gain a few seconds. The stalling tactic served its purpose, allowing Tommy to cut loose with a thunderous right hook to Gunn's head, blasting him into the ropes, dazing him. He stepped towards Tommy and unleashed a punch into the centre of his face, splitting his nose open in a shower of blood. The referee looked over with concern as did Dave, but he held back from interceding, at least for the moment.

Tommy appeared unfazed by the injury, simply wiping his bloodied face on his arm. He unleashed a flurry of stiff jabs, lefts and rights before cracking him with a murderous hook. It connected just above Gunn's left eye, forcing him to bob and weave as he circled sideways. He tried to defend his head, but another right from Tommy slipped through.

Tommy was focused now and imbued with a newfound sense of purpose. He delivered a solid blow to Gunn's mid-section and watched him collapse to his knees. The referee signalled for Tommy to return to his corner and Gunn took the mandatory eight count before rising to his feet, slightly stunned. Tommy returned to the fight with a sledgehammer right that further opened up the cut to Gunn's eye. The number and power of further blows sent Gunn back up against the ropes.

Tommy followed up with blows to his face but the assault was curtailed with a crushing body blow. He felt a rib crack and wobbled back in pain. He could hardly breathe and Gunn had no intention of letting him, pounding away at his body with bone-crushing punches.

Tommy lashed out wildly, catching Gunn with a succession of blows to his face. Both coaches shouted from their respective corners as the fighters hammered away at each other. It had become less like a boxing match and more an all-out brawl, with only their willpower keeping them on their feet.

Tommy increased his intensity and found an opening to Gunn's solar plexus, filling it with a flurry of blows. Gunn's legs were beginning to buckle, an observation that increased the ferocity of the attack.

Gunn fell back against the ropes as Tommy continued. His body had now become a temple of pain. His bulk that had made him the favourite now only made him a bigger target for Tommy to focus on.

Gunn battled back slightly, a rally that moved them towards the centre of the ring. Right hooks led to uppercuts, and body blows were followed up by jabs. When Gunn tried to protect his now-battered face, he received a flurry of blows to his ribs and an unexpected haymaker sent him to the floor. He tried to get back up but his legs wouldn't respond, instead forcing him to collapse onto his back.

Gunn lay still. His eyes closed as Tommy danced back into his corner and waited, bouncing, eager to keep the fight going. The referee began the count but Gunn remained unresponsive.

Tommy echoed the count in his head, using each second that passed as a mental step towards his victory. Gunn's eyes slowly opened and remained still.

The referee reached ten and waved his hands over Gunn's motionless body. Tommy ran to the middle of the ring, pumping the air with his gloves.

Dave parted the ropes and moved to the centre, greeting

Tommy with a huge hug and gentle slap to the side of his face. Alan wasn't far behind him, climbing though the ropes and grabbing his brother in a bear hug. The crowd were all on their feet, acknowledging the courage and spectacle of the fight.

Tommy moved towards Gunn and held out an outstretched arm for him to link onto. Gunn acknowledged the gesture and used Tommy to lever himself up to a standing position. They embraced, recognising each other's spirit and determination. The respective coaches met up and shook hands, exchanging a few uplifting words to each other.

Tommy Myers moved back to his corner and basked in the adulation he was receiving. He was in pain, physically and mentally exhausted, yet oddly alert. Dave had taken him under his wing and put faith in him to become a winner. They'd worked their way up from the bottom, Tommy pushing himself so hard in training sometimes that he would puke. He had won other fights, but this one meant so much more.

This had been the one that could take him from amateur to pro; from nobody to somebody.

His dad had always told him he would become a name that people remembered and feared. Reputation meant everything; he had learnt that growing up.

This evening was going to change his life. He could just feel it.

"You realise what you're up against, don't you? Evil. Evil is a spiritual being, alive and living, perverted and perverting, weaving its way insidiously into the very fabric of life."

Exorcist 2: the Heretic

Chapter Five

Newcastle Upon Tyne,
Tyne and Wear

Karen wiped along the bar, making idle chat with the remaining customers as she went. It had been a slow night for a Friday but probably had something to do with either Roxy Music appearing at the City Hall or Tommy's fight in Newcastle. She would have been going to his fight herself if not for one of the bar staff calling in sick an hour before her shift was due to start. Karen swore if she found out that Julie had phoned in sick to go and see Bryan Ferry, she'd fucking kill her.

It wasn't so much that she minded helping out. Most of the time she enjoyed it, especially if she got to pull a shift with her mam. And the money certainly came in handy. It was just tonight of all nights, when she had been planning to watch Tommy fight, she felt as though she'd let him down.

His middleweight bout was in the Carousel Club. Most of the regulars would be there, cheering him on as their idol and inspiration. They certainly all spoke of him that way in the pub, often regaling other punters with his feats of sheer animalistic aggression and determination. To listen to them you would think he was a deity demanding reverence. She wondered if they would feel the same way if they had seen him afterwards, having to be carried up the stairs because of his broken ribs and unable to take a piss properly because he couldn't hold his dick in his swollen fingers. There was no doubt that Tommy was a good fighter. She heard the talk around the pub of him being a contender for the middleweight championship in a few years. And he certainly had the reputation to go with it. Few people, unless they were from outside the area, spoke out of turn about Tommy Myers.

Dave had trained him well. Karen's girlfriends swooned over him, describing what they would like to do to him in detail if he ever happened to be injured and needed nursing back to health at their house for some inexplicable reason. She would pretend to gag, reminding them he was her brother.

Sticking her head into the snug and finding it empty, Donna collected the few remaining glasses and headed back behind the bar. She rang her cloth out under the tap, by now ignorant to the smell of stale beer and cigarette ash that emanated from it. Moving out front, she swept her hair behind her neck and began polishing the mahogany surface, straightening high-backed bar stools as she went and saying goodnight to some of the customers as she moved round.

As the last of the regulars waved goodbye to her and moved outside Karen glanced up at the clock, noting it was just after ten. She finished cleaning one of the tables and made her way towards the door to lock up, placing glasses on the bar as she went. She was just about to slide the bolt into place when the door swung open, causing her to stumble back onto the floor. Eric Doyle staggered in and immediately outstretched his hand in a helpful gesture.

"Shit! I'm really sorry, Karen. Didn't realise you were there."

"What the fuck, Eric?" she fired back, slapping away his hand as she picked herself up. "What are you doing here this late? And besides, you know you're barred."

Eric nodded, wobbling back against one of the tables. "I know. I was hoping to see Tom and see if I could straighten things out. If only he'd let me explain…"

"Well, irrespective of that, I can't imagine he'd be interested in listening to you when you're pissed."

"Come on, Karen. You know I'm not a thief… it's just complicated. I would never betray Tom, he's always done right by me."

"You have to admit it looked a bit dodgy, Eric," Karen said. "It's understandable he jumped to that conclusion, even if it's not true."

He took some unsteady steps closer to her. "What do you mean – *even if it's not true*? You don't fuckin' believe me? You've known me for years. I'm no thief. I just got into a bit of trouble and was going to straighten it all out… I thought I'd have a little more time."

"Look, it's got nothing to do with me," Karen responded, taking a step back. "All I know is that I'm tired, fed up and I want to lock up, so can you just go and come back tomorrow. Tom's not in anyway, so…"

Eric moved forward again. "It's your fuckin' brother, isn't it? He's fuckin' turned you against me. He never liked me, that little bastard. Thinks he's *the big I am* doesn't he? With his boxing and his fights. He's a fuckin' nobody. I shit guys like him back in the day."

She waved her hands dismissively. "I'm not interested, Eric. And it has nothing to do with Tommy. His dad runs the pub, so any problems you have you need to speak to him."

"I know, *I know*," Eric said defensively, his tone softening. "I'm sorry. Listen, why don't we go and get a drink? End the night on a high note, eh?"

Karen turned towards him, a sad look on her face. "I'd love

to, I would. But like I said I'm tired and just want to go home. Maybe another time."

"Another time," Eric repeated quietly as he steadied himself against the bar. "Just don't get tired of fuckin' me off, do you?"

She walked away, shaking her head as she went. Eric moved quickly, quicker than she would have expected given his inebriated state. He grabbed her right arm and forced it up behind her back, marching her towards the back of the bar and in the direction of the cellar.

He slammed her up against the wall. "You've always thought you were better than me, haven't you? With your little bodyguard looking after you, strutting around here like you own the fuckin' place. What was Tom thinking giving you a job? Probably only because he's banging your slut of a mam. Is that what you are, Karen, a slut just like your mam? I've seen the way you've looked at me all these years... flirting and being all friendly. When really this is what you wanted."

Eric span her around and kissed her roughly, his tongue sliding over her cheeks before finding her mouth and forcing its way inside. Their teeth clashed, causing Karen to wince at the sharp nerve pain. She pushed on his face and turned it away, his rancid breath still hot on her neck.

She could feel the terror rising inside her, clawing its way from the pit of her stomach and all the way up her body. Her mind was reeling. Had she left the door open or locked it? Could she break free and make a run for it? If the door was locked, he would catch her before she could unbolt it.

The last customers had left just prior to Eric's arrival and Tom and her mam had done what they always did the nights of Tommy's fights and gone to the cinema, predictably nervous and unwilling to watch him get hurt. For a surreal moment, she remembered specifically them saying they were going to see *The Deer Hunter*. She felt it was an unusual detail to remember given her situation, wondering if her mind was somehow trying to distract her from the realisation spilling over her. What about the neighbours? Would they hear her if she called out? Desperate, Karen considered trying to calm him down again.

"Eric, let's just go back into the bar and get you a drink... we'll have a chat."

He looked at her with a quizzical yet amused expression. His hand was clasping her chin so tightly that his fingers dug into her cheeks.

"You had your chance to talk, love. Now it's my turn to stimulate a conversation."

His hand shot down between her legs and pushed against her so hard she began to slip towards the top of the cellar stairs. He grabbed her by the neck and pulled her back towards him, his tongue lolling out of his mouth as he kissed her again so hard he bit her lip.

Karen tipped her head back and stared at him, confused and desperate. His eyes appeared black, his fully dilated pupils giving him a crazed countenance.

"Eric, please. Stop."

"Shut the fuck up!" he demanded.

Her eyes remained locked with his and, in that moment, she saw her fate. She slammed her knee up into his groin, causing Eric to stagger back and cry out simultaneously.

Pushing him back further to create a gap, she ran through the door leading back into the pub. Glancing to her right, she spotted a corkscrew sat on the bar as she raced past. But defending herself wasn't foremost on her mind. Escape was the only objective.

The environment once so familiar to her had suddenly become an alien landscape, full of obstacles that seemed intent on hindering her race to freedom. She tripped over stools and crashed into tables on her way to the door. Glancing up she saw she hadn't locked it after Eric's arrival. Relief washed over her in waves so powerful she thought she might burst into tears. She could make it. Just a few more feet and she would be out.

Her relief was snatched away by the feel of his hand on the collar of her shirt. He yanked on it so hard she fell backwards and into a table, her flailing arms trying desperately to break her fall but finding no purchase.

"No you fucking don't!" Eric ordered, leaning down and grabbing her again, this time by the front of her shirt.

He began pulling her back through the door and towards the stairs to the cellar. She reached up and grabbed at his hand, trying to prise his fingers open. A few buttons popped free from the top of her shirt, exposing her bra. He stared at her now-exposed cleavage, his eyes full of salacious malice.

Karen felt bile rising in the back of her throat. "Please, Eric. Don't," she begged before screaming, "Get the fuck off me!"

"Oh, I'll get off on you all right," he leered, heaving her up before reaching into his jeans pocket and pulling out a switchblade. "I always thought you'd be a good fuck, now I get the chance to find out." The snick of the blade popping free sent a shudder down Karen's body. He directed the knife towards the remaining buttons on her shirt and began to flick them free, one by one. Once all the buttons were removed, he ripped it from her body and tossed it on the floor behind him.

"I brought this knife to use on Tom, but seeing as he's not here... would be a shame for it to go to waste."

He pulled her close to his face, the smell of beer and brandy fetid on his breath. She clawed at his face, digging her nails into the top of his right cheek and dragging them down as hard as she could.

He released his grip on her and the knife before grabbing at his face, a guttural moan emanating from him.

"*You fucking bitch,*" Eric hissed, slapping her hard.

She felt herself wobble backwards through the force of the blow and realised she was teetering at the top of the cellar stairs. The echo of her terrified breathing in her ears, her unstable swaying at the top of the stairwell – all of it was as though time had decided to pause and allow her to take in the enormity of what was about to happen. Life's cruel illustration that no one really has control over their own life. Fate comes unbidden to all, regardless of the choices made that we think point us in a particular direction. We have no control. We just play the parts chosen for us by a capricious and uncaring god.

Everything around Karen snapped back into focus and she found herself falling down the stone stairs, feeling every bounce on the concrete and hearing the sound of a few ribs breaking as she fell. Maybe even an arm.

The bottom came up to greet her, hard and solid. She raised her head slowly, feeling dizzy and saw Eric smiling as he moved towards her, unbuckling his belt.

She lay motionless, looking up at him and hoping this would be enough. That he would be satisfied with the sight of her bleeding on the cellar floor. But the expression on his face told Karen that this wasn't even close to enough for him. He reached the bottom of the stairs and grabbed her twisted, broken body by the hair, pulling her across the floor as though she weighed nothing at all.

The cold of the concrete on the base of her back took her breath away.

"Please," she sobbed.

"Shut up!" he said, his voice chilling and devoid of the warmth it had held earlier.

Eric covered her mouth to silence her moaning, his free hand grabbing at her skirt and pulling it up around her waist in rough motions. The movement caused pain to shoot up her left arm. She knew it was definitely broken.

She felt him pull her knickers to the side and, in that moment, felt every fibre of who she was as a person begin to snap, bit by bit. Everything she had dreamt of being, every aspiration she had ever had, slowly ebbed away like water trickling down a plughole, disappearing into nothingness. Her final thought as she felt him painfully force his way inside her was of Tommy and how she wished he had been here. He had promised to always protect her. So, where was he now?

Eric kept trying to kiss her, but she moved her face away until he grabbed her hard by the chin and held her head still, forcing his tongue into her mouth. He kissed her so hard she felt herself baulk, the smells emanating from his breath only making the sensation worse.

She tried to push him off her, but his weight combined with her broken arm and physical condition after the fall left her weak and unable to put any real purchase behind her efforts.

She had known this man for years. Had talked to him on an almost daily basis after school and college, had worked with him behind the bar and had even had nights out drinking with him. Tommy had always been suspicious of him, but Karen had only ever known kindness – or what she had perceived as kindness – from him. Granted, he might have been a little obsequious and overbearing, but had never given her the impression he was a monster and that he hated her so much. All that time, his fantasy of doing this to her had been fattening in his mind like a maggot in dead flesh.

She felt her muscles being pulled and ligaments tearing as Eric forced her legs open and beyond what was natural; a sheering sensation as he pushed himself further inside her, his groin crashing into her so hard she thought her pelvis, already compromised from the fall, was going to break.

He began to pound into her harder, his breathing coming in short, staccato bursts. At the same time, the fabric of her world was tearing wide open. Her mind bizarrely went through a myriad of circumstances where sex had always been something which had left her with a goofy grin all over her face and on a physical high that seemed to last an entire day. She heard her voice in those moments as she had screamed, "*Yesyesyes, moremoremore*" and she saw herself in the best kind of spotlight – one that was powered by affection and love.

Only this wasn't sex. This was unwanted. This was violation. This was rape. And the voice in her head wasn't screaming phrases of enjoyment or pleasure. It was screaming for someone to find her, for someone to save her. It was screaming, "*Nonono, stop,stop,stop!*"

It was screaming, "*I wish you would just hurry up and kill me.*"

She felt his whole body tensing as he prepared to climax, the idea of him finishing inside her causing her to taste vomit in the back of her mouth. It forced her to dig deep inside herself and find strength to push him away, but it wasn't enough to shift the weight that pinned her. All she succeeded in doing was making him grip her chin so hard she felt the cheekbone on the right-hand side of her face crack.

She felt his body shudder and his thrusting slow as tears streamed down her face. His breathing had become panting as he buried his face into the crook of her neck, his hot breath like fire on her skin.

Eric lifted his head, a look of satisfaction on his face. "There, it wasn't all that bad, was it?"

Karen stared at him, unable to speak. Her mind had turned into a blank canvas, devoid of thought or logical processes. He pulled himself out of her and stood up, standing over her as he buttoned up his jeans.

"Would you like me to help you up? Second time tonight, eh?" Eric held out his hand but she ignored it, shaking her head slowly.

"No," she heard come as a reply, but was uncertain as to whether it was her who had said it. The voice that had vocalised it sounded hollow and bland.

She struggled up to her knees, feeling a dampness between her legs that she was certain included a fair amount of blood from the trauma she had suffered. Rising unsteadily to her feet, she wrapped her arms around her to protect her modesty as best she could, waves of pain-induced nausea rising with every movement. Karen pulled her skirt back down and straightened it out with her one good hand, experiencing a desperate compulsion to look smart as though it would dampen out the horror of what had just happened.

She saw herself move past Eric, and up the cellar stairs. But it was as though she was watching a movie of herself doing these things. She felt detached from the world around her, moving on autopilot to somewhere currently unidentified.

Reaching the top, Karen looked down and absentmindedly picked up her shirt and the knife he dropped when she'd attacked his face. Moving through the door into the pub, she could hear Eric calling out her name, his voice echoing in the spaciousness of the cellar. His footsteps began to resonate on the steps as he made his way toward her, his voice piercing her brain like individual needles every time he spoke.

She was leaning against the bar pulling the tattered remains of her shirt around her shoulders as he moved besides her, her legs shaking so violently she truly believed if she didn't have something to rest against she would collapse.

"Can I get you anything?" Eric asked, his voice suddenly soft and gentle. He placed his hands on her shoulders.

The change in his demeanor and vocal tone caused a feeling

to rise in Karen she didn't know could exist. How dare he sound so caring and tender after what he had just done. He didn't get to be *that* man after he had possessed and punished her in one, despicable act. He didn't get to be kind and nice. Not now.

Not ever again.

Tommy walked up the path at the rear of the pub, clumsily fishing a set of keys out of his pocket with a swollen hand. He preferred to use the back door after a fight in order to avoid anyone seeing him. Looking the way a boxer often did after rounds of being punched in the face lent itself to questions. The last thing you wanted to do when your jaw was so swollen it hurt just to swallow was speak. Besides, he just wanted to get in, wash up and collapse into bed with a bag of frozen peas on his face and as many extremities as he could manage. His pain was intertwined with satisfaction. Gunn had been a challenging opponent and was a good fighter. Tommy knew it had been his determination more than his skill that had pushed him through to victory. That said, it was satisfying just the same. His future was just around the corner. He could feel it.

He reached the door and placed his keys in the lock, surprised to find it already open. Noting the time, it was odd but not out the ordinary that it was unlocked. He stepped inside and secured the door with a flick of the latch, the familiar and comforting smell of hops greeting him like a close friend. It was a smell that always reminded him of his Mam. It made him feel as though she were still around, allowing him to imagine seeing her appear from the cellar having just changed a barrel or popping her head from around the bar and greeting him with that beautiful smile that she'd always had on her face. Even at the end, he had only ever seen that smile.

Tommy had just taken his first, aching movements up the staircase when he heard a voice coming from the bar. He considered ignoring it as it meant talking to someone and breaking the rule he had of ignoring people post fight. He changed his mind when he recognised the voice as Eric's. Though he couldn't stand the fat bastard, he was curious to know what he was doing in the pub after closing, especially as he was barred.

Letting out a sigh of annoyance, Tommy moved painfully back down the two stairs he had managed to climb and hobbled towards the bar.

It took him a moment to register what he saw.

Her broken arm hanging uselessly by her side, Karen turned and plunged the knife deep into the soft flesh of Eric's belly. He staggered back, the look on his face one of shock and disbelief. Karen remained still and let the knife fall from her hand.

She stared into his surprised eyes and momentarily considered what she was doing. He had done something to her that could never be erased. Every time she looked in the mirror she would see his face and be reminded of what he did. On the cold, concrete floor of a public house cellar, he had forced her to become someone new. Someone different. Someone broken.

Karen didn't notice Tommy coming up behind her. It was only when he touched her on the shoulder and she flinched away with repulsion that she turned to see who it was. She found herself unable to speak, the words lodged in her throat.

Tommy backed away, his hands up submissively. "Hey sis, it's only me."

His eyes flashed over her, noting her open shirt, crumpled skirt and battered body. She could see his mind processing the scene before him, trying to connect the dots.

He glanced over at Eric leaning against the bar, digesting the details of his bleeding stomach wound and then looked back at Karen's disheveled appearance and haunted, vacant expression.

"She fucking stabbed me," Eric blurted out.

Tommy felt the pain in his body rapidly fade like footprints being erased by a receding tide. He could work out what had occurred. He didn't need Karen to speak the words. The look of desperation on Eric's face as Tommy stared at him confirmed it. He had always been suspicious of this man. Tommy approached Eric before he had chance to speak again, his discomfort all but masked by adrenaline. He landed a flurry of blows to Eric's face before he had chance to defend himself, the inertia of them carrying him from the side of the bar and spinning over the top of a table behind him.

He pulled himself up into a kneeling position and held his hands out as though requesting parlay.

"Tommy, wait. You don't understand..."

"I fucking understand all right."

Tommy closed the distance between them and pulled him up from the floor, delivering a blow to his stomach and an uppercut to the underside of his jaw, shattering it in one punch.

Eric slipped from Tommy's grip and slid to the floor, his smashed face making him look like a caricature of himself as he curled up into a fetal position.

Still high on adrenaline, Tommy span round to see Karen crying quietly and rocking in a seated position. He took a few calming breaths and moved over to her. Placing a comforting hand on her shoulder was his first reaction but he hesitated, instead choosing to sit beside her. He didn't speak. What could he say?

A few minutes seemed to stretch out before him, the only sounds the occasional car passing by outside and Eric's moaning in the corner. The subsidence of adrenaline in his body forced him to acknowledge the pain that was now surging across his body, both from his earlier fight and exertion here.

Karen's cries had settled into a low sob, her laboured breathing most likely from her broken arm and cracked ribs. To compound all her physical symptoms, she felt humiliation washing over her like a smothering veil. It enveloped her entire body, wrapping itself tightly around her person like an elastic band – leaving her room enough to breathe but not enough to break free from its grip.

Tommy stood and moved to Eric's prone body on the floor. He kicked him in the side with his foot, trying to rouse him.

"Oi, get up ya bastard. I haven't finished with you yet."

Receiving no response, Tommy kicked him harder before kneeling by his side. He grabbed him by the collar of his jacket and lifted him up, only then noticing the pool of blood that had been collecting beneath him. Laying him back down, Tommy rolled him slightly to the side, again taking stock of the wound to his stomach and the extent of his blood loss.

Karen's assault must have caused more damage than he'd thought. The enormity of the whole situation began to unfold before him. They had a problem.

His mam had instilled in them all that they had to look after one another. After she'd died, that was the one thought careening through his mind, every day in everything he did.

Protect your family.

Tommy was a fighter. That's what he'd been doing tonight, what he'd been doing every day since his mam had been taken from him. This was no different. Dave had taught him that in the ring options present themselves all the time. Look carefully enough and the secret to that knockout blow, that points-scoring flurry will be there, so blindingly obvious that you wondered how others could have ever missed it.

This was no different. The solution was in front him. Overinflated, dramatic and full of consequences – but nevertheless, it was there.

"Where is it?" he asked gently, standing up. "Whatever you used… where is it?"

Karen lifted her head and looked at him, initially confused. She slowly raised her unbroken arm and pointed along the base of the bar.

Tommy glanced in the direction of her shaking hand and scanned the floor, his eyes finally resting on the bloodied knife. He retrieved it and stepped back towards Eric's body, looking intently at the dead man's face as though absorbing his every facial feature for future reference.

Karen stared at him, her first words spoken since the attack coming out in a broken staccato timbre. "Tommy, what are you doing?"

"Protecting you," came his stoic reply. "I always said I'd protect you and I meant it. I wasn't here to save you from this. I don't know how I can help you get over what happened, if that's even remotely possible. But I can save you from the repercussions… I killed him."

Karen struggled to her feet, wincing through the pain as she hobbled towards Tommy. "You can't… I won't let you."

"Karen, I have to. Don't you see? I can't ever bear the thought of you going to prison for this. I can't imagine any jury in the world would ever convict you, but if there's even a chance… I can't take that risk… I won't."

Karen began to cry again, this time from the overwhelming emotion she was feeling at Tommy's gesture. He couldn't take this for her.

"No, Tommy," she pleaded. "We'll work something out."

Tommy curled his fingers around the handle and threw it

back onto the floor, watching as it bounced and settled beside Eric's body.

"There's nothing to work out. This is how it has to be to save you. Remember that time you stole that jewellery and the cops came knocking at the door?"

Karen nodded, tears streaming down her face.

"I told them it was me, even though they knew it wasn't. I mean, what does a teenage boy want with necklaces and bracelets at 17? Dad knew it was you, Donna knew. But I wasn't going to let you get arrested for it, because I promised I'd look after you. And one day, you'll be the one who takes care of me, just like we said all those years ago lying on my bed. But until that day comes, it's still my turn. You'll have to report what happened to you. I can't do anything about that, but him dying... that's on me. I can say I came in, saw what he had done, we fought, he went for a weapon and in the struggle I stabbed him. Are you listening to me? It's important you say nothing. Can you do that? I'm doing this for you to keep you safe. Do you understand?"

Karen nodded slowly, her slight frame shaking violently Tommy wanted to hold her until it stopped, telling her everything would be okay. But he knew it would never be okay again. This was where their lives had changed irreparably.

Tommy smiled lovingly at his sister and knelt by her side. "I would do this for you every day of the week and twice on Sundays," he said with a smile. "But first we need to get you an ambulance, then we need to phone the police. Eric attacked you. I came in and stabbed him. Okay?"

Karen nodded again.

"Okay," Tommy confirmed. He walked over to the phone behind the bar and picked up the receiver. He took a few deep breaths and looked back at Karen. He'd been right. His future was lying just around the corner. He just hadn't foreseen this.

He gave her a slight smile and dialled the numbers.

Someone answered after two rings.

"Hello, please state the service you require?"

"Police… there's been a murder."

* * *

"You are sentenced to eight years."

Just like that, I stopped being Tommy Myers and became FF8282.

Investigation, remand, trial, involuntary manslaughter, and rehoused courtesy of Her Majesty's Prison Frankland. Did I regret it? Nope. That fucking nonce got what he deserved. Karen testified about what happened. Nearly destroyed me seeing her have to go over everything that fuckin' piece of shit had done to her that night. I don't know if it made a difference. I wasn't found guilty of first degree murder due to the fact there was no evidence I premeditatedly intended to kill him. However because I was a fighter and had obviously given him a good hiding before I 'stabbed' him, the judge concluded that, despite the mitigating factors of him having raped my sister and my high emotions at having discovered it, my actions could have likely led to his death with or without a weapon. I was found guilty of manslaughter and sentenced to eight years with the possibility of parole – which I couldn't complain about, given that it holds the maximum sentence of 25 years. It could have been worse. Thinking about it, that all depends on your definition of worse.

Did I regret going back to the pub that night? Well, that's a bit more complicated. Did I want to throw my life and a shot at a professional boxing career away? Not at all.

But the point is, decisions lead to consequences. Karen's decision led to the death of a man. That action led to my decision to protect her at all costs. At the end of the day, it's always about whether you can live with the consequences of your actions.

Was I scared the moment I stepped through the doors of a custodial establishment? Of course I was. Not that anyone would have ever known. Anyone who says they were never scared the first time that cell door slams shut is either stupid or a liar. And I'm neither of those things. But that first day... when you're put in the cuffs, taken from the dock to the cells and eventually transported to the van – that's scary. And the fact is, you know there's worse to come.

You're strip-searched, given your prison issue clothes and a few other bits and pieces and then ushered into the reception wing with the other new prisoners. Bit like first day at school, only with robbers, rapists and murderers.

From the reception wing you're then transported to the medical wing. When I say medical wing, I mean a cell along a corridor filled with tormented souls and depressed individuals. This cold, unwelcoming abode was my home for the first evening in order to keep me under close observation. The first 24 hours are when you're considered most likely a suicide risk, so they put you there for your safety.

A handful of paces across in either direction, the mauve-coloured room had a bed with a mattress seemingly carved from rock, a square steel table and steel chair, a matching steel washbasin and an open lavatory with no lid or flush. A wall with a window encased with thick, black iron bars caked in dirt was my only oracle to an outside world.

About 20 minutes after arriving there, the steel grille on my door had flipped open to reveal a grinning man.

"Now then, Myers. Delivery for you."

The guard pushed a pillow through (when I say pillow, I mean rock), a mauve pillowcase, a green sheet and a brown blanket.

"Thank you..." I said, leaving a pause for him to fill in the blank with his name.

"Evans. Andy Evans."

And with that I was left to fall asleep and be woken every hour by a fluorescent light being switched on and a set of eyes observing me through the letterbox. Every hour, on the hour. Good ol' suicide watch. The irony being the hourly interruptions made you want to commit fuckin' suicide.

The following morning Andy reappeared and escorted me to the showers. Now, when I say shower I mean something akin to being licked by a small cat... or perhaps a kitten. The shower room consisted of a large, stone-floored room with four push-button showers that issue a trickle of lukewarm water that lasts about 30 seconds before you have to press the button again. I must have pressed that thing over a 100 times, savouring each and every drop of water on my body as though it was the last time I would experience it.

After my kitten-licking shower, I was moved to the main block where my sentence began for real. Andy reappeared and gave me some toothpaste, toothbrush and a green towel, striking up a conversation where he told me working there was just a part-time gig for him and that he had aspirations to be a pathologist or coroner. I wished him the best of luck with it and considered myself fortunate the guards I had met so far seemed fairly decent. To be honest, most of them were okay, some even going so far as to be almost professionals who did their jobs admirably. But there are always the ones who think they're the big man on campus: those who humiliate, belittle and try to make your life as miserable as possible. The occasional torch in your face in the middle of the night, running keys along the bars of the cells, but on the whole fairly standup men just doing a job. I guess some just see extra opportunities to dish out punishment as just desserts for you being there in the first place.

The chaplains were also good to get to know. In those first few weeks, despite knowing how to handle myself, I had questions, uncertainties and they've seen it all before which makes them the best people to ask. And who better to ask for a favour than a servant of God? Granted, they can't break the rules but at least they exercise some common sense, are accessible and you don't have to fill out a fucking form to see them like you do anyone else.

As for your routine, breakfast is served at 0800 and you work until 1100 when you get your association time. You know the kind of thing. Nearly an hour of mooching around a furlong square enclosed by a high brick wall with what is laughingly referred to as a garden in the centre. Searched when you go out, searched when you come back in and that's your freedom for the day. Lunch and a couple of hours association time in the evening where you can play pool, make a phone call, that kind of thing and then lock up at 2100. And that is pretty much it. Every. Fucking. Single. Day.

Newspapers are a blessing and a curse. They keep you sane but make you miss the outside world. Buying stuff through the canteen was something I quickly got the hang of. Toiletries, tobacco, batteries, fruit, tins of food... these were the only things that made you feel remotely connected to the outside. You would pin so much happiness on receiving your whole order, that when something got fucked up you would honestly be devastated. Appreciate the little things – that's one of the first lessons I learnt.

So I did all of that and I boxed. Once word got out that I'd killed a man (allegedly) then other inmates started showing me a little due reverence. I didn't court it, but nor did I reject it. Fuck that. If people wanted to bow down to me then let them... Mam would have killed me for that kind of arrogance. But in prison, if you can get that kind of attention then it goes a long way to keeping you safe. That said, it also means others want to challenge you. Which is a huge pain in the arse.

Enter stage left: Charlie Woods.

"But I'm telling you, and I'm telling everybody at this table that that's a shark! And I know what a shark looks like, because I've seen one up close. And you'd better do something about this one, because I don't intend to go through that hell again!"

Jaws 2

Chapter Six

1978
HMP Frankland,
Brasside

Tommy walked the well-trodden path back to his cell, passing door after door. The atmosphere was oppressive, filled with humidity and the exhaled dreams of dispirited men.

He'd already learnt to tune out the constant babbling and chatter that made up the baseline, monotonous sound of prison. Those first few weeks he thought he'd go insane from the cacophony of noises that constantly filled the air around him. But, like living by a motorway, you eventually get used to the sound and it becomes a comforting blanket when you feel alone. That was the one thing Tommy had yet to get used to more than a year down the line; he was in an establishment stuffed floor to ceiling with other men and yet he still felt lonely.

Once in his cell, he threw himself down on the bed. Being in prison was like living in a biosphere. Everything was pre-engineered and constructed to deliver a certain environmental element or activity at a certain time of day. Even the lighting was artificial, electrical and automatic. No slow awakening to the sounds of birds singing in the distance or being roused by the soft glow of the rising dawn. Just circuit breakers triggering an illusionary day and night. All scheduled, all timetabled, all like clockwork.

HMP Frankland held 108 single cells. His home comforts now consisted of a bunk bed, toilet and sink all bolted to the wall, wrapped inside molded concrete and brick to create a bespoke living habitat that was a mirror image of the next. Monotone paintwork and the sounds of desperation reverberating off the thick, cold walls completed the aesthetic.

The prison itself was a brand new, Category A facility, having only opened the year prior to Tommy's incarceration. From the outside it looked like a medieval castle minus the turrets. If you didn't know better, you could be fooled into thinking it was a tourist destination, given that it blended quite subtly into the surrounding architecture and villages of Newton Hall and Pity Me situated nearby. Tommy had always found the village name of Pity Me amusing. The history books claimed that it was simply whimsical given its desolate and exposed geographic locale. His Mam had told him that the name originated around 600 BC when the coffin of St. Cuthbert had been dropped off on the way to Durham, prompting the saint to implore the monks to be more careful and take pity on him. Tommy had always preferred that version better.

Inside, HMP Frankland consisted of four wings housing male prisoners over the age of 21 and whose sentences were four years or more, life or something specific that branded them high risk. High risk of what Tommy wasn't sure of and didn't particularly care, but he imagined it meant they were nutters. Stabbings and various versions of physical mutilation were commonplace, proving beyond a shadow of a doubt that prison represented the epitome of Darwin's evolutionary phrase: survival of the fittest. Step up and you'd be fine; be soft and you're fucked.

The services on offer to guests of Her Majesty were a healthcare centre that had a four-bedded ward, a dental suite, an X-ray department and a suicide crisis suite. Inmates got the chance to educate themselves to whatever level they desired, take lessons in carpentry, assist in the charity workshop, visit the library or go to the gym. In all honesty Tommy had begun to think fondly of it all, allowing himself to accept that Hell had become home.

* * *

Many of the prisoners already had Tommy pegged as someone who would not take kindly to being fucked about. This was both down to his physical presence and the suspicion that he had killed a fellow prisoner, Stuart Caplin, shortly after his arrival. Most of them kept a friendly but tentative distance and it suited Tommy just fine. It allowed him a better chance to keep his head down and do his time whilst he worked out what to do once on the outside. That was the decision that had occupied his mind from the moment he'd landed in here and was the one circling his brain now.

"That's an intense face you've got going on, Magpie," Charlie Woods said from the door of Tommy's cell.

Charlie had called him that since day one as a reference to his place of birth. Tommy didn't mind. On the contrary, he thought it showed affection for him rather than an insult. Not that he would have necessarily said anything if it had been insulting. Charlie Woods was small and wiry but had a look in his eyes that you knew meant that if you fucked with him it was your life. In for two counts of murder, the details of which he'd never shared, Charlie had immediately taken him under his wing. There was no hidden agenda with him and he went through the do's and do not's, the must have's and must avoids – claiming he saw a little of himself in Tommy and with it, saw potential. Charlie was also what was called 'a listener'. Certain prisoners

59

are trained by the Samaritans to assist fellow inmates who might be finding prison hard or contemplating suicide. Tommy was neither of those things, but it made Charlie someone who was easy to talk to and was non-judgmental. Two things almost impossible to find inside and rare to find on the outside.

"Get yourself to church, Magpie," had been one of the first pieces of advice he had given him.

"Why?" came Tommy's reply.

"Because it's 45 minutes out of your cell in a wide open space. That's why," said Charlie.

Tommy sat himself up, leaning back on his elbows and smiling.

"It's my thinking face. If it bothers you I'll stop," Tommy replied with a smile.

"It looks more like your *having a shit* face. Honestly, I'm more worried about you having a mental hernia from over-exertion," he said, gesturing for Tommy to move over on his bed so he could sit down.

"So, did you have a think about our conversation yesterday?"

"I did mate, it's just hard to get my head around, you know? I spent my life pushing myself in one direction and I know that life has gone now but..."

"But?" Charlie repeated.

"... but you still dream, don't you? You like to tell yourself you had a plan. I mean, some people choose their path don't they, whether it be burglar, bank robber or fuckin' rapist. I didn't choose this, it was chosen for me. I don't regret what happened to me that night. I'd do it every night – it was the event that made me do it that I regret, that I hate I couldn't be there to stop it. But choosing this lifestyle is something completely different to what I had in mind. I'm tempted to raise that fucker Eric Doyle from the dead just so I can kill him again."

"Well, you let me know how that goes for ya, kidda," Charlie said as he rose from the bed and started pacing around the cell. "Listen, when you walk through those doors it doesn't matter who you are, Steve McQueen or Charles fuckin' Bronson. Anything you were outside those walls becomes irrelevant the moment you're assigned that number. All that matters is what you do in here... what you make of yourself *in here*. You did that, even though you didn't want to. Killing a man out of rage or revenge is one thing. Killing a man because you need to is something else entirely. Stuart Caplin wanted to make you his bitch, you stepped up and ended him. Everyone knows it was you – whether you scratch another notch onto your cell wall or not – and no one fucks with you because of it. That's power my friend, true power. Forget that you could have been heavyweight champ. Focus on what you are, which is fuckin' dangerous with power. We'll make it so that when you step foot out of these doors, you'll be a fucking legend."

"It was middleweight... I was a middleweight."

"I know that, Magpie. Just heavyweight champ sounds more... *butch*," Charlie laughed.

Tommy found it hard to disagree with his logic. Boxing had taught him to evaluate every situation and find the opportunities and weaknesses. You don't have time in the ring to study your opponent leisurely, you do it quickly, you don't have time to berate yourself from being tagged unexpectedly from a right hook you didn't see coming. You have to quickly learn from your mistake and avoid making it again. Once the fight is over and you've survived, that's when you sit down and consider your options.

This was no different. Charlie had given him law books, history books, classic novels and books on world history. He'd laughed, wondering what the fuck he was supposed to do with them. Charlie had responded with a "What the fuck do you think? Read them."

Tommy knew knowledge was power. Physical prowess and a hard punch could get you so far, but that wasn't where real strength lay. Keeping your eyes open and hands working brought knowledge your way. And Tommy had slowly come to learn that there was no knowledge that wasn't power. He knew you can't do time and come out fat – you train and you learn, making your mind lean. So he started studying hard, determined to come back stronger than he'd ever thought possible. This revelation also allowed him to see that with it came status. And no one could survive in prison without that. Status brought with it challenge. But challenge bred conflict.

Already he knew he was no longer the same person anymore. Eric's death had left part of him broken, something he would have never openly admitted to anyone. But breaking his soul had perfected his spirit. He unearthed a part of himself he hadn't even known existed. Both he and Karen had suffered that evening. And though Tommy would never dream of comparing his struggle to hers, he knew one thing their suffering had done for them both: it had birthed insight. He hadn't seen Karen since his sentencing but knew she would feel the same. The only difference was that his comprehension had allowed him to feel a burning rage and hatred. Hatred for Eric and what he had done to his sister; spite for what he had made Tommy do that night.

Tommy had taken that hatred and funnelled it into survival. It had served him well, but he was determined not to let that fury consume who he really was. It was fine using it inside to survive, but Karen would expect the real Tommy to return home. If she even wanted to see him at all when that day arrived.

"Remember what I told you, Magpie," Charlie announced as he made his way out of Tommy's cell. "If you let it, this place'll eat you alive. Make yourself unpalatable and you'll do just fine."

Tommy let Charlie's words bounce around his head as he lay back onto the bed that was too short for him and allowed the soft, restless sounds of his surroundings lull him into a fitful sleep.

"Total submission. That's what I like in a woman – total submission."

I Spit On Your Grave

Chapter Seven

Newcastle Upon Tyne,
Tyne and Wear

The room felt bereft of warmth, despite the heating being on.

Karen pulled her knees higher towards her chin and wrapped her arms around them, creating a protective circle that she wanted to believe nothing would be able to penetrate.

Was this her life now, eating anti-depressants like Smarties and spending week after week in therapy? She wanted so desperately to get some context to everything in her head, but it was as though her soul kept refusing permission.

It had been months since the attack and yet Eric's face was there, in her mind, as clear as day. When she did manage sleep, the nightmares were bad enough, having to relive the assault on a nightly basis. At times it would be as though it was just that, a nightmare that hadn't really happened. When it would replay in her mind, sometimes Tommy would arrive earlier and save her. Sometimes he would arrive during her rape and temper some of the horror of the attack. Sometimes he never arrived at all and she would have to endure it all again.

Tommy.

She felt guilt at having not been to see him yet. After everything he had sacrificed for her the least she could do was to pay him a visit; tell him how much it meant to her. But it was too soon. Her brother was still entangled in thoughts relating to Eric and until she could work out how to separate the two, she didn't think she could face him. She could barely find the strength to stay awake most days, never mind coping with more emotional stress.

Karen felt like she hadn't eaten a proper meal in weeks, her appetite virtually non-existent at times. She constantly had a headache – everything ached – and she still had trouble with infections. The thought of going to the doctor only to be told she had the clap made her feel sick. That would have been his final fuck you to her after everything else – damaged her mentally, affected her physically, contaminated her personally.

She had moved into the bedsit shortly after the attack, unable to bear being in the same building as where it had happened. At every turn in the pub, she'd seen him, been able to smell him, heard his voice to the point she thought she had been going insane.

Her mam and Thomas had understood, despite their sadness and guilt at not having been able to protect their daughter. It wasn't their fault, she knew that. What happened most likely wouldn't have happened if they'd been there, but who's to say it wouldn't have happened another time.

Fate didn't like changes to its destination. Inflexible, immutable, it would always ensure that it played out. Karen believed certain events in your life had to happen, that try as you might, life would ensure key events unfolded however much you might wish to change your destiny.

Besides, she had needed to move out for no other reason than if she heard one more 'well-meaning' customer tell her she would get over it and she was lucky to not be sharing a cell with her brother.

Her therapist had told her that there would come a time when she would begin to be able to resolve certain elements of her assault. The manner in which they would manifest themselves would be unique to her. The biggest hurdle she needed to overcome quickly was that she'd somehow brought it on herself. She needed to believe that, because when you already know it but someone tells you that *you didn't bring it on yourself*, then that's exactly what you *do* think happened. The subconscious battle is more difficult than those you can see.

She also needed to know it hadn't altered her perception of intimacy. At the moment, she couldn't imagine anything worse than someone slobbering all over her, but she somehow knew that was only a short-term thing. What Eric had done had left her irreparably damaged in the sense that she felt worthless. She no longer had a role to play in the production of life she had previously inhabited. She found herself turned on by men, music videos and sex scenes in films, but it only made her feel guilty. More than that, it made her feel undeserving; that she had no right to feel sexy and attractive, even if only for a moment.

Karen wanted someone to love her in the way that poets promise love should be experienced – without compromise and inhibition. Eric hadn't won by giving her the mentality that all men were evil. She knew that wasn't true just as she knew there was someone out there for her, as clichéd as it might sound. All she needed to believe was that there was a future for her and that she had a place in the world.

What she knew with absolute certainty was that she would never feel powerless again or at the mercy of someone else's whims. Karen was determined, no matter how long it took, to take back control of her life. Eric had unlocked a part of her psyche that she hadn't known existed: a section of her mind that was calculating and full of more determination than she had ever believed possible.

She had no idea how to channel it into something constructive. She wasn't even certain she could. But, if she were to somehow manage it, Karen knew that she would be reborn as someone different. Like the caterpillar who is forced by nature to endure a process only to become something entirely new on the other side, she would find a way to embrace this evolution.

She needed to become something else.

She would become *someone* else.

"Stanley, see this? This is this. This ain't something else. This is this."

The Deer Hunter

Chapter Eight

1979
HMP Frankland,
Brasside

Tommy had risen to the usual sound of his alarm clock – lights on, guards screaming for everyone to get up. After using the toilet and splashing water over his face, he'd settled back down on the bed and thought the same thoughts he had for the last 398 days – what was he going to become now.

It was less worrying about how prison might change him – he expected that to be the case and knew it had already. How could it not? Spending every day looking over your shoulder and ensuring you projected an air of authority and assertiveness was tiring. It was an act at first – then the transition fully developed.

Wear a mask long enough and it becomes your true face.

Tommy started about his daily ritual: worrying about what he would do when he was free. It was another transition that he'd accepted without even knowing he had. It wasn't as though the local Boy Scout service was going to employ him once they got wind of his criminal record; no one would touch him. He knew that his options were now mostly limited and, in all probability, illegal. That said Tommy knew that you could be in the gutter but still be looking at the stars. Boxing had been his route to them once. Now Tommy Myers knew he walked a different path.

As though in response to thoughts of his future reputation, four men appeared at the open door of his cell. The three stood at the back looked like rejects from The Rolling Stones, the leader more like Charles Manson. His thick beard, uncombed light brown hair and intense blue eyes gave him a feral quality that made people do whatever he wanted them to. The muscles bulging through his shirt probably helped though Tommy had always guessed that the image Peter Rooney projected was far removed from his actual persona. He always had an irresistible urge to point out that his nose was way too large for his face and his ears looked like they were ready to leap from his head, but he resisted. Why wind him up more than he needed to?

"Wakey, wakey, Myers. Rise and shine," Rooney said.

"Wow, worst alarm clock ever," Tommy replied "Mind you, could be worse... better than coming too soon which is something I'm certain you know all about, eh? You're doing your rounds early. What's the matter? Piss the bed?"

"You think you're such a clever bastard," Rooney stated loudly. "You need to be careful that mouth of yours doesn't get you knacked."

"So, where you lot off?" Tommy asked. "To the gym to pump each other?"

Rooney smiled. "You think you're so funny. Big man, strolling around this kitty, thinking he owns the joint. Well, people are getting a little tired of it, Myers. They think you need ta be taught a lesson."

Tommy stood. "Firstly, a lot of people happen to think I'm *very* funny. Second, I could do with brushing up on me algebra... is that the kind of lesson you're talking about?"

Rooney stepped towards him so that their noses were

almost touching. "You fuckin' little shite. I'll snap you in half."

Tommy grabbed him by the collar of his shirt, fast enough that the men behind Rooney were slow to respond. "Listen to me, fat man. You're in my house now. Find someone else to mug off or your boys'll be carrying you out of here."

"Go on then, ya fuckin' prick. I fuckin' dare ya. Even you're not that stupid. He'll have you fuckin' kneecapped."

Rooney said the words but knew his bravado hadn't come across as intently as he had desired. He couldn't deny that he was slightly intimidated by Tommy Myers but would die before he would let him know.

"Who will, your boss? The one you strut around saying owns most of Newcastle? You're deluded mate. Jack Hudson's a fuckin' joke and always has been."

"You listen to me..." Rooney started.

"No," Tommy interrupted, pulling him even closer but maintaining a contrite expression. "You listen to me, you fucking idiot. And listen closely. You cannot possibly comprehend the immensity of the fuck I do not give about you and your boss. Tell him I won't be bullied or scared. If he wants me he can wait another 7 years until I'm out and then tell me to my face like a fuckin' man. Until then – fuck off!"

Tommy pushed him out his cell so hard Rooney fell to the floor. One of his men, who looked like David Soul, took the opportunity to show his master how loyal he was by marching towards Tommy brandishing a wooden cosh that had been hidden up his sleeve.

Tommy suddenly felt like he was back in the ring, having to make lightning-fast decisions in a heartbeat. He felt a familiar sense of ferociousness wash over him, the last few days' laments at his fate finding the outlet they'd been waiting for.

Tommy lunged forward without a sound and grabbed Soul by

both wrists, tightly enough so that he dropped the weapon and pulled them apart wide enough to accommodate his forehead that he slammed into the bridge of his attacker's nose.

Rooney's other two lapdogs ran into Tommy's cell, hoping to overpower him.

Tommy zeroed in on Soul who was still dazed from the head-butt and put him down with a single punch. He knew it left him momentarily exposed to the others, but it was an acceptable risk. Dave hadn't only taught him boxing, but street fighting savvy: when fighting multiple opponents, better to finish off one than hit two and not take either of them down.

If you're one and they're many, your priority is to even the odds... always.

Tommy kicked the first of the two men in the kneecap, hearing a satisfying crack. Before the man could even start screaming, Tommy was up and driving his left elbow into the face of the second assailant. His screams came out as muffled gags as he reached up to hold his now shattered jaw in place.

Four men down, 12 seconds: two incapacitated, one un-conscious, one humiliated.

Tommy could hear the guards sprinting up the corridor and took standing position up against the bars of his cell, acutely aware of what was about to happen. He was shaking with adrenaline, his stomach churning. Tommy had the same philosophy in here as he had outside – keep your head down and stay out of trouble. But he hadn't been able to stick to that when free and there was even less of a chance inside. The whole establishment was rigged, designed to ensure you accept you are whatever put you in here in the first place.

The persona of a criminal.

If that was how it was to be, so be it Tommy thought to himself.

As the screws raced into his cell, pulling him down and pinning him to the floor, Tommy knew what he had to do. He would let Charlie help and guide him so that he could understand how the criminal fraternity worked. He would absorb everything this place had to throw at him and turn it up to eleven.

"You will make my strength your own, and see my life through your eyes, as your life will be seen through mine. The son becomes the father, and the father the son."

Superman – The Movie

Chapter Nine

HMP Frankland,
Brasside

Tommy fidgeted nervously at the table. He looked around to see the other inmates receiving their visitors, embracing them with hugs and genuine smiles of pleasure to see not only a loved one, but someone from the outside world.

All he wanted to be was ready for Karen's visit.

His dad, brother and sister had been to see him every month, but Karen had stayed disappointedly absent. He understood why, but still found it hard to shake the sadness he felt at not seeing her. He had been her anchor to the world, and her his. Serving his time would be a lot easier knowing that his sister still cared about him.

He glanced around the visiting room again, feeling himself becoming more nervous by the minute. Put him in a ring with a 200lb opponent and he had little fear. Sit him in a room awaiting his sister's arrival and he wanted to run away.

As if on cue, he saw Karen walk through the doors. She exchanged a few words with the on-duty screw who pointed in Tommy's direction. He saw her glance over and forced a smile, an expression he reciprocated with less effort.

He stood to greet her as she made her way towards him, weaving in between the other tables and their occupants. She was dressed in stirrup pants and a bright pink jacket with shoulder pads over a white shirt. The jacket made her look like Sue Ellen from *Dallas*. Her big, permed hair had changed from its original blonde to auburn. Her skin was pale and she looked like she'd lost weight, but other than that, she looked good.

There was an awkwardness they'd never experienced. Karen seemed unsure.

"Hi, Tommy."

"Hi." All this time and that was his greeting? "Please, take a seat," gesturing to the empty chair opposite him.

They sat at the same time, Karen placing her jewel-encrusted black bag on the floor beside her. She glanced up at Tommy but only held eye contact intermittently. They sat in silence for a few seconds, the discomfort rising until:

"Good journey?"

"It was okay," Karen said. "It's a nice day out, so no bother really."

"That's good," Tommy replied.

A few more silent beats passed.

"How's Dad?"

"He's okay," she said. "Keeping busy. Business is going well, so he and mam are working all the time. Can't complain, I suppose."

"I like your hair, Kaz," Tommy said absentmindedly, struggling to keep the conversation going.

"Thank you, I fancied a change. It was a bit of a whim actually…"

"Why didn't you come and see me?" Tommy blurted out. He

hadn't intended to, but the words just seemed to come from nowhere.

Karen looked shocked and confused, as though searching for the right answer. "I don't know," she replied quietly. "I honestly don't know."

"I've missed you, sis" Tommy said earnestly. "I could have used you early on."

"I know. I just didn't know what to say, especially after… well, you know."

Tommy nodded, "How are you bearing up now?"

"Okay, I suppose. I've been seeing a psychologist to try and sort it all out in my head. And the doctor gave me some tablets to help me sleep… still have nightmares."

"You seeing anyone?" Tommy asked and then immediately regretted his thoughtless approach. "Sorry. None of my business."

She smiled lazily. "No, it's okay. I am, actually. We don't live together or anything like that. I like my own space and he respects that.'

"Fair enough. You working?" he asked, desperate to shift the subject away.

"Ah, you know. This and that, nothing major but it pays the bills."

"What pays the bills?"

"My work."

"I know, I mean, what work?"

"C&A… and other things."

"What other thing?"

"Some other time, Tommy," she said avoiding eye contact, avoiding the issue.

"I'm sorry, Kaz. Not doing well, am I? I don't mean to push. I'm sorry for a lot of things."

Her eyes moistened. "You have nothing to be sorry for. It wasn't your fault. It was mine. I should have listened to you all those years ago. I should have locked up earlier. I should have taken those self-defense classes Mam was always on about… shoulda, woulda, coulda – the list is endless."

He smiled with gratitude at Karen's words, feeling some sense of closure more than a year after that night. The more time distanced him from those events, the more he viewed it as a time that took his and Karen's lives in a new direction. Not the one they'd wanted, but the one they've been given. And they had to adapt and survive and do everything they had done and were doing to continue to overcome it and evolve.

"What's it like in here, then?" Karen asked.

"Ah, ya know. Every day is pretty much the same – wake up, have breakfast, association, dinner, association, tea, association, bed."

"Plenty of sleep and play time then… no different than when you were at home," she joked.

"Aye," Tommy replied. "Only in here you don't have to tidy up after yourself and sleeping is more like being dead only without the commitment."

Karen smiled. Her eyes lit up and, in that moment, he saw the sister he loved and had missed.

"So, what's happening in the world, sis? We get the newspaper and TV, but they restrict what we can watch. Anything particularly exciting?"

"There's this new puzzle thing called a Rubik's Cube, which is basically a square block with colours on it and you have to get each side all the same colour… impossible. A big volcano exploded in America, killed loads of people. Errr… there's this serial killer who's been murdering lots of people over there too... I don't know... lots of stuff."

Tommy smiled back, "Never mind, I was just curious. So, Alan and Faye... how are they doing?"

"Okay. Alan is, well... Alan. Doing his dodgy deals, getting money from God-knows-where. And Faye, she's now working behind a bar in town. Following in our parents' footsteps, senior manager I think. To be honest, I don't see them that much now that I don't live there."

Tommy shuffled forward in his seat, "I didn't know you'd moved out?"

Karen's cheeks flushed, surprised, "About a year ago now. Just after you were sent here. I couldn't stay there anymore, Tommy. Everywhere I looked I saw..."

She looked past him, into the distance, before re-focusing.

"I had to get out. Mam and Tom helped me find somewhere near town. Sorry, I thought you knew."

Tommy shook his head, "No, but I understand."

She held his gaze for the few moments before turning to look around the room, squirming in her seat.

"What?"

Her eyes were moist when she turned back to him, "I don't know how to tell you," she said, feeling her heart break. She knew his would. Of all the places to have to-

"I always asked your dad to tell you, but he said he could never work out the best way..."

"Let me know what?" He was getting a nauseous sensation in his stomach he hadn't experienced since the day his mam had died. "What's happened?"

"It's not what happened, it's what *is* happening right now.

You, being in here, when you should be out there... with your son."

The words hung in the air, waiting for Tommy to fully comprehend them.

"*My son?*" Tommy asked, more to himself than to Karen. "When... w-I mean, *who?*"

"Remember Susan Bullock? The girl you were seeing before... here? Her."

Tommy slumped back into his chair, winded.

"Your son, Tommy. A little boy called Daniel."

"Daniel," he repeated quietly, his eyes beginning to fill. He let them well up to the point where they were ready to flow down his face before quickly wiping them on the sleeve of his shirt and glancing at the screws, then the inmates. No one had seen.

"How old is he?" he asked, his voice breaking slightly.

"Five months," she said with her first genuine smile. "And he's gorgeous, Tommy. Looks just like you. Big blue eyes and that charming smile."

Tommy ran his hands through his hair, caught between wanting to laugh with excitement and shout out in anger. He felt the opposite of how he had felt when he'd found out his mother was dying. He suddenly wanted to race over to the guard and shake him, begging to be let out of here. He knew it would never happen. But that only made the pull of his desire stronger.

"Do you have a picture?" he asked.

"Sorry, not with me. I wasn't expecting to tell you today. Just seeing you sat here, looking alone... I thought you needed to know so you could see you have something to look forward to when you get out."

"You think Susan'll let me see him?" he asked. "A criminal?

Don't be stupid, Kaz, that'll never happen," he spat.

"He's not with her," she fired back. "He lives with us. Susan gave him up, didn't want him. Smackhead. She came to the pub after you were locked up and told us she was pregnant and that it was yours. She said she didn't want to keep him and what would we do to persuade her otherwise. Your dad mortgaged the pub to raise money for it. She had him, was paid and gave him to us. She's never even bothered to see him. Probably can't even remember she had him. Was a wrong 'un that one, Tommy."

"Jesus, she sold ou- my son?!" he said incredulously.

He could understand why Susan would have wanted nothing more to do with him after his arrest, especially if she'd known she was pregnant. There was no love lost between them in that respect, yet he couldn't help but wonder what could have happened that meant her own flesh and blood – *his* flesh and blood – would become less important than a quick fix. Tommy regained his composure.

"He lives at the pub?"

"No, he lives with me. My mam is babysitting him. You should see your dad with him, Tommy. Dotes on him, that one. And don't worry, I've kept my relationship with George separate on purpose. Daniel's my prime concern and George understands. The only man who should be in his life is you and as long as I have breath in my body that's the way it'll stay."

Tommy smiled. "George, eh?" he said with a smile.

"Yes," she couldn't help but break a smile saying his name: "George."

"I'm happy for you, Kaz, I truly am. And thank you for telling me that, it means a lot."

"Well, given the bombshell I just dropped it seemed only right you know that your son is safe and only has family in his life."

The bell sounded.

Karen reached over the table and took hold of his hands, "I'm sorry you had to find out like this – in here – but I wouldn't forgive myself if you'd found out later. I don't want you to be angry or sad, I want you to be happy knowing you have a little boy who looks just like you and who'll be waiting for you when you get out. So you'll look after yourself in here."

Tommy squeezed his sister's hands tightly before standing up, "Bring a photo next time. If you want to come up again, that is."

Karen rose from her seat.

"Of course I will. I'll come back soon. Sorry I didn't come before. I was scared and nervous and didn't know if you'd be happy to see me. But Daniel has helped me, Tommy. He helped me find light after what happened and gave me a purpose, someone to look after like you looked after me."

He nodded. One of the guards gestured for him to begin filing out of the room.

He fell in line with the others and looked back one last time to see Karen walking out. As he made his way back to his cell, he realised that nothing he'd endured so far was anywhere close to the suffering he now felt. Not anguish at what the world had done to him, but anger at where his actions had led him. It was something else to keep him awake that night and many others.

Act Three

1980s

"Whatever doesn't kill me makes me stronger!"

Runaway Train

Chapter Ten

1982
HMP Frankland,
Brasside

Mark Chapman was laughing as he struggled to free himself from Tommy's headlock

"Get off me, ya fuckin' idiot,"

"Don't let him out 'til he says, Tom," Andy Ross shouted from the bench.

"Tell me who she is and I'll let you go, Chappy," Tommy said, pressing and twisting the knuckles of a clenched fist into the top of his head.

"Ow, that fucking hurts. You daft bastard," Mark said, grabbing a fold of Tommy's thigh skin between his fingers and pinching hard.

Tommy quickly released his grip and pushed him away with a friendly shove, before rubbing at his thigh, "You fucking nipped me…" his voice broke into laughter. "I've fought men in the ring bigger than the ones who used to shag your mam and you beat me with the puff's death grip?"

Andy was chuckling as he stood up to jostle his friend.

Chappy was still rubbing the top of his sore head. "Chappy, what have we told you?" he said, pointing over the group of men lifting weights on the opposite side of the yard. "No nipping. You'll turn on those big bastards over there."

"Fuck off, ya big flamer" Chappy said, shoving him back gently.

"So," Tommy said. "What's her name? Seriously."

Chappy smiled a wry smile. "She's called Mary. I was seeing her before I was banged up… didn't think she would speak to me again but she started writing to me and said she wants to come and visit."

"Mary," Tommy said sadly. "That's a good name." He felt his heart swell as he inhaled, his thoughts drifting back to his mother and the huge smile she always had upon seeing him.

Given his circumstances, Tommy considered himself fortunate to have met such honorable men. Chappy was originally from Durham and was serving a life-sentence for the murder of his wife and her lover. Tommy noticed this prison seemed to have a thing for crimes of passion.

Andy came from Redcar and was serving a nine-year sentence for armed robbery. Tommy had always thought he didn't look like a bank robber. He had a baby face and a smile that seemed to stretch from ear to ear, not the grizzled, weary look one imagined a serial thief would have.

Between the two of them and Charlie, Tommy thought life could have been a lot worse for him, especially given the reputation he appeared to have preceding him. It was good to know he had loyal men watching his back. After all, if you didn't have loyalty, you had nothing worth a damn inside.

The cold wind blowing through the yard quickly dispelled his reminiscences. As the three of them made their way towards the door to go back inside, Tommy spotted Charlie sitting on a bench alone. He looked lost in thought, his gaze directed towards the horizon as though trying to focus on something distant. It was a 'prison look' that wasn't out of place in here, but Charlie was a mate.

"I'll catch you lot up," Tommy said, waving them off as he headed in Charlie's direction.

"What's up, old man?" he asked sitting down beside him. "You're here but your mind's somewhere else."

"Yeah," he said. He didn't break his focus.

"Anything I can help with?"

"Not unless you can turn back time or teleport me out of this fuckin' place," he snapped, before gesturing apologetically to Tommy, with outstretched palms to the sky.

Tommy wasn't offended, "Well, in the absence of being able to do that… unless it's in one of those books you keep giving me."

No reaction.

"Seriously, what's up mate?"

Charlie handed Tommy the letter grasped in his left hand. Un-crumpling it, he pulled it from the envelope and scanned the contents; he glanced at Charlie while skimming: still no movement. He re-read the last few lines before folding the letter and placing it back in the envelope.

"I'm so sorry, Charlie. Did you know?"

"That she was sick? Yeah I knew," he said despondently, wiping at his eyes. "Gill used to visit me at first, every weekend. Like clockwork she was, always punctual. Lovely visits they were too. We'd talk about the old days, she'd tell me what she'd been up to and what was going on in the world… truly lovely."

He took the letter from Tommy, his grip tightening as he continued.

"But then she fell ill and the visits became less often until she couldn't manage it. She rang me a few months ago saying she was going into a hospice, Conrad House, and that she loved me and was glad I couldn't see her. She wanted me to remember her as she used to be. That was the last I heard until I got that letter."

"My mam was in Conrad House," Tommy stated. "It's a good place, she'll have been well looked after." He placed a hand on Charlie's shoulder, almost trying to make the grip on the letter loosen and help him relax.

Charlie turned to him, "You never said your mam had cancer."

"It never came up. And to be honest, I never like talking about her, not like that. I like to think of her as young and beautiful, not ravaged and dying."

"I get that," Charlie said with a nod. "Sorry, Magpie."

"Nothing to be sorry about, my mate."

"Listen, Gill and I had drifted apart long before she died. She visited me and we had a laugh, but after I was sent down she wanted to move on with her life. I was angry at first. So *angry*. But as time went by, I understood she needed to do that... she couldn't wait around for me. We had no kids, she was still young and I was going to be in here for a long time. But I loved her and I'm just sorry I never got the chance to tell her I was sorry for fuckin' up her life by fuckin' up mine."

"I can't even guess how you must feel right now," Tommy said. "Just know that I'm here for you, like you've been for me."

"I know, cheers mate."

Tommy saw the remaining few prisoners heading back into the cellblock as the alarm sounded the end of their 45 minutes as free men. Once the courtyard was empty, he always felt a sense of loneliness wrap itself around him like an uncomfortable blanket. He couldn't imagine he would ever get used to it and wasn't certain he wanted to. They stood up and headed for the door. Their pace was slow, hands in pockets, eyes to the ground.

Charlie pulled on Tommy's arm, indicating for them to stop.

"Listen to me for a minute, I want to tell you something. Break the pattern of history. Don't be like me, getting letters about loved ones who've passed away whilst you were rotting in some jail cell," he said.

He held Tommy's arms by his side, his grip tightened.

"Don't be told where to stand, what to do, what to think. Don't wait for people to keep empty promises – remember it's always up to you to take what you need. Nobody is going to give it to you. You have to claim the power to change your own destiny."

There was a look in his eyes, an expression on his face that Tommy hadn't seen before. They'd had serious chats, but this was... *intense.*

"You need to be willing to risk everything you have for all that matters. Get yourself in the mindset that everything comes with a price, but that if you're willing to pay it, then you'll get what you want. Life hits hard, Magpie. It hits harder than any of us will ever be able to, even you. So don't hit harder, just keep going. Keep moving forward and you'll be fine."

"Charlie, is everything okay? What's...?"

Charlie gripped him by the shoulders. "Just promise me you'll remember what I just told you."

"I promise," Tommy said, gripping his friend in a similar manner. "Now, come on, old man. Let's get inside and prepare ourselves for the culinary delights awaiting us."

Charlie smiled, looking up to the clouds, "Lord, please hold me back from such temptation."

As they made their way inside, Tommy heard a noise overhead and looked up to see an unkindness of ravens swooping over the prison and perching themselves along one of the turrets.

Their calls and squawks echoed in the expanse of overcast sky, leaving Tommy with a foreboding feeling as the metal door back into HMP Frankland slammed shut behind him.

"To the last, I will grapple with thee... from Hell's heart, I stab at thee! For hate's sake, I spit my last breath at thee!"

Star Trek 2 – The Wrath of Khan

Chapter Eleven

1984
HMP Frankland,
Brasside

"Anyone for another cuppa?" Tommy asked to the group. Charlie, Chappy and Andy all shook their heads.

"Fuck ya's then," Tommy smiled, as he poured some hot water into his cup and gently teased the teabag in it.

It had become a regular Thursday afternoon thing for them to all meet up at Tommy's cell for a cuppa and a few joints. The screws generally left them alone as did other prisoners, aside from the odd one who would drift past and try and engage Tommy in conversation as though having spoken to him gave them immediate standing in the prison.

"Ah, ya fucker," Andy announced, throwing his cards down on the table. "You cheating bastard, Chappy."

"*What?* I beat you fair and square, ya daft twat!" he replied as he swept up his cigarette winnings. "When are you gonna learn? I am the master whereas you are simply the apprentice."

"Master this," Andy retorted, flicking him the bird.

"Gentlemen," Tommy interjected. "Now-now. Andy, everyone knows you're shit at cards; Chappy, stop winding him up."

"Yes, boss," he replied with a pretend salute as he stood up.

"Fuck you," Andy said with a laugh.

Tommy had just sat down next to Charlie who was busy shuffling the cards for another game when John Donnelly appeared in the cell doorway. Tall and slim with the build of a long distance runner, he was eight years into a 14-year stretch for murder. Tommy always had time for John. He was taking an Open University degree in English Literature and was hoping to take a law degree, ambitions Tommy admired. Even in here, you could better yourself. All you had to do was want it.

He always made Tommy smile when he'd tell of how the press got it all wrong whenever they reported his crime in the media.

"They always say I shot my wife's boyfriend when I found them shagging and that he was a Freemason."

"And he wasn't a Freemason?" Tommy had asked him once.

"Of course he was," had come the reply. "I just didn't shoot him. Fuckin' stabbed him 27 times."

He stood in the doorway looking agitated, bouncing from foot to foot. "You guys need to see this. Someone just tried to shoot President Reagan."

They all rose simultaneously and headed in unison to the recreation hall where there was already a congregation around it. In prison, you were insulated from events in the outside world, so major news stories tended to get everyone excited.

"… minutes ago at the Washington Hilton Hotel when shots were fired at President Reagan. Here you see the President coming out now. You just have to watch… don't know if we can hear this or not…"

Five shots rang out on the footage, apparently recorded earlier that afternoon. Tommy saw multiple agents bundle the president into his car whilst others wrestled the unknown assailant to the ground. Lying immediately in front of the skirmish were three people prone on the floor, one was definitely alive as he was moving, but the others Tommy couldn't tell.

"… he was a young, white male… one, two, three persons on the ground. Brady, Jim Brady the White House Press Secretary is the one closest to the camera…"

Everyone in the room was silent. A bit of shoulder-nudging was going on to get a better view of the screen. Even the guards were transfixed.

"Come on, lads," Tommy announced. "Let's get back to the game. Even the president can't keep me from my cuppa."

They all laughed and headed back the way they had come. Charlie reshuffled the cards while the rest of them sat down. They had just started their first hand when Chappy called for their attention.

"Heads up, lads," he announced from his position by the door. "The Osmonds are on their way over."

"Oh, for fuck's sake," Tommy stated. "This is going to be fuckin' cold before I get chance to drink it." He stood and looked in the direction Chappy was indicating.

The Osmonds was Chappy's derogatory term for the brothers heading their way. Phil, Stuart, John and Peter Armstrong had been sent to Frankland four months ago and were looking at life for armed robbery. Chappy had given them the nickname because they all had long, dark, immaculate shoulder-length hair and slight overbites giving them a goofy expression. Tommy knew they worked for Jack Hudson and thought it was most likely they got nicked committing a robbery on his instruction. He also knew they would still be loyal to him. Tommy appreciated that, even though he thought they were a pack of knobheads.

"Oh look, it's the long-haired lovers from Liverpool," Tommy said loud enough for them to hear.

"You're a funny fucker aren't you, Myers?" Stuart Armstrong said with a growl.

"Gee, I've never heard that before," he replied sarcastically. "This better be important… my brew's getting cold. And we're busy." He indicated towards the deck of cards laid out on the table.

"I can see that, I just don't give a shite."

"Well, in that case, what can I do for you?" Tommy asked, cradling his cup of tea between his hands like a precious object.

"I've got a message from Jack Hudson."

"Would you like me to read it out for you?"

Armstrong stepped forward, his brothers remaining behind him like obedient lap dogs, awaiting instruction. "You know, I should just fuckin' knock you out, ya cheeky little fucker. I don't know why he even fuckin' bothers with you. Everyone knows he hates you. The only reason he shows you any respect at all is 'cause he knows ya dad. You can guarantee that once he croaks, you'll be top of his shit list."

"That's fascinating, and when that day arrives we shall definitely see. But until, then I'll ask again, *what the fuck do you want?*"

"Hudson wants to meet with you."

"To talk about what?" Tommy asked.

"I don't know. That was the message, I've passed it on."

Tommy waited for a moment, watching them and exaggerating a shrug. "Well, what do you want, a Blue Peter badge? Trot on."

Stuart smirked and began to walk away. Phil and John

followed him whilst Peter stepped forward, jabbing his finger in Tommy's face. "You'll fuckin' get it one day, you smug prick."

Tommy closed the distance between them. "Point your finger at me again and I'll fuckin' bite it off."

Peter took a few steps back, his face flushing in embarrassment at his obvious intimidation. He quickly broke Tommy's gaze and hurried to catch up to his brothers.

Charlie moved up behind Tommy and clasped a hand on his shoulder. "You okay, Magpie?"

"I'm good, Charlie."

"What do you think that's all about?" he asked with concern in his voice.

Tommy paused. "I'm not sure,"

"You never told me Hudson knew your dad?" Charlie said.

"Yeah, they grew up together. I wouldn't say they were best mates, but I think they got on well when they were young. Dad ended up distancing himself when Hudson got into the whole 'I think I'm a gangster' business. Didn't want his family exposed to it all I suppose. He'd talk about him over dinner and tell us stories of what they used to get up to when they were kids. He's not a gangster, he's just a bully with an enormous set of balls."

"Well, just be careful, Magpie," Charlie instructed. "Bully or gangster, he knows a lot o' people in here and out there."

Tommy turned to face him. "Hey, it's me!" he said with his arms outstretched.

"That's what scares me," Charlie replied wryly.

* * *

Tommy woke just before dawn. He remained motionless on his thin foam mattress and stared up at the ceiling where a thin sliver of pre-dawn daylight was visible. He watched it grow slowly wider, indicating an abstract passing of time.

He let Armstrong's message roll around his head. Jack Hudson had tried to do Tommy over twice since he'd been banged up. Once by Rooney and then another time by some second-rate, hard man wannabe called Damien Peck who'd tried to shiv Tommy in the shower only to end up with a broken nose and two broken ribs. Tommy had been warned if he caused any more trouble he would be upgraded to Cat A status. Cat A meant he would be considered a threat to the public and his security conditions would be beefed up, meaning an end to weekly catch-ups with the boys and the freedom he currently enjoyed, though he used the word freedom subjectively.

He couldn't imagine Hudson wanted to chat to him about his injured henchmen, but as to what it might concern Tommy was at a loss to guess. He knew one thing though: he wasn't going to spend his life in prison. Once his sentence was up, he was going to be out and stay out. He would stay out for his family – for his son.

He'd die before he'd end up in the nick again.

All good things, he thought to himself.

All good things.

"Don't push it! Don't push it or I'll give you a war you won't believe. Let it go. Let it go!"

First Blood

Chapter Twelve

HMP Frankland,
Brasside

Jack Hudson looked every inch the businessman. Dark blue suit, purple tie and shoes polished to within an inch of their existence, his appearance belied his actual occupation. Business was something he dealt with on a daily basis, but most people would classify drug-trading, prostitution and loan-sharking as criminal rather than *business*.

He stood and smiled as Tommy walked into the visiting area. His slicked back, black hair and dark brown eyes made him look more like a predator than a friendly acquaintance. Tommy thought it just made him look smarmy.

"Tom, how are things?" Jack said in his clipped, London accent as he held out his hand.

Tommy stared at it for a moment, uncertain whether to show defiance at refusing to take it, or courtesy at accepting the conciliatory gesture. He opted for the latter.

"Jack," he acknowledged. "And it's Tommy, not Tom. My dad's Tom." He held Jack's grip slightly longer than was comfortable, wanting his visitor to know he held no sway over him in this place.

"Right," Jack replied, sitting down the moment Tommy released his hand. Tommy knew Jack wasn't in the least bit intimidated by him, but then Tommy wanted him to know that neither was he.

"So, to what do I owe this dubious honour?"

"Your dad always said you were a direct kind of guy," Jack said with a chuckle that made Tommy's skin crawl. "So... I have a business proposition for you."

Tommy laughed louder than he intended. "*Seriously?* Why on earth would I accept a job from *you?* You tried to have me killed twice."

"Tommy... *Tommy...* I didn't want you killed, just taught... a lesson. I realise now that I went about it all wrong. I should have made this visit back then. You have to understand Eric was a friend of mine. His death came as a bit of a blow."

"Your *friend* was a rapist who got what he deserved. I'm sorry Jack, but I don't feel bad about Eric Doyle. Not one bit. He ruined my sister's life and mine simply by being a fuckin' nonce."

"Nonce is a little harsh," Jack said.

"You think?" Tommy replied. "He used to perv over Karen when she was still at school, leching over her like a dog on heat. Given the opportunity, he would have probably raped her then. So yes, nonce is pretty on the money."

Jack held his hands out, submissive. "Tommy, I didn't come here to fight, I came here to talk. Let's put the past behind us and look to the future. Your future, when you're out of here."

Tommy looked at him suspiciously. "I'm all ears."

"Okay, I was thinking that once you've done your time you should come and work for me. You've already proved you can handle yourself and I know you're a quick study, so why not put those talents to good use on the outside and take up a position with me?"

Tommy smiled. "You know Shakespeare, Jack?"

"A bit," he answered, slightly confused. "Why?"

"Brutus and Casca are both honourable men... who killed Caesar?"

"Your point?" Jack demanded with a smirk.

"My point is that I don't trust you. And without that, there's nothing to build a relationship on."

"A relationship? Why, Tommy Myers... are you proposing to me?"

"You know exactly what I mean," Tommy chastised. "Therefore, I appreciate your kind offer but, regretfully, I'll have to decline."

Jack held his smile longer than natural. He finally nodded and leaned across the table, clasping his hands in front of him. "Clever bastard aren't you? Is that how you've been spending your time in here? Expanding your brain?"

"Well, there's not much else to do. I thought I'd educate myself so that, when I get out of here, I can start up a business of my own."

"Doing what *exactly*?"

Tommy gave a knowing smile. "I haven't quite decided yet."

"I see," Jack said. "Well, if you'll allow me to give you a small piece of advice: when you get out and if – and I emphasise *if* – the opportunity arises for you to start up a business, whatever it may be, make certain you have yourself surrounded by people who'll steer you right. Don't make the mistake of getting into businesses you don't understand or can't control. It can make you look weak... vulnerable... stupid. And you can upset certain people if you make the wrong deal, speak to the wrong person, make the wrong turn.... you understand?"

"I understand," Tommy replied, having maintained his smile throughout Jack's diatribe.

"Excellent," Jack said with excessive enthusiasm. He stood up and held out his hand. "Until we meet again, young Tom."

Tommy slowly rose from his chair, hiding his irritation at Jack's repeated shortening of his name. He took his hand and shook it forcefully, tightening his grip with every shake.

"Appreciate the visit, Jack," Tommy said before releasing his hand.

"You're welcome," came the reply. "You look after yourself here. It'd be terrible if something happened."

As Jack left the visiting room, Tommy was seething at the threat just made.

He was still feeling indignant when he returned to his cell and lay down on his bed. Even the sudden pull of tiredness failed to quell the anger he felt.

The gauntlet had been thrown: Jack Hudson had made it clear. He was in charge.

But he didn't know Tommy Myers.

"It lies to her. It tells her things only a child can understand. It has been using her to restrain the others. To her, it simply is another child. To us, it is The Beast."

Poltergeist

Chapter Thirteen

HMP Frankland,
Brasside

Tommy stared at the sombre clouds in the distance as he sat on the bench in the recreation area. It was the rarest of occasions that he sat by himself, Andy, Charlie and Chappy having yet to arrive. He thought it was unusual, but paid it little mind.

His view on either side consisted of red-brick buildings whose only purpose seemed to be to shield all human life from the sun. Being able to look out and see that the world still turned on its axis allowed Tommy to believe this wouldn't always be a way of life for him. Gazing about his surroundings, he noted the faces of all the men in the yard. Each of them here for different crimes, all of them wishing they'd taken an alternate path.

He considered how much he'd changed. Being in prison was somewhere he had never imagined in his darkest dreams he would end up. But life breaks in mysterious ways and here he was, doing time for killing a man who hadn't been deserving of existence.

Being here, a man had to adapt in order to survive. Tommy knew he was already different to the amateur boxer who'd arrived. He had known the moment he'd walked through the doors that he would need a different skillset to keep him going in the face of adversity. He had known the moment he'd found out he had a son that he had to survive if he wanted to be part of his life. And he would.

Self-preservation is the driving force behind all human beings. Tommy had always known that but had seen it as a tangible reality in prison, a conceit that drove the men in here to dream up honour, bravery, strength and integrity. They were the only currency that had any worth in prison and ironically, were nearly always bullshit.

Men in prison had to believe such things because without that belief, they would be as vulnerable as that lone gazelle on the plains of Africa, ripe pickings for a predator.

Tommy was determined to be different, not only for himself but for his son. He wouldn't let what he had done define him.

He knew he'd need work once he was released, especially if he wanted to provide for Daniel. He also knew it wouldn't be easy to come by as no one particularly wanted to employ an ex-criminal. He'd need to choose his path – whatever that was. If that idiot Jack Hudson could do it, so could Tommy Myers. Only he would do it better. He wouldn't be the bullyboy that Hudson was, who ruled those around him with fear and intimidation. Tommy's mam had always said you attracted more flies with honey than vinegar.

He had all he needed right here. The law books he'd consumed had given him insight he'd been ignorant of before, with Charlie himself being a steady voice in this madness around him. Dave had already taught him how to fight with his body a long time ago. Charlie had been teaching him how to fight with his mind. If he used them well, Tommy knew he could really achieve something exceptional.

He remembered a line from Bram Stoker's *Dracula* as he stood to stretch his legs.

'*The strength of the vampire is that no one will believe in him.*'

As he slowly made his way around the perimeter, he failed to notice the four men walking towards him.

Before he knew what was happening, Tommy felt himself being pulled backwards so hard he stumbled to the floor.

He looked up – the Armstrong brothers were forming a circle. "Watch your step, Myers. You're prone to hurt yourself," Peter said.

Tommy rubbed the dirt from the palms of his hands and stood, noting the positions and posture of the men around him. "I thought you lot normally had a cappella practice at this time of day."

"See, there's that *funny fucker* attitude that's going to get you into trouble, Myers."

"So that's why you're all here," Tommy said casually. "To provide the trouble."

"Got it in one. Now you can walk out of here or be carried out. In the words of the family you're so fond of using to take the piss out of us, I'm leaving it all up to you."

"Amusing," Tommy replied as he swung a fist at Peter's face. He managed to dodge it, the blow striking him on the right shoulder instead. Stuart moved in and lashed out with a backhand sweep of his right arm but Tommy ducked and had it behind Stuart's back into a hammerlock before he knew it. He punched him in the head with his right a few times before pushing him away.

Peter came at him again, swinging big haymakers – none connected. Tommy bobbed and weaved until he saw an opening and landed a solid series of jabs to his face before knocking him out with an uppercut to his jaw. John jumped over him, charging at Tommy with a knife, screaming in rage. Tommy blocked a slash of the knife with his elbow and followed through to with a whack to the side of John's face. Wobbling and dazed, he slashed out at Tommy, catching along the side of his ribs.

Tommy moved to intercept but Phil grabbed him from behind, sinking a choke hold on him and squeezed hard. Tommy strained, resisted, reached up and grabbed two of Phil's fingers, pulling them in a direction opposite to the one they were designed to go. He heard a satisfying snap and felt the hold slip enough for him to writhe free. He spun around and hit Phil twice, hard. He watched his eyes slowly roll into the back of his head and then focus again.

John prepared to charge at Tommy a second time, the knife held down by his side. He noted Tommy taking a few steps back and stared at him, puzzled at his expression until he heard the charge of footsteps behind him and realised that whatever they had been intending to achieve today, their time was now up.

Two guards grabbed John and pushed him to the ground, kicking the knife out of his hand and forcing his arms up behind his back.

Tommy looked at the three brothers littered around him on the floor and let out a huge sigh as he dropped to his knees. A guard raced up and grabbed him, pulling him to his feet but with slightly less force than they'd used to push John to the ground. Tommy considered whether they'd seen it all and knew he'd defended himself and not been the instigator.

Either way, there'd be consequences. *Fucking Jack Hudson.* He didn't need to be a genius to know he was behind it for turning down his offer.

Jack would learn Tommy Myers was a new breed of criminal. One he would never would see coming.

Because of that shit in the yard, I ended up in segregation 'for my own good'.

Yeah, right. Being alone was fine, I was used to that in Frankland as all the cells were single occupancy. The smell of shit, crappy food and sounds of screaming smackheads were something else. That said, it's amazing what you can get used to when you have to.

I look back now and think that, despite the fact that it made me fuckin' hate Hudson even more, being in segregation gave me time to reflect and focus my thoughts on what I was going to do when I was out of here. Granted it was annoying being 'on the book' and having my every move, visit and visitor recorded, but I knew it was only temporary. They weren't going to keep me in there forever and didn't, letting me out about two months later. I still got to see the lads when I was in there, just with a few more conditions. It also turned out that the reason they hadn't been in the yard that day was because they'd been involved in an altercation in the canteen with a few of Hudson's other boys already. I was never able to prove it, but it was all a distraction so he could ensure I was alone when Donnie fuckin' Osmond and his brothers jumped me.

People still came to see me, my dad, Donna and Alan. Faye had moved to London and was working for a solicitor. I asked Dad to pass on my regards. I hoped I'd get the chance to visit her one day with my son. Karen came every other month, telling me stories of Daniel and how fast he was growing up. Looking at Karen as she spoke made me realise that Eric's death had given her some closure. Justice if you will. Not legal justice and certainly not emotional justice, but something that made her believe he had suffered for what he did that night.

If he'd have been banged up for it he would have suffered, that's for sure. He would have probably found himself on the receiving end of the odd cock or two and it would have had some sort of symmetry attached to it – the hunter becomes the hunted type of thing. But that wouldn't have made Karen feel any better whereas his death gave her the finality of knowing she would never have to bump into him in the pub or walk past him in the street or, as it turned out, never do it to anyone else again.

Being in segregation was a pain in the arse, but it gave me perspective. I was able to see my entire future stretched out before me like a road that had yet to be built. I had new determination; I knew where I was going.

"If my calculations are correct, when this baby hits 88 miles per hour... you're gonna see some serious shit."

Back to the Future

Chapter Fourteen

1985
HMP Frankland,
Brasside

"Your solicitor's on the phone, Myers," the guard shouted into Tommy's cell.

Tommy closed the book he was reading slowly and placed it beside him on the bed. Since being in prison, Tommy's favourite book was *The Count of Monte Cristo*. He found Alexandre Dumas's book about wrongful imprisonment cathartic, imbuing him with a sense of kinship to Edmond Dantès and his dual desire to be reunited with his loved ones and quest for vengeance.

Tommy made his way to the payphone, the one source of access to the outside world any of them had. He scanned over some of the graffiti scribbled in amongst random telephone numbers. Apparently the warden gave really good blowjobs and could be contacted on 0191 7523781.

"Hello."

"Tommy?" the man's voice at the other end asked. "It's Robert Grayson."

"Aye, what's up?"

"Well, some new information has come to light I thought you might be interested in. I'm not entirely certain how it can benefit you in regards to your sentence – if at all – but I'm going to do all I can."

"Well, what is it?" Tommy asked more impatiently than he intended.

"It turns out that Eric Doyle was a more prolific rapist than we knew. Two women have come forward with information that he assaulted them in the early seventies."

Tommy took a moment to process the information... "Hang on a minute. You're telling me that he'd raped other women *before* Karen? And this is only coming to light now *because*...?"

"...because for whatever reason – fear, intimidation by Doyle, humiliation – the women felt they couldn't come forward before. It turns out one of them overheard someone talking in their local about Doyle having been killed and she knew nothing about it. Once she knew he was dead, she went to the police which encouraged the other woman to come forward."

Tommy put his head back against the wall and uttered a quiet, 'For fucks sake,' clenching his empty hand in frustration. "Hudson."

"Jack Hudson?" Robert asked.

"Jack Hudson," Tommy repeated. "It's all down to him. Doyle was his man. He must have known what he'd done to those other women, or at the very least had a fucking idea. Yet he did nothing and just kept a rapist on his payroll. A rapist who ruined my sister's life and pretty much fucked up mine. So basically, if they'd come forward sooner then I wouldn't be in here because he wouldn't have been at the pub that night because he would have been BEHIND FUCKING BARS!"

"Tommy, calm down. I can appreciate you're upset-"

"Upset? That's a fucking understatement."

"Okay, I know it is. The point is that now we know, we can push for an early release."

"I only have just over a year left. What's the fucking point?"

"The point," Robert stressed. "Is that it's a year earlier. Granted, you did stab a man but with your good behaviour – and I use the word loosely I might add – I'm confident we can have you out by the end of the month."

"Allegedly," Tommy said.

"Excuse me?"

"I allegedly stabbed him. Beat him definitely... allegedly stabbed him."

"Of course. Okay then, I'll be in touch. You stay out of trouble, Tommy."

"I can do that," he replied with as much confidence as he could muster.

There hadn't been any real trouble since that incident with the Armstrongs. They had stayed out of his way once they'd been released from the health centre and no one else had really attempted to challenge him. He tried never to be smug or arrogant and had no intention of his reputation ever being someone who was thought of as a bully, but if it allowed him to finally be left in peace, then he could live with it.

There was a click at the other end of the line before the dialing tone sounded. Tommy placed the phone back on its receiver and turned to lean back against the wall. The sounds of institutionalised life around him blended away, leaving him in a vacuum of thought. He dared not hope that Robert's call was anything other than a shot in the dark, a million-to-one chance. If he put too much belief in the fact that something could come of it, Tommy had a suspicion he would end up bitterly disappointed.

Seven years had already passed, during which time Tommy had not so much given up hope that something would occur to lessen his sentence but had chosen to accept reality.

He'd been found guilty of killing a man, whatever the reason, whatever the facts.

But hope was seeing there was light despite the darkness.

He just prayed it wasn't some bastard with a torch.

"Going in one more round when you don't think you can –
that's what makes all the difference in your life."

Rocky IV

Chapter Fifteen

South Shields,
Northumberland

Karen felt irritated. She knew she shouldn't. The news that
Tommy was being released should have been the only thing
occupying her mind. After almost a decade, her brother, the
man who had sacrificed so much for her, would be a free man.
Yet her feelings of elation were tainted with guilt she couldn't
shake. It had haunted her for so long.

The thin walls of the flat allowing the raucous laughter to filter
in from next door weren't helping her mood. She was worried
it would wake Daniel. She knew it was more than frustration.

Karen knew how her family perceived her. How others saw
her. Closed, distant, curt and temperamental. They would put
it down to *the incident* as it was known nowadays. In part that
was true. Eric Doyle had taken everything from her in a matter
of minutes. She'd been made to feel worthless, as though she
didn't deserve to be in the world. The scars of that night had
been left to fester in her soul, scabs that she would pick at
from time to time if she needed to feel something real; anger or
pain, it didn't matter. She'd tried therapy, support groups and
medication, all of which had helped put her back together, but it
was almost as though some instructions had remained missing,

taken that night. Edges of her were jagged and sharp, elements of her being that she now intended to use against those who would do harm. Eric had tried to make her his possession and, after that night, the remodelling of her soul had continued in his absence. So she had channelled that, forging it into something else; something unexpected. And in doing so, she had experienced an epiphany.

Karen had realised that the most popular game in life is playing the victim. It's a bestseller, with so many people now playing it that they've probably forgotten how it started or that it's even a game.

Early on, Karen had found something seductive about the victim game, taking comfort in its repetitive familiarity and routine. Attending therapy had only served to reinforce this sense of being the victim, as so many others around her were playing it too in one form or another. But then, one day, she had decided she didn't want to play anymore. Throwing her toys out of the pram, Karen decided that she would check the rulebook. And sure enough, there was no rule stating that you had to adopt that role.

So she decided that instead, she would approach it simply as a game. *The game*: maintain clarity about how you got there and why you were playing and you could know yourself. Know your enemy.

As time had gone by, she had begun to feel strong to the point of arrogance. She began walking friends home so she could return alone, mentally daring anyone to try to touch her again. She had wanted someone to approach her to show them that never again would she be the vulnerable one – never again would she be the one who trembled in fear at a man's touch. She would become the dominant one, the one calling the shots. And she had in many ways. Sexually, she was never submissive, always certain of what she wanted and how she would get it. If they weren't up to the task then they were gone and she found another one. Granted, she had taken some risks on occasion, looking for that next thrill greater than the last and temporarily becoming ignorant of consequences, but as time had gone by, she had learnt to temper that recklessness with confidence and assurance.

Conversely, it had allowed her to embrace the darker side of her soul and the more aggressive facet of her nature. When it came to Daniel, she was loving and caring. When it came to her girls, she was loyal and rewarding. To those she loved and cared about, she would protect them no matter what the cost.

When it came to business, she was ruthless and merciless. She intended to show this world of men that women were not there to service their every whim, to be at their beck and call. She intended to show them the day of the woman was coming and that they could be just as successful, ambitious and powerful as them. Life had made her that way. She knew everyone had two sides to their personality; dark and light, good and evil. She had just never given it that much thought and couldn't work out if she'd always been a bad person pretending to be good, or now a good person trying to be bad. Either way, it didn't matter. Jekyll was asleep and Hyde was awake.

She would show Newcastle what a woman was really capable of.

"Can I borrow your towel for a sec? My car just hit a water buffalo."

Fletch

Chapter Sixteen

1985
South Shields,
Northumberland

"So, in front of the entire planet, Nik Kershaw tripped over as he started Don Quixote," Alan said. "Biggest music event this year… shit – of any year – and he nearly falls over. I was gutted for 'im. Wasn't as bad as Simon Le Bon hitting a duff note during *A View to a Kill*, mind. But Queen… they were something else."

Tommy's brother was giving him a brief rundown of everything eventful he had missed while banged up. He didn't have the heart to tell him to go easy as he'd only been out for four hours. Or to tell him that they'd had access to a television and newspapers in the nick for fear of disappointing him. He was so enthused in his storytelling that Tommy decided to let him be. He actually found it calming, especially after the persistently similar conversations day after day he'd experienced in prison. It was nice to have someone talking about something other than cigarettes, weed and how they weren't supposed to be in prison (everyone's innocent in there, you know?).

Strictly speaking, Tommy hadn't been inside for that long for so much to have changed, yet he knew he'd have to find his place in society again – he didn't like having to catch up with it all.

Puffball skirts and political strife, that seemed to sum up the decade. Northumberland had become a cliché – a huge boiling pot of people and headlines. Football was the thing; Jack Charlton resigning as manager of Newcastle United just as the season had begun and some lad called Paul Gascoigne from Gateshead who had had a fantastic debut for the Magpies against QPR. Apparently, he was going to be even bigger than Charlton.

It was the fashion that had Tommy most confused and fascinated. It seemed to have gone from conservative to being all about size, colour and experimentation as far as he could tell: yellow mascara, hair to the sky and shoulder pads not far behind. The men were just as flamboyant with their mullet hairstyles, jewellery and Ray-Bans. His brother had brought him a pair of blue Converse Chucks upon his release, telling him that they would help him to blend back in. He'd accepted them graciously and actually found them comfortable but decided to avoid taking the full plunge by tight rolling his jeans and buying a gold chain as thick as his middle finger.

Arranging to meet Daniel was the first thing he'd done on his release. Turning onto a non-descript street, he had slowly made his way up the slight incline towards number 151 and noted the pebble-dashed properties either side of him. It wasn't a bad part of South Shields and had always had a canny reputation as far as Tommy could recall, but already he wanted better for his son. He felt slight guilt at his internal criticism of his sister's living arrangements, knowing that Karen had done her best for him and that he had no right to even comment on the location or flat she lived in – she was doing what she could, doing her best.

But fucking hell, he couldn't remember having ever been so nervous, in the ring or in prison. The anxiety he had felt in the pit of his stomach as he'd knocked on the door had been almost overwhelming. Combined with the emotions of being free – something he hadn't yet got used to – he had struggled to put one foot in front of the other.

Tommy hadn't been certain what to expected. His son, having never set eyes on his father since birth, was unlikely to run into his outstretched arms like an episode of *The Waltons*, though he hadn't quite been prepared for him to scream and wrench his body in what looked to Tommy like terror.

The visit hadn't lasted long with Daniel so upset. Karen had told him to give it time, that it would be a big shock for someone to meet a long-estranged parent when they were an adult, never mind six year-old child. He completely understood but still felt upset that it hadn't gone like he'd foolishly imagined it would.

As he'd sat there on Karen's walnut-coloured leather lounger and looked around her front room, trying to understand why someone would want to sit on a bean bag chair, his mind drifted towards his brother telling him about the sequel to Star Wars on the way here. Alan had taken great glee in spoiling the ending for him by telling him that Darth Vader was Luke Skywalker's father. Tommy had laughed incredulously, thinking it was insane and also perhaps the cleverest twist ever in a science fiction film, yet now he could relate in the most bizarre way. A father estranged from his son, tells him the truth about his identity and ends up getting screamed at. That was pretty much the experience Tommy'd just had, only without the lightsabers and heavy breathing.

After saying his goodbyes to Karen, he'd met back up with Alan and they'd headed off towards The Horse & Hammer. This time his anxiety had been at returning to the scene of a crime mixed with excitement at being home for the first time in what seemed like forever.

He paused for a few moments at the double-doors leading into the pub, the nauseous feeling returning with a vengeance.

He could hear the muted sounds of Midge Ure's *If I Was* mixed with the chatter of merry punters resonating out towards the both of them.

"You okay, bro?" Alan asked.

Tommy nodded. "Aye, just getting my head right, that's all. Been a long time…"

"I know," Alan agreed. "Come on. Fortune favours the brave."

"Or the foolish," Tommy replied with a laugh.

They both pushed through the doors simultaneously and stepped inside. Tommy was immediately hit with a tidal wave of noise and colour, the contrast of it all compared to being in prison almost causing sensory overload. He saw his dad and Donna stood amongst a crowd of people he recognised from his childhood and beyond. All were smiling, some were clapping and a few were stepping forward to greet him. Midge Ure was replaced by Howard Jones' *Like to Get to Know You Well*, the irony of the song not lost on Tommy as he moved forward to shake the outstretched hands of those around him. The applause for him got so loud it almost drowned out the music.

Alan smiled and gave him a solid pat on the back before making his way to the bar, parting people politely as he went and shaking the occasional hand. Tommy couldn't help but smile at seeing his brother being the social raconteur. Once upon a time, Tommy Myers would have regaled the audience with tales of his boxing triumphs and battles to the death. Now all he had were stories of a road less travelled and what you could get in prison for a packet of 20s.

Shaking away his self-pity, he headed in the same direction as his brother, nodding and smiling at people as he went. If all he currently had were tales of woe, Tommy decided that he would use tonight to make new stories.

"...So she's screaming *I'm so fucking wet, give it to me now, I'm dripping!* but I shook my head and said there's no way you're getting my umbrella."

The series of tables roared with laughter at Alan's joke, some spitting out their alcohol uncontrollably. Tommy's dad and Donna were wiping away tears, some of their other friends were commenting the joke was, 'fuckin' classic' and stating, 'nice one, mate'.

Tommy rose from the table and headed towards the bar, still chuckling to himself while Alan immediately launched into another joke about an Eskimo having broken down in the North Pole.

A blue, cigarette-created haze hung over the entire pub like an independent atmosphere. Tommy was still trying to take in the various fashions that seemed to be coexisting, spotting people obviously modeling themselves on Madonna and Michael Jackson. He returned a smile to a girl as he moved past her, commenting on how nice she looked. Her bolero-style jacket, tutu, gloves and tights made a nice change to the prison-issue blues he was used to seeing, though he was struggling to understand the guy with a black derby hat and long braids that had colourful ribbons tied onto the ends. Having not quite caught up with popular culture, he wasn't certain if he dressed after someone famous or was just making a unique fashion statement.

He signalled to the barman – someone he didn't recognise – and took some money out of his pocket as his dad sidled up beside him.

"I'll get this," he said, putting his hand over Tommy's and directing it back towards his jeans. "You don't pay for any drinks tonight."

Tommy put the five-pound note back in his pocket. "Thanks, Dad."

"You're welcome, young 'un. I'm just glad we're all together."

"Well… almost all, eh?" Tommy replied.

"I know," recognising his reference to Karen's absence. "She's just never really been able to feel comfortable being here after… well, you know… I take the blame for that."

Tommy clapped him on the back. "You can't think like that, Dad. We didn't know… no one did. He was a serial rapist for fuck's sake – a real fucking predator. It's not like it was going to be on his application."

"I know," his dad said nodding. "But still, I have to live with that. Dave and I should have seen it."

Tommy's face lit up at the mention of his old boxing coach. "Dave! Where is the old bastard? I thought he'd be here."

"I invited him, but he said he was busy. Said he'd catch up with you tomorrow."

Tom leaned over the bar as the barman arrived in front of them. "Another round for us all, Phil. Can you get one of the girls to bring it over?"

The barman nodded and began preparing their drinks. Tommy's dad reached into this pocket and removed a packet of Bensons, offering one to Tommy before lighting his own.

"Already had enough things in my life wanting to kill me. Don't need to willingly start something that'll add to the list."

"Fair enough. So," his words came accompanied by a plume of exhaled smoke. "Work? What ya gonna do?"

Tommy shrugged. "I don't know yet. I've got a few ideas, but no one's going to be banging at my door to offer me work are they?"

"How do ya fancy the door here? We could use a new lad and it's not like I need to check you out, is it?"

"I don't know, Dad. Might draw a bit of attention, having your son on the door right after he's been released from prison."

Tom laughed. "I couldn't give a fuck what it draws. I'll employ whoever I want. Anyway, could use someone I can trust. Big drug problem around here now."

"In here?" Tommy asked.

"In here, down there," his dad said, pointing in the direction of Newcastle. "Everywhere. You missed it all being inside, what with that, AIDS and Third World poverty, everything's going to Hell in a hand basket."

Tommy frowned, this time in surprise. "AIDS?"

"Apparently, it's going to kill us all," his dad replied nonchalantly. "Some disease killing all the gays and smackheads. Making people scared to shake a bloke's hand in case he's a fuckin' gay. Bollocks to that, I say. I'll shake whoever's hand I want. I don't believe for a minute you can catch it from touching someone. That fuckin' iceberg advert doesn't help, mind."

"I know what it is, Dad. We had newspapers in prison, you know. I'm just surprised you do."

"Cheeky wee shite," his dad mocked. "I know stuff, an' all. All fuckin' scaremongering if you ask me. Anyway, enough of that shit... job? Interested?"

Tommy took note of Phil with the tray of drinks destined for their set of tables and stepped away from the bar. He considered his options, which currently consisted of very little and nothing.

"All right, Dad. Cheers!"

"Cheers yourself. You're doing me a favour and I can't lie, it'll be good having you around here again. Which reminds me – do you have a place to stay yet?"

Tommy shook his head. "Not yet. I was just going to bunk down with Alan."

"Nah, stay here, Tommy. Spare room's all made up in case you said yes anyway."

His dad moved away and kissed Donna on the cheek as he sat back down next to her, leaving Tommy smiling to himself. He'd only been out for eight hours and already he had a job, a roof over his head, had met his son and was having a good laugh. The first genuine good laugh he'd had in a long time. His mind drifted towards Chappy and the lads still in Frankland. He knew some of them were up for release in the next few months and let himself hope they could all be together again one day. He realised in that moment how much he actually missed prison and the world it had provided him. He'd taken what could have been nothing and made something out of it. Every choice he had made in there about how to survive had been his and his alone. He would have to start the whole process again now... find a new way of surviving in what was now a brave new world indeed.

As he sat back down and began listening to Alan rolling over into another joke, he let those thoughts clear from his head for a bit. All that could wait, but it was an exciting prospect.

"Well, if you're waitin' for a woman to make up her mind, you may have a long wait."

Pale Rider

Chapter Sixteen

South Shields,
Northumberland

Tommy stamped his feet in an effort to keep warm. His dad had always said if you move your feet, your body will take care of itself.

He hadn't remembered it being this cold last night, but then that was probably a combination of alcohol and the desire to stay in one place. As the others left he'd turned down invites to accompany them to The Ritzy or Dobsons. He felt comfortable drinking in his old home, but wasn't quite certain he would feel the same in town, at least not yet. Instead he'd said his goodbyes, staggered up the stairs and collapsed onto the bed in the spare room, finding himself lulled to sleep by familiar creaks in the floorboards and smells from the bar.

The remainder of the day was spent relaxing and just taking in his newfound freedom. He felt no inclination to rush anything, except the opportunity to do nothing. Aside from speaking to Karen and asking about Daniel, he'd read newspapers, watched television and dozed. There was no shame in that, he thought. By the time the evening arrived, he found himself excited about working, his dad advising him that, providing he didn't kill anyone on the door, they would sort out something more official later. One black bomber jacket, white shirt and black tie with matching trousers later and he was smarter than he'd ever been in his entire life.

It was quiet for a Saturday night, Tommy had been informed by his fellow doorman, Ronnie Gilding. He was told it usually started off like this but would be bouncing in a few hours. Ronnie went into the dos and don'ts of working on the door and how to handle himself if 'shit gets out of hand'.

"Judge the punters on two things:" Ronnie was saying. "Whether they look like they're going to be difficult or ill-suited to the other people in the pub. And I mean the women as well. Some of them can be a fuckin' nightmare… scary shit to watch them fight, Tommy. Scratching at eyes and pulling out fuckin' hair… nasty stuff. And don't get me started on the toilets, fuckin' hell. Tammies 'round the U bend, fuckin' bottles in the cistern. At least bloke's bogs only smell of piss."

Tommy laughed. He hadn't the heart to tell him he was an ex-con and that bloke's toilets smelling of piss was nothing compared to some of the things he'd witnessed. His dad had either not mentioned his son was just out of prison or Ronnie was playing it down. Either way, Tommy was already enjoying his company.

"Served in the Green Howards during Operation Banner in '69 and saw some fucked-up shit, yet the things you find in the female toilets is enough to make me want to be back in Northern Ireland!"

Tommy had already learnt that, aside from serving in the army, he had a wife called Noëlle, two kids and a dog called Buster. Ronnie said he'd lived in the north of England all his life and intended to die here.

"The troubles really brought it home to me. I thought I would die never seeing my family again. I swore that once I was home, I was staying put. Terrible things happened over there… we did terrible things. No wonder they don't like us."

Ronnie excused himself to visit the toilet, giving Tommy the opportunity to step away from the door and gaze up at the night sky. Not until that moment had he realised how much he'd missed something so simple as the ability to look up and see the stars.

Standing here now, Tommy felt small, insignificant. It was humbling to learn that your place in the universe wasn't quite what you thought it was. He took a deep breath, savouring the night air and the way it chilled his throat and lungs. He felt alive... renewed. He had a second chance to do things differently. It wouldn't be the difference he had imagined growing up, but it would still be one people would talk about.

Just like his dad had always told him.

* * *

Tommy barged through the crowd of people at the bar. Ronnie was behind him and moving off to the right so that they could flank the two young lads currently engaged in what was about to either become a passionate kiss or one hell of a fight. Neither of them looked old enough to be in the pub, but Tommy let that one slide. He must have missed it by letting them in and made a mental note to be more observant in the future.

Ronnie marched up behind the one on Tommy's right and grabbed him by the collar, firmly but carefully so as not to knock him off balance. As he was moved away, Tommy intercepted the other one who he'd noticed was about to use the opportunity of his challenger's exposure as a chance to get in a cheap shot.

"Woah, I don't think so, sunshine," Tommy announced.

The lad struggled against Tommy's grip on his arm. "Get the fuck off me, man."

Tommy spun him round and pulled him in close. "Come on, fella. I think you've had enough tonight," Tommy shouted above the sound of Kenny Loggins claiming his feet were loose.

"Do you know who the fuck I am?" the lad shouted back at Tommy as he was being marched out of the pub.

"Nope," Tommy replied. "Should I?"

"Yes, you fuckin' should. My dad owns this city, this pub and will own your fuckin' arse when he finds out about this."

"*Is that a fact?*" asked Tommy. "I'll quake in my boots later on."

The lad broke free, holding his arms out, gesturing a plea to Tommy's good nature. "Come on, mate. Let's call it quits, bygones be bygones, and all that shit."

Tommy shook his head and held the door open. "Not tonight."

"Always one big lad who thinks he's harder than the rest, isn't there?" the lad said to the people stood near him. "Your mam obviously didn't teach you manners, big fella. Probably couldn't speak with all those dicks in her mouth."

Some of the customers nearby smiled but they were strained, partly because of the poor taste of the joke and mainly because a number of them knew who Tommy was and what had happened to Mary Myers.

Tommy immediately felt a red mist descend. The people in the bar could practically *see* it. He charged at the lad and punched him hard in the face, his nose exploding on impact. He staggered back and stumbled out the doors to the street.

"I'd fuckin' go on home if I was you, mate."

The lad wiped his blood on the sleeve of his shirt and made a wobbly attempt at standing up, achieving his goal on a second attempt.

"You've just made a big fuckin' mistake," he said in a stunned tone. "My dad'll fuckin' kill you, you *cunt*."

Tommy tried to smile as he chastised himself internally for

his stupidity. "Well, it won't be the first mistake I've made and certainly not the last. Go on, fuck off home. There's a good boy." Tommy waved him away as he spoke.

The lad smiled at Tommy before spitting a mouthful of blood onto the floor, staggering off up the road.

Ronnie appeared with his friend in tow, clapping him on the shoulders in a friendly manner and telling him to sod off elsewhere, an instruction he obliged without any fuss.

Tommy looked at him incredulously. "How come I got the twat and you got the three-toed sloth?"

"Luck?" Ronnie replied. "You okay?"

"Yeah," Tommy said with an accompanying nod. "I'm fine, just didn't want any trouble, that's all."

"Don't be too hard on yourself, he had it coming. This town has gone to shit in the last few years. There's drugs everywhere, every dickhead in Newcastle wanting to have a go every time they have a few beers, Jack Hudson thinking he rules the roost and some mysterious person called Ren trying to strong arm him by buying out the prozzies. Can't get away from it, even in here. Used to be a decent boozer this, now every weekend there's some fuckin' idiot smacked up to the eyeballs or dealing speed. Feel sorry for your dad and Donna. Usually throw out four or five a night, tonight's been an exception. Must be because of you, new face and all."

Tommy smiled as Ronnie continued. "Yup, there'll be a gang war if we're not careful. And on top of that, there's all these blokes getting their bollocks handed to them… literally."

"What do ya mean?"

"I mean, physically *handed to them*," Ronnie emphasised with his cupped hands and a chuckle. "Someone is cutting off bloke's nuts and leaving them to bleed to death. None have, but I bet they're falsettos for life."

"Jesus," Tommy replied.

"Jesus, indeed. Don't feel too sorry for them, Frankland. Turns out all of them have a history of beating on women, prostitutes mostly, but still..." He let the words hang in the air for a moment before concluding. "Someone obviously has a bit of a hard on for men who beat women."

"Frankland?" Tommy quizzed.

"Yeah, thought you needed a nickname. I know where you've been, lad. Everyone around here does. You were a legend before you got nicked. Used to come and watch you fight and a good fighter you were, too. Wasn't right what happened to you and your sister, but no one felt bad for that nonce Eric. Did the world a favour, but it is what it is... what happened to you happened and, for that, you need a good fuckin' nickname,"

Tommy smiled at Ronnie's compliment. "Fair enough. Not Frankland, though. Bad enough I've been there, I don't want other people knowing it."

"All right then... Frank."

Tommy wrinkled up his brow as he thought about it. "All right, I'll have that," he said with a nod.

"Oh, and by the way, the lad whose face you just remodeled?" Ronnie said heading back inside the pub.

"Yeah?"

"That was Jack Hudson's son."

Tommy grimaced at Ronnie's revelation as the door slowly closed in front of him.

"Bollocks," was Tommy's only response.

"I enjoy being afraid of Russia. It's a harmless fear, but it makes America feel better, Russia gets an inflated sense of national worth from our paranoia."

St. Elmo's Fire

Chapter Seventeen

Newcastle Upon Tyne,
Tyne and Wear

Patrick Campbell felt irritated. The girl he'd just had sex with had been just how he liked them; young, pretty and fresh. Yet she'd been sedate, boring and uninteresting, cumulating in nothing more than a complete waste of money. His usual provider of girls had never let him down before, so he felt angry and disappointed that they now seemed to be getting him girls who didn't know what they were doing. What's the fucking point in that? A girl of her age should have been lapping up the opportunity to fuck someone like him, a bloke who knew what he was doing, not a young lad who would rather stick it in a sock for a posh wank than in a pretty girl. She'd taken the beating better than he'd expected mind. Instead of wanting to leave afterwards she'd stayed, though he thought that was more out of fear than desire.

He rose from the chair to admire his 6 foot 2 inch naked self in the full-length mirror hanging on the wall opposite. He had a broad chest, thick neck and big arms – three areas of his body he was proud of. He should be, given the amount of time he'd spent at the gym building them. His dark hair would have touched his collar had he been wearing clothes, slightly longer than regulation but something he rarely got pulled up on.

He turned to the side and noted the slight bow to his shoulders that was a result of only training the vanity spots of his body. He knew it was there and regularly cursed himself for having been so foolish as to not train his back in the same fashion as his other areas to maintain symmetry and balance. He knew no one would ever mention it out loud to him though, a little like his hair, not unless they wanted to be fucked up and charged with child abuse, whether they'd committed it or not.

He was one of Newcastle's best detectives, had worked hard to get to where he was and would be damned if he was going to put with up the lowlifes that seemed to surround him on a daily basis. If he could get them banged up, he would.

"Frame 'em, fuck 'em," was the motto he often sported to his friends.

He walked over to the bed and began kicking the mattress to rouse the pretty blonde girl lying prone across it, the duvet barely covering her naked body. The bruises would fade. It wasn't as though he'd cut her or anything.

"Oi," he shouted. "Wake the fuck up and get the fuck out."

She stirred slowly, prompting him to reach over and pull her up by her hair. "I said wake the fuck up and *fuck off!*"

She immediately started screaming as he dragged her across the floor by the hair and unlocked the front door to his apartment.

"What the fuck you doing? I've got nee clobber on!" She grabbed and scratched at his hand but was unable to loosen his grip. He threw her out onto the landing and marched back over to the bed, picking up her strewn clothes and shoes as he went. He strode back to where she cowered in the entrance, desperately trying to cover her modesty with both hands.

He threw her belongings at her along with £50, laughing as she bent down slowly out of embarrassment and pain.

"Here ya go. Take your money. Don't make me tell you to fuck off again."

"You're nowt but a fuckin' bastard, ya know that?" the girl said through the tears now freely flowing down her face and mixing with her makeup.

"Aw, look at that. Didn't know I'd been shagging a member of Kiss," he said in a mocking tone. "You were shite anyway, love."

He slammed the door in her face and smiled as he heard her burst into tears, the sound of her sobs rising and falling with the movement of picking up her clothes and money. He knelt down in front of the glass table in the living room and finished off the lines of coke he'd racked up last night: always a few for the morning. He wiped his nose and realised he hadn't even bothered to get her name as he made his way back into the bedroom and opened his wardrobe. He began humming Madonna's *Like a Virgin* as he selected a dark blue suit and matching tie. He had a big meeting with his boss today, not his constabulary boss who thought he ran the town, his actual boss who *knew* he ran Newcastle. It was his job to make certain that all the old fuckers and up-and-comers who thought they were still or could be in the game were put in their rightful places.

There were no business takeovers, hits or deals without Jack Hudson's say so. Patrick's job was to make certain it stayed that way. Step out of line or attempt to grow a brain and you ended up on the extremely shitty end of a long stick that stretched all the way to prison or the Tyne. It was always their choice. He always hoped someone would pick the Tyne option just so he could enjoy drowning some dozy fucker. Jack always said it was bad for business when your ex-employees started floating up the Tyne and appearing in Teesside.

One day perhaps, he thought to himself… one day.

So, I'm out of prison and things are going well... better than expected, actually.

I thought it would take me a while to decide the path I wished to walk, especially given that most of them were illegal in nature. It wasn't that I was afraid of becoming a criminal, more that I was afraid of the effect it would have on those around me

Would I have done it differently knowing what I know now? Hard to say. You have to appreciate that there was more at stake than my just remaining out of prison. It was a moral thing, an ethical decision. My mam always used to tell me that you don't do things because someone would do it for you, you do it because it's the right thing to do.

And anyway, I was actually enjoying the slightly less legal side of life! I was no Scarface or Al Capone, but just a few weeks out and I have a few deals going on, a few little earners here and there for squaring out some lowlifes. Mind you, one of those went completely tits up due to Alan being a dumb arse. Didn't realise my brother knew so many 'interesting' people and slowly learnt that he was quite the entrepreneur.

Why would I decide to turn to crime immediately after being released from prison? Well, that's the million dollar question isn't it? You can look at all the textbooks you like and read all the studies: genetics, routine activity theory, strain theory. All of them will throw a different reason at you for why someone becomes a criminal and all can be debated at length and leisure (other than the Gage theory; Phineas Gage was a railworker who suffered an accident when a tamping iron was blasted through his frontal cortex, permanently altering his behaviour. I have never been shot in the head, so that one's out... for the moment).

But the one reason people often fail to notice is the most obvious one – that I became a criminal because I could.

As a boxer I was on the path to fame and fortune. Then I

was in prison. Once I was a free man, I had few prospects and little enthusiasm for anything resembling the rat race. I knew that I could make more money if I once again turned my talents to what I knew I could do. It had worked for boxing, so why couldn't it work for something else? And I now had a son. He didn't know me, but I was working on it. I wanted a life for us both. Crime wasn't intended to be a permanent solution to my financial situation, just a temporary one. If I earned enough money, I could take him away and we could start somewhere fresh. Without the baggage that stuck to us like shit living in Newcastle. That was my plan, but you know what they say about best laid plans...

Anyway, the 'tits up' scenario: he comes to me one night saying that one of his mates had gotten into a bit of bother when he was out in Middlesbrough one night. Got into an altercation with some lad and had the shit kicked out of him. He asked Alan if he knew anyone who could sort the lad out for him. Alan tells me and Ronnie that the lad lives in Brotton... the arse end of nowhere. I couldn't even find it on a fuckin' map. And it's so far outside Middlesbrough you wonder how anyone could be fucked travelling there and back on a night out.

But anyway, we drive to Brotton, which takes the best part of an hour with Alan in the back of the car. We pull up outside this house that looks the same as all the others in the street. Reminds me of Karen's house actually, all pebble-dashed and Stepford Wives. We sit there, balaclavas on, asking Alan if it's the right house.

"Yeah, definitely, he said it was 183. 183, I'm certain."

We get out the car and pull the balaclavas down, sending Alan to the driver's seat for a quick getaway. We're sneaking around the back, trying to work out which house it is. We find the one we want and we're through the gate, up the garden path and to the back door. Ronnie says he can see there's someone in. We saw a fire burning through the split in the curtains.

We nod to each other, I kick in the door and we both steam in.

"Come here you little fucker. We've got a message for you."

A little old man and his wife are sat on the sofa, cups of tea now flying out of their hands, she's screaming, he's screaming, the fuckin' dog starts barking and Alan, the dozy bastard has sent us to the wrong house.

Turns out it was the one next-door, 185. He couldn't read the writing properly.

We offer sincere apologies, slowly back out of the house and I go and slap my brother for being such a prick.

My first foray into the world of crime and we nearly give an old fella and his missus a heart attack.

Lesson – don't listen to your brother.

We went back the following week to finally sort it out and the house was empty. Little fucker had heard all the commotion in 183 and moved out.

"Sorry I'm late. There was this big problem... and I'm late because of it."

The Sure Thing

Chapter Eighteen

South Shields,
South Tyneside

Six weeks had passed and Tommy was finally beginning to feel like a citizen of the world rather than a lodger. He'd seen Daniel on two more occasions since his release and, though he was a long way off having his son embracing him with open arms, he was no longer hysterical in his presence which Tommy saw as a huge step forward.

He had also made it his personal mission to clean up The Horse & Hammer. He'd been on the course for his doorman's license and filled out the requisite forms, but still had a few weeks to go before he was legal. His dad had no problem with him staying on the doors providing he stayed out of trouble, the response being that if he could break Jack Hudson's son's nose on his first night, then it couldn't get any worse. He was yet to see any retribution for that, but he knew it would be coming. Especially now he was interfering with Jack's drug trade.

Tommy knew Jack supplied most of it in and around Newcastle. It wasn't just the Horse that faced difficulties, every pub and club was experiencing the same issues. It was most prevalent in town where people would go and watch *The Tube* on City Road, pop over to the Egypt Cottage and Rose and

Crown in the hope to see one or two celebrities who invariably went there after filming. They'd get tanked up, do some speed or coke and then be off their tits for the remainder of the night.

Tommy had offered some suggestions for the pub his dad had been receptive to. The first was implementing an ID policy at the door, something rarely done before. Ronnie had his grumbles but started to come round when results had begun to manifest. Tommy's logic was that those people willing to show ID and even carry some on them in the first place were less likely to cause trouble. It was a thin argument and one that Tommy knew was flawed on many levels, but it seemed to be paying off. They had caught a few lads in the toilets in pairs who would immediately plead their innocence. Ronnie would say either they were doing Gianluca Vialli or they were preparing to suck each other's dicks, either way they were done for the evening. They would often plumb for the former and be on their way.

Granted, the women were just as bad as the men, but with them always going to the toilet like Noah's Ark it was a little more difficult to challenge them directly. Tommy always thought that women were more subtle than blokes as they had nothing to prove ego-wise.

Another reason for his positive mood was that he had already started making a bit of a name for himself. It had been one thing to be respected inside. Tommy had expected little upon his release, yet word was out that he'd done Hudson's son, was trying to rid the pub of drugs and had an honest but brutal approach to problems. Not that he'd been in many fights, but the few that had occurred he had dealt with swiftly.

Tommy knew that status was like herpes – you either had it or you didn't, but once you got it you had it for life. It was all about your next move, about out-boxing your opponent or die trying. Tommy needed to make certain he didn't let it go to his head.

Get to know and get along with those in the area with power, earn enough to make yourself a legitimate presence but not enough for anyone to start coveting what he had, stay loyal and ultimately he knew that it would pay off. He would be respected for all he had achieved since being released from prison and feared by those who knew what would happen if they tried to take it from him... All he had to have was something worth taking. Cleaning up the pub was a good start. He knew it would rattle Hudson's cage, but he cared little about that. It was making a stand and showing Jack that he wasn't scared of him. The fact it was his family home made it personal though. Jack had grown up with Tommy's dad which made it all the more galling that he'd allowed his dealers to do business in the pub. He could have asked them to avoid it for old time's sake, but Tommy imagined greed had played a part... or power. Show his dad that he owned him and everything around him and it would keep him in line. His mistake had been to overlook his son.

Tommy had already started making a little money, not just from working on the door but through dealing in cigarettes and tobacco. Ronnie said he knew a guy who was looking to shift some contraband he had brought over from Spain and he had given him Tommy's name as someone he could trust. He'd taken up the offer without a second thought, despite hearing Karen's voice in his head reminding him of his responsibility towards his son. It was because of him he was doing it. No one was ever going to offer him a 9-5 job sat behind a desk, were they? He knew how it worked – once an ex-con, always an ex-con.

It was Daniel who was occupying his thoughts as he stood enjoying a cup of tea on the door of the pub when he heard someone calling his name from up the street.

"Oi, Myers. Long time no see, ya lunatic."

Tommy narrowed his eyes, filtering out the glaring street-lights. With no recognition forthcoming, he waited until the man was closer before speaking.

"All right? I have to apologise, I've no idea who you are."

"Not surprising, mate," came the stranger's reply. "Been a long time… you'll be pleased to know I don't make jokes about people's mams anymore. Stopped being funny when I lost my own."

Tommy's brain clocked around a few cycles before it stopped at a particular memory.

"Stephen Bennett! Jesus, it's been a fuckin' dog's age mate. How are you? Sorry to hear about your Mam."

"Ah, thanks. Long time ago now. Anyway, welcome back. Glad to be out?"

"Takes a bit of getting used to but I'm getting there," Tommy said. "You coming in?"

"I am indeed, my old mate. It's nice to see someone who has a brain about them on a pub door, not like the usual Neanderthals you get. No offence, mate," Stephen said, pointing to Ronnie.

Ronnie furrowed his brow. "None taken."

Tommy opened the door and ushered his old school friend in along with a few other customers who had arrived behind him.

Ronnie nodded in Stephen's direction. "So, who's the clever bastard?"

"Someone I used to know at school. Used to bully me until I smacked him in the face and we became friends… funny how it sometimes happens that way."

Tommy drained the last of his tea and placed the cup on the floor only to find himself almost lying in the road as Alan came bursting out of the doors of the pub, smacking him with them on the back.

"Jesus, Alan!" Tommy shouted. "Watch where you're fuckin' going."

"Sorry, kidda," he replied.

"What's the hurry?"

Alan was almost jumping up and down with excitement. "I've got some news I think you'll be interested in. Something *big*."

"Is this news going to be from a better source than the fuck-up the other week?" Tommy asked.

"Funny," came his response. "For your information, yes it is."

"Well, spit it out then."

"I heard that there's a big score going down at the docks... alcohol, cigarettes, the whole nine yards." Alan paused and cast a glance around the street to ensure no one was close enough to hear. "I say we pay it a visit and steal the fuckin' lot."

"Just us?" Ronnie queried.

"Just us," Alan answered gleefully. "It would be a piece of piss. One of us stays in the car, the other two transfer the stuff over and we're off. No one would ever know we were there... until the morning when they find all their shit gone, that is."

Tommy leaned back against the wall, his face pensive. "When?"

"Tomorrow night," Alan said.

"Whose shit is it?"

Alan hesitated. "Jack Hudson's."

Tommy waited a few beats before smiling. "No guns," he instructed.

"No guns," his brother replied.

"In that case, count me in," Tommy stated. "Ronnie?"

"As it's you asking," he said after thinking for a few moments. "Then yeah, I'm in."

"Nice one," Alan said. "Right then, Popeye and Cloudy, I'll let you both crack on cleaning up the streets."

As his brother disappeared back through the pub doors and into the mixture of Cyndi Lauper and cigarette smoke, Tommy frowned. "Popeye who?"

"The French Connection," Ronnie said with a laugh. "Film about two cops who take down a huge drug-smuggler in New York."

"Ah," Tommy said knowingly. "More like The Geordie Connection."

Ronnie laughed again as he nodded to the couple making their way towards the pub. He held open the door for them, eliciting a smile in return as they passed.

Tommy couldn't help but smile himself. Everything was going perfectly. If tomorrow paid off he would have stuck it to Hudson and the man would have no idea.

"And the check is in the mail, and I love you, and I promise not to come in your mouth..."

To Live and Die in LA

Chapter Nineteen

Newcastle Upon Tyne,
Tyne and Wear

The drive to the Port of Tyne had been uneventful. Traffic had been light, the sky clear. It was only when they'd arrived at their destination that the weather changed, as though sending a message of foreboding. The wind picked up and developed a cold bite as it blew across the Tyne, tingeing the air with a combined smell of oil and seaweed.

Tommy sat in a black Ford Capri nestled between two cargo containers, waiting for Ronnie and Alan who'd gone to scope out the docks and make certain there were no surprises. He fidgeted in his seat, attempting to get comfortable. He knew it was less to do with the car and more to do with the left-hand drive. It had been years since he'd driven, but adding insult to injury Alan had pulled up in a Capri 2.8 Turbo and thought it would be straightforward him just jumping behind the wheel. Tommy had told him he couldn't give a shit that it was a limited edition, had a turbocharger and anti-roll bars in case they got into an accident. Bring back a good old Morris Marina had been a reply that elicited boos from his companions.

Coal was the port's usual export, but everyone in the region knew that it was branching out into bulk and conventional cargo, looking for investors in order to make it into a terminal for rail, cruise and passengers. Tonight, the only import Tommy was interested in was the one that was already docked and waiting to be unloaded. Alan had told him that Hudson wasn't expected to take delivery until tomorrow, so that gave them a good window to liberate some of its contents. He had no intention of being greedy. One thing being inside had taught him was that greed wasn't good. Greed made you so cocky you never saw the shank coming. They only needed to take enough to make a profit, nothing more.

He heard them before he saw them, silently bemoaning their lack of stealth. Alan appeared on Tommy's right before remembering it was a left-hand drive and moved around to the other side.

Tommy shook his head. "Jesus, it's your fuckin' car."

"It's not my car. I borrowed it from someone who stole it from someone else. It's a very layered story. I have yet to decipher its exact origins."

"Whatever," Tommy said. "So, how we looking?"

"Copasetic I think. The container is there, only the one guard patrolling the docks. His rounds take him about half an hour then he spends most of the night in his cabin. Unless we make too much noise or royally fuck up, we're good."

Tommy nodded, his hands gently squeezing the wheel. "Okay then, where do you want me?"

"Our box of tricks is just over there," Alan said pointing in the direction of the container in question. "You back up to it, we'll pick the lock, empty what we can into the boot and then Bob's your uncle."

"Our uncle's name is Reg," Tommy replied with a smile.

"Funny," Alan acknowledged. "Just start the car."

Tommy's eyes grew wide in faux-shock. "Oh, check out the big balls on Alan."

He started the car and slowly idled out of his hiding position. Ronnie and Alan jogged in the same direction, their heads swinging side to side regularly to check for witnesses to their forthcoming infraction of the law.

Tommy noted the container they'd stopped beside and swung the car around, reversing until Alan gestured for him to stop. He turned off the engine and climbed out, popping the boot catch as he went.

"So, do your stuff, Houdini," Alan said, nodding towards the container.

"You're a cheeky bastard, you know that?" Tommy said. "Just because I've been inside, doesn't mean I know how to pick locks."

"I know, I'm just kidding," Alan said with a smile before reaching into his jacket pocket and removing a small black, fabric wallet. He unfolded it and removed two thin implements; one long and pointed, the other the same thickness but bent over at a 90-degree angle at the top making it look a little like a straight hook.

He jointly inserted them into the padlock and rotated them independently of one another, his head cocked to one side as though listening intently. After a few moments there was a click audible enough for Tommy to hear, prompting Alan to remove the picks and place them back into the wallet.

He turned and winked at his brother before lifting the clasp on the padlock and letting it drop to the floor.

"Don't get cocky," Tommy warned.

Ronnie sounded a low grunt of agreement before moving forward and taking hold of the door opposite to Alan. They both nodded in unison to indicate they would pull together. The doors swung open slowly with a low squeak and slight release of pressure as the air temperature within dropped to meet the temperature outside.

Tommy hesitated. He considered that this was the moment when he would go from being a small-time grifter to a professional criminal. He knew in the back of his mind that he was already a criminal, but this would cement it. This was the game-changer. After tonight, he would be earning his money illicitly and illegally and there'd be no going back.

But dreams sometimes end abruptly and try as hard as you might, you cannot keep hold of the threads they dangle in front of you. They coalesce and disperse into the ether as quickly as a whisper and then, though you can still sense something of their original intention, they're gone. That was what his life had been; a dream that had become a nightmare that had morphed into something else.

An opportunity or a reckoning he had yet to decide.

Ronnie shone his torch inside and flicked it around so they could scan the contents. Crates of cigarettes were piled high alongside bottles of Jack Daniels, Bells whisky and Jim Beam bourbon. Tommy nodded at their success in securing what looked to be a huge payload. Alan clapped his hands together and rubbed them in childlike glee before loading the boot with cigarettes.

Tommy glanced over at Ronnie who looked slightly apprehensive. He moved over and stood beside him, scanning the dock as he went to ensure they were still alone.

"You okay, big fella?"

Ronnie swallowed. "Yeah, no worries Frank. I guess the situation just caught me off guard for a second. I mean, it's Jack fuckin' Hudson we're ripping off. Crossing the rubicon here, mate. If he ever found out..."

"He won't find out," Tommy said with as much assurance as he could. "There's only the three of us and Alan's informant who knows and he won't say anything. Besides, Jack'll probably think it's this Ren person I keep hearing mentioned. He's the one trying to fuck up Hudson's life, not us. We're just liberating him of a few belongings to see us on our way. Little earner for us, no big loss for him."

Ronnie looked at him intently, as though seeking confirmation in his eyes for what he'd just heard. Appearing to get it, he smiled before making his way into the container and picking up two crates of whisky.

"Best get crackin' then," he said with renewed enthusiasm.

Tommy joined them and together they began taking what Jack Hudson had thought belonged to him. The wind had picked up again, though with less force than earlier, rubbish and leaves now scattering across the dock, fluttering and quivering instead of circulating in a maelstrom.

Tommy unloaded his crates into the car and shivered, buttoning up his jacket. The boot was already full with the back seat looking crowded.

"Alright lads, that'll do. Quick in and out, that was the plan."

Ronnie and Alan nodded, prompting Tommy to slam shut the boot and climb into the car. Ronnie slid into the back seat beside their cargo whilst Alan re-secured the lock on the crate. No one would know anything had occurred, until they opened it up that is.

By that time, the sun would have risen and they would be far from here.

As he left the port and turned onto Newcastle Road, Tommy Myers allowed himself to take a deep, cleansing breath. His first major steps into the world of crime had been taken.

And it felt good.

"If one receives evil from another, let one not do evil in return."

Enemy Mine

Chapter Twenty

Newcastle Upon Tyne,
Tyne and Wear

Patrick Campbell studied Jack Hudson intently whilst he prepared drinks for them both. Campbell considered him one of Thatcher's clichéd Essex men: entrepreneurial, insurgent and weary of the failed quasi-socialist politics of the post-war decades. He, like many people who voted Conservative for the first time in 1979, was restless for change. He understood it to a certain extent.

Already halfway through the eighties and the decade had pronounced itself as extraordinarily exciting when compared to its predecessor. With the promise of mobile, handheld technology for making phone calls, home entertainment systems and the wearing of seatbelts in cars set to become mandatory, they were living in a time convulsed by a social, cultural and political counter-revolution. It was an ideal opportunity for men like Jack Hudson to capitalise on an already established power base.

The eighties suited him down to the ground; from the violence on the football terraces to the riots on the inner-city streets, Jack Hudson had made certain he was exactly where he needed to be, every single time. He had learnt everything he knew from watching his old man. Ray Hudson had been an all-round nasty bastard. Never one to shy away from a dodgy deal, the odd murder and knocking his wife around, when he'd died, no one had been particularly heartbroken. His wife had remarried almost straight away, using her deceased husband's illicitly earned wealth to carve out a comfortable future for herself, forgetting she had a small boy who needed her love and attention. That child grew up to realise the world only made sense if you forced it to.

By the time his mother Iris had died, Jack was a young man, angry at the world and intent on showing others that the only way to survive was to take what you wanted, answer to no one and ensure that anyone who disagreed with you either fell in line or fell off the radar. What happened to his stepfather remained an unsolved murder, though Patrick didn't need a slide ruler and a pencil to work out what had happened to him.

The more he thought about it, the more Campbell could see how Hudson's current self-professed ownership of Newcastle was inevitable. Now was the time for innovation. Pop music, inspired by the 'anything is possible' attitude of punk and the David Bowies of the world had already changed the way music would forever be made. Wall Street was churning out stockbrokers by the day who believed they could do anything with money that didn't belong to them, a conceit that Campbell could only see biting everyone back in the arse in a few decades. Jack Hudson was thriving in a world that was coarse and reactionary, choosing not to change what existed in their somewhat superficial society but rather to prosper in it. And Patrick Campbell was just fine with that, as it meant he could also take what he wanted. Money, young girls and power were there for him to indulge in. He dared anyone to try to stop them.

Jack Hudson slamming his whisky down on the table broke Campbell's reverie. Its contents splashed over the side of the glass, causing Patrick to jump ever so slightly.

"I want to know who had the fuckin' sack to rip me off and I want to know now," he demanded.

"At this moment we're not sure, Jack. It wasn't professional as they only took what they needed by the looks of it… left the good stuff at the back. But they weren't amateurs either as they got in and out quickly without being seen."

Hudson snarled as he spoke. "Well, it's not fuckin' difficult to not be seen on the docks in the middle of the fuckin' night, is it?"

"I guess not," Patrick agreed in a slightly condescending tone. "The point is, we have no idea who it was. Maybe this Ren person who's been moving into our territory."

"Our?"

"Yours," Patrick conceded. Hudson's dark eyes were trained on him, causing him to feel a prickle of unease at the intense gaze. "We're following up the usual leads, so I'll let you know if we get something."

"Not *if*, sunshine, *when*. That's what I pay you for remember?"

Patrick recognised it as a statement rather than a question. "Of course. You'll be the first to know."

"You're fuckin' right I will!" Hudson spat venomously. "And as for this Ren character, fuck him too! Thinks he can muscle in on my girls, on my businesses and take over. Not gonna happen. I've been doing this for a long time and one thing I've learnt is that you have to squash these up-and-comers immediately before they get a foothold. They're like cockroaches, Patrick. If you don't kill them off, you'll find five more the next time you turn around, all of 'em thinking they got what it takes to be a big shot. So, same as with the dock issue, you find out who it is, you tell me, understood?"

Patrick nodded. "As for Myers, I've had a few of the lads keeping an eye on him. He's made it his mission to clean out the Hammer and he's succeeding. Pretty much lost all your business in there, Jack. Quite a presence is young Thomas."

Hudson sat down and reclined in his leather chair, looking Campbell up and down. "Not easily intimidated that one. Being inside did the opposite of what it does to most blokes. Instead of making him a nonce or fuckin' girl it made him fearless. They all fuckin' loved him apparently. One of those 'loyal and honest' hard men you hear so little about. Killing Eric did wonders for him. Like he needed to be any more difficult to take down. Ever see him fight?"

Patrick shook his head as he grabbed Hudson's glass and poured them another drink. Jack took it with a conciliatory nod and continued.

"He was good…one, tough bastard that Tommy Myers. I think losing his Mam at such a young age did something to him. Hardened him to life's tragedies and challenges. The fight he had the night Eric died was amazing, beating the living shit out of each other they were. Remember 'The War'? The Hagler/ Herns fight? It was like that. From the minute the bell went, they were smacking the shit out of each other. Would have been one of the greats if he hadn't taken the blame for that skank."

Patrick pulled a puzzled expression, but remained silent.

"Come on, Campbell. Everyone knows she killed him. Myers just took the blame. Inseparable those two, even as kids so it was obvious he would take the fall for her. No way he would allow her to go to prison, too honourable. Threw away a promising career for a silly bitch. Can't imagine she was even a good fuck."

Patrick laughed. "A few of the lads dated her and apparently she wasn't. Seems a waste really, to die for that daft slag."

"Indeed," Hudson agreed, smiling thinly. "Well, anyway, He humiliated my son and though he probably deserved it and is a cocky little shit, he's my boy so I want Myers watched until he oversteps the mark, which he will. They always do. And when he does, I'll fuckin' have him. Keep an eye on that brother of his too. He thinks he's a clever bastard and has a big gob."

Campbell finished his drink, placed his glass on the edge of the desk and took Hudson's silence as an indication for him to leave.

As he made his way to the door, he momentarily considered how he had gone from believing in the law to being someone who bent it to suit his own ends. It seemed so long ago he couldn't remember when he had approached the crossroads in his life that had subsequently defined his existence. All he knew was how it felt to him being on the other side of that line,

It felt like fun.

We did a few more jobs after that, different places, different marks. We'd steal money, goods, belongings but never with the intention to hurt anyone. The way I figured it, Jack Hudson had it coming. For too long he'd been lording it over Newcastle, believing it belonged to him. Christ, he probably believed he could command the flow and eddy of the Tyne if needs be. As I saw it, his line of work had brought drugs into my family home, to the very place my son may well spend time with me if everything went the way I would like it to. Eric Doyle had worked for him and had ruined my sister's life… ruined my life. The reason Dad had sacked him in the first place was because of Hudson which he'd seen as a personal slight on his character.

It hadn't mattered that they'd been friends growing up, Dad had insulted him by firing Eric therefore Dad had no longer benefited from his protection. Not that he'd ever paid for it. I think it had been out of loyalty and respect for Mam to be honest. Nor for one second do I think Jack sent Eric over that night to rape Karen, that was all his fuckin' perverse doing. But I couldn't get away from the fact that Jack knew what he had done and had offered no support aside from the odd semi-compassionate statement. And yet despite all of that, I wasn't going to follow his path and be the bully, the ex-con who ruled over people with fear and violence. There was no need for it.

Actually, that's not entirely true. There was this one incident that didn't go as well as I would have liked. Ronnie and I were having a few beers one night in town. Nothing too lively, just a chat and a laugh when we notice this bloke staring over at us. Ronnie's giving him the evil eye, I'm just ignoring him. We finished our drinks and head off to the Metropolitan Bar.

We're walking through Elswick Park and there he is following us, so I tell Ronnie to stop. When he asks why I say that he'll have to walk past us as there is nowhere else for him to go. We stop and turn around and he pauses for a minute and then carries on towards us. As he passed us he said that he was a friend of Jack Hudson's son and that his mates were out to get us for what I did.

I laughed and told him where we were going and that if that was the case, they could meet us there. And sure enough, when we're leaving our little skulker is there with two of his mates. No sign of Jack's lad, but anyway they give us the proverbial 'we're gonna fuck you up' speech and let us believe they've balls big enough to come in a dump truck. I lunge for our little friend whilst Ronnie knocks one of his mates out. The other one starts laying into Ronnie, with some decent punches I have to say. Obviously had a few lessons in his time. Anyway, I grab Skulker, smack him around a bit and grab hold of his ear, telling him if they don't fuck off I'll tear it from his head. He throws a few colourful metaphors at me whilst his mate uses the opportunity to carry on laying into Ronnie. So I begin pulling at his ear and it literally starts coming away from his head. I actually didn't realise ears were so fragile and I've had a few blows to mine over the years. But the fuckin' thing's coming off like peeling wallpaper. He's screaming like a fuckin' girl, I'm yelling for his mate to stop or his friend'll end up with more than a passing resemblance to Vincent Van Gogh. Eventually Ronnie's guy gets the message and I let go of our mutual friend who's virtually crying. They're trying to pick up their unconscious third wheel, he's trying to hold his ear on… it was almost comical. Felt bad afterwards knowing that I'd probably disfigured him for life, but as with all things it seemed like a good idea at the time.

It's not that I'm against violence, on the contrary, I love a good bust up if they deserve it or I'm in a ring. But it sends out the wrong message. Granted, you don't want the police to know you're behind a crime, but you want the public to have at least a feeling, heard a rumour or know someone who knows someone who knows someone… that way you can build the respect without the fear. Never drop your guard, never break the act. I learnt that in prison. Fear and respect aren't necessarily mutually exclusive; you can have both at the same time but it takes work. In this case, it was the people of the North East.

Damn right I wanted to take Newcastle off Jack Hudson. I

wanted to rip it off his fuckin' skin and leave him bleeding in a corner. But these things take time. I needed to be patient and wait for that big score, the one that would really tip the scales and show him who was boss. Trouble was, all the time I was thinking it would be me it was actually someone else. Behind the scenes, there was someone manipulating a lot of things that, at first glance, didn't seem connected, but when I stood back and looked at the big picture it was like seeing a masterpiece for the first time. Not that the end result had been achieved, far from it. But I could see all the little things that had been put into place and realised that it had all been happening right under everyone's nose and no one, including me, had noticed.

I have to say, knowing that there was someone sticking it to Jack Hudson was a satisfying feeling. Not better... subtler. It had been done in such a way that even Jack hadn't realised. You could see how it was going to all play out, how this Ren character was planning to take it all away from him, piece by piece.

Of course, lying dying on a cold, concrete floor does wonders for your ability of hindsight. All I could do was marvel at the skill and brazenness of the whole plan.

All I could do was lie here and consider how I'd been working in parallel with the same objective, yet never appreciated the links.

All I could do, bleeding out in the town that I loved, was think I should have realised sooner.

"The dreams of youth are the regrets of maturity."

Legend

Chapter Twenty-One

Newcastle Upon Tyne,
Tyne and Wear

The lights in the interview room were harsh, reflecting off every surface around Alan Myers. The mushroom-coloured, plasterboard walls gave the room a muted feel, the air thick with stale sweat and disparate souls who'd had lie after lie forced out of them. Alan could feel the tension in the air despite his being alone.

He'd been minding his own business when he'd been arrested making his way back to the Horse & Hammer after an afternoon session in town. It had been the usual fare with lads he'd known for years - a bit of banter and leads on potential jobs. Granted, he'd been a bit drunk but nothing too lary which is why at first he had been a little confused by the arrest. But as the alcohol had worn off and the reality of the situation had dawned on him, he'd realised it was more likely something to do with his and Tommy's extracurricular activities. What was puzzling was how the police could know he had anything to do with anything. Unless one of the lads had ratted them out, but he just couldn't see it. They were afraid of Tommy for a start and he couldn't imagine any one of them would want news getting back that one of them was a grass.

He and Tommy hadn't done any jobs in the last few weeks specifically to avoid drawing attention. The only other person who knew anything was Ronnie and there was no way he would have said anything. Under the intrusive lights in a small room a million scenarios played in his head, allowing doubt to burrow into his mind where it now nestled like a parasite.

At that moment, Patrick Campbell entered the room. He took a few moments to study his guest before closing the door slowly behind him and taking a seat opposite Alan. He paced a manila folder on the table and clasped his hands together, rocking his chair so that it was resting on the two back legs.

Alan began to fidget, noting that his interviewing officer had no pen out to make contemporaneous notes with. He had a funny feeling that the recently introduced Police and Criminal Evidence Act was going to be conveniently absent on this occasion. Certainly a solicitor was. Unable to make direct eye contact with the man sat before him, it was all he could do to not be sick. Campbell's stare was unwavering and intense as though he were trying to read Alan's mind.

"Did you know that the first modern police force was formed in Newcastle in 1836? This particular branch was part of the amalgamation in 1974 when the merger occurred between Northumberland and Durham Constabularies. Durham was actually one of the first county police forces to be set up. Lots of history in this job…lots of details that make you proud to be a Geordie. Did you know that the world's first house to have working light bulbs installed was in Gateshead? Joseph Swan's house; a physicist and chemist."

Alan didn't speak, mostly because he had no idea what to say in response to the detective's unorthodox approach to interrogation.

After a few minutes uncomfortable silence, he returned his chair onto four legs and pulled it forward. When he spoke his voice was soft and welcoming. "Mr. Myers, do you understand why you've been brought here this evening?"

Alan tried to regain some conversational ground. "Apparently for a history lesson."

"No," Campbell replied, his tone suddenly shifting from encouraging to self-assured. "You're here to learn a different lesson."

"Oh aye, and how's that then?" Alan asked, hoping he had intonated enough irreverence at his situation. He was terrified but he had no intention of letting the man before him know if he could help it. He felt as though eyes were locked onto him somewhere behind the one-way glass, watching him, studying him the way a spider does a fly trapped in a web.

Alan cleared his throat and pushed the image out of his mind.

"Do you like chess, Mr. Myers?" Campbell asked.

"Why? Are we about to play?"

"Oh, you've been playing for a while now. You just didn't know it. And you've lost. So this is all going to be about honesty. Just you, me and the truth."

"Did I say chess? I meant draughts. I like draughts," Alan said, trying to deflect his growing anxiety with humour. His mouth was dry and the nauseous feeling was growing more intense. He had to work hard just to meet Campbell's gaze.

"Ah, ah," Campbell said patronisingly. "Remember, we said honesty. To make it easy, I'll start. The robbery at the docks a few weeks ago. You're here to tell me that you know who carried it out."

Alan sat back in his chair, his brow peppered with sweat. "I don't know what you're talking about." He was going for indifference, but was certain he missed it by a long chalk.

"Tut, tut Mr. Myers. Remember the key word here... honesty.

I believe you know who was there that night. I know things, all sorts of things. History, culture…"

"And?" Alan croaked.

"… and people like you," Campbell continued.

"I don't understand," Alan said, blinking frantically.

"I see you. I can always see people like you. You think you have it all worked out, trying every angle to stick it to the man, to the establishment. You feel hard done by because you're way down the social strata and believe life owes you something. And if you can't get it freely, you'll take it from others. You think people like me dance to your tune. Well, I hate to spoil it for you sunshine but you can't play with people like us. You're a little fish in an ocean and I'm fuckin' Jaws."

Alan tried to find words but instead found himself staring stupidly into Campbell's eyes. He waited a few more beats for his accuser to speak again but Campbell remained silent, instead forming a smile so wide Alan could think of nothing but the Cheshire Cat from Alice in Wonderland.

"My apologies," he suddenly announced, his change in demeanor taking Alan from anxious to afraid. "Where are my manners? I'm Detective Campbell and as I said I'm investigating a robbery carried out a few weeks ago. Sources tell me you might be in a prime position to assist in my investigation."

Alan blinked in the face of Campbell's assuredness. "Your 'sources' are mistaken Detective. I'm a local lad, but I don't know of any robberies. I know the area but not much else. Keep my nose clean, or at least I try to."

Patrick Campbell gave a condescending nod and leaned across the table, prompting Alan to shift back instinctively at the gesture.

He felt his face begin to blossom as he bounced the words *calm down* around in his head, over and over again in the hope they would help slow his racing heart.

"A little bird told me you know things," Campbell continued. "That you could help me identify the individual or individuals responsible."

Alan shook his head. "Like I said, I don't know anything."

"Mr. Myers, we both know you're lying. It's in our mutual interests for you to tell me what you know and then we can both go home. Why would you want to protect these people?"

"I don't know what you're talking about," Alan said, feeling himself deflate as though popped with a pin. He made an exaggerated scan of the small interview room. "Aren't I entitled to a solicitor or something?"

Campbell laughed softly. "You're not being charged with anything. We're just talking. Why? Do you need one?"

Alan shook his head. "No, I was just curious. So, what now?"

Campbell studied his suspect intently, noting every facial twitch and tick. He knew Alan was lying, despite not having any actual evidence. It was all supposition and conjecture, a whispered comment here, a late night conversation in the station there. Tommy Myers had a reputation that preceded him, not only because of his promising but short-lived boxing career but also from his time in prison. Blokes who had served time with him all said he was loyal, upstanding and not someone you fucked with unless you had a desire to end up on a ventilator.

In all honesty, Campbell thought Tommy Myers was becoming a bit of an obsession for Jack. Patrick thought he should be focusing on this Ren character who seemed to be slowly infringing on his businesses, but he'd have none of it. Ever since he'd returned from Frankland that day having seen Tommy, he had a suspicion burning inside of him that Myers was going to be trouble.

The man had spent a good part of a decade inside. Hard time like that did a lot to a man, never mind strengthening their

159

resolve. Jack knew that Tommy had become an intractable force who would move for no man, therefore the only course of action would be to implicate him somehow and remove him from the playing field before he became an immovable object. It had been Patrick's idea to bring in the brother. He knew they were close and would never willingly give up Tommy. But Patrick knew it didn't have to be voluntary for them to get what they wanted.

"Okay, Alan. Do you mind if I call you Alan?" Campbell's question was more of a statement. "Well, Alan. I know your brother was involved in the robbery at the docks, I know your brother was involved in the post office job…I know your brother has been involved in quite a few little infractions. I was hoping we could come to some sort of arrangement, you and I about the whole thing, an agreement for which Jack Hudson would be extremely grateful."

Alan was now the one who leaned forward across the desk, his eyes full of anger and hatred whilst his body tried to sustain the bravado. "You think I would roll over on my brother? You don't know the Myers family very well at all, do you? Just to clarify once again, I have no idea what it is you are talking about, but in the event I did I'm not a grass. You've no idea what we've been through, the things that have happened to us. I'm bound to him through more than just blood, he's my role model. My little brother who had the chance to become a boxer, my little brother who served time for taking out a nonce who raped my step-sister, my little brother who endured all of that and came out of prison with the drive and determination to make something of himself. I know about you, Campbell. The whole of Newcastle does, how you're in Hudson's pocket, his lackey. Don't go threatening me with things you can't prove. And on that note, if you've nothing to charge me with then let me the fuck go."

Campbell smiled at Alan Myers, considering how he had managed to not smack him in the face but also admiring his loyalty.

Fucking Myers family are all the same, he thought to himself.

But as far as Campbell was concerned loyalty may well lead to bravery, but bravery led to self-sacrifice.

He held Alan's gaze before speaking. "Well then, I guess we're concluded." His tone was dismissive, his smile like that of a crocodile welcoming prey under the illusion its mouth was a cave.

"I'm free to go?" Alan asked, his momentary anger being replaced with a cramp beginning to radiate out from his stomach and down to his bowels. His body was telling him he needed to be out of here, that the whole situation was wrong.

"You're free to go," Campbell confirmed with an exaggerated smile. "Just need you to sign a release form and you can be on your way. See the custody sergeant on your way out and he'll draw up the paperwork."

Alan nodded hurriedly and made his way out of the door, anxiously looking behind him in case it was all a big joke and Campbell was waiting to arrest him for trying to escape. But he was just sat in the chair, his arms folded across his chest as though waiting for something.

He quickly turned away and headed towards the counter at the front of the station, announcing as he approached Campbell's indication he needed to sign something before he could go.

The sergeant stretched over to his left and grabbed a pad that he placed in front of Alan alongside a pen.

"Just sign there," he said pointing to the bottom of the form.

Alan scribbled his signature, returned the pen to the sergeant with a nervous smile and made his way as quickly as he could out of the police station door.

A few moments later, Campbell appeared from the interview room and moved to lean on the counter Alan had just vacated.

He signalled to his colleague to hand him the pad of release forms and reached beneath the top one Alan had signed only minutes earlier, pulling out a piece of blue carbon paper.

He held it up to the harsh, artificial light and examined the perfect replica of Alan Campbell's signature.

"That'll do nicely," he said with a conciliatory nod towards the sergeant. "That'll do just fine."

"We're all pretty bizarre. Some of us are just better at hiding it, that's all."

The Breakfast Club

Chapter Twenty-Two

South Shields,
South Tyneside

Steven Bennett turned his collar up to combat the cold northeasterly wind blowing in from across the Tyne. There never seemed to be any common ground in Newcastle in regards to the weather; warm summers, no dry season and freezing cold winters. With 25% of the land surrounded by water and the North Sea, it didn't surprise Steven that the weather was as inclement as the population. Given what he was about to do, he was glad it was so bitter. It reflected his mood towards the Chief Inspector who had issued the arrest warrant.

There was no way that Tommy's brother would have ratted him out. Yet, there it had been in black and white. A signed confession that Tommy Myers was responsible for the robbery at the dock a few months ago alongside a few other crimes – selling of stolen goods, drug dealing, GBH – in exchange for a waiver from prosecution for his involvement in them.

Steven didn't know Tommy that well, despite the fact they had become close at school after he'd stopped behaving like a dick. They'd ended up becoming quite close actually, but as with all things, life got in the way once they left school and they drifted apart. Steven had kept tabs on him, followed his boxing career with keen interest and had been saddened and surprised when he'd been sentenced for the murder of a man. Having gotten to know Tommy when they were young, he knew he had extremely high moral standards and that if he had killed a man there must have been a good reason, if there was such a thing.

Everyone suspected Campbell worked for Jack Hudson but there'd never been any proof, only rumours that no one dared challenge. Campbell having been Alan's interviewing officer only lent credence to his theory. Steven couldn't prove anything, but nevertheless he intended to do all he could to give Tommy a heads up.

He took a deep breath and knocked on the side entrance to the pub. The sound of someone unlocking the door followed a few moments later.

"Is Tommy in, Mr. Myers?" Steven asked informally, removing his helmet. He didn't know Tommy's dad personally but felt that a friendlier approach might make the conversation he was about to have a little easier.

Thomas looked slightly confused as he replied. "Er, yes... he's upstairs. Can I ask what this is about?"

"It's probably better that I speak to Tommy first."

"Okay," came the hesitant reply. "You'd better come in then."

Thomas widened the door to allow Steven access. He gestured for him to make his way up the stairs before closing it behind him. As he followed, a sense of unease formed in Thomas' mind. He knew his sons had been participating in businesses that were less than legal, but also knew they were far too careful to do anything that would get them arrested. There was no way Tommy would ever run the risk of being sent back to prison, therefore the presence of the police in his home had him anxious.

Steven had paused at the top of the landing before turning

towards the living room and in the direction of the sofa. Nodding politely at the officer, Thomas made his way to his son's room on the second floor.

Steven placed his helmet beside him and glanced around the living room, finding himself slightly impressed. It was more sumptuous than he had imagined, high ceilings and huge bay windows that gave the room an airy feel. The floor had thick, brown carpet that held the imprint of Steven's feet where he had trodden. The Pye television with a polished, wood effect surround was on in the background, playing something he recognised as *Return of the Jedi* via the Ferguson Videostar connected below it. Given the film had only been released the year previous Steven knew it was a pirate copy, something he would have questioned Thomas about on any other day.

But this wasn't any other day.

* * *

Thomas gently knocked on his son's bedroom door, aware that he had been working on the door last night and wouldn't have gone to bed until late. He heard Tommy coughing before hearing him call for whoever was outside to come in.

The room was swathed in a subtle darkness, the dust in the air disturbed by Thomas's entry visible in the beams of sunlight forcing their way through cracks in the curtains. He moved over and sat on the end of his son's bed.

"Everything okay, Dad?"

"The police are downstairs. They want to talk to you."

Tommy's expression remained impassive. "Did they say what about?"

"No, just that they were here to see you." He paused for a moment before speaking again. "Listen Tommy, I let you stay here because you're my son and I know you need to find your feet, but I hope you haven't brought more shit into our house."

"What, aside from going to prison for murdering a man who raped your wife's daughter? Not recently, no."

"Sorry," his Dad replied. "I didn't mean that."

"It's okay," Tommy said reassuringly. "Ronnie and I have been careful. I've no intention of going back to prison, trust me. I have no idea what it's about."

"Son, you know I'll stand by you no matter what. We have to do what needs to be done to get by in this world. Nothing comes to us for free and what we do have we have to fight to get and keep. I don't question what it is you do as it's none of my business. All I ask is that you keep it out of here."

"And that's what I've done, Dad."

"So, why are the police downstairs, Tommy?"

"As I said, I don't know," he said confidently. "But why don't we go and find out."

He climbed out of bed and pulled on some trousers and a t-shirt, running his hands through his hair in a crude attempt to make himself more presentable.

Leaving his Dad sitting on the edge of his bed, Tommy made his way slowly down the stairs and into the living room. It took him a few moments to register the face of the man on the settee.

"Steven," Tommy stated followed by a surprised pause. "I don't see you for more than fifteen years and then see you twice in a few months. I didn't know you were a copper."

"Almost ten years now, mate."

Tommy nodded casually as he sat down in the chair opposite. "Don't worry, I won't hold it against you. It's not your fault most of your mates are dodgy bastards."

Steven made a conciliatory nod.

"Right. So, to what do I owe this dubious pleasure?" Tommy asked.

"I'm here to give you a heads up about a rumour I've heard."

Tommy remained impassive, casually picking at fluff on the arm of the chair. "And what rumour is that?"

"A rumour that you were involved in a robbery at the docks a few months ago."

Tommy let the statement hang in the air for a moment. "Says who?"

Steven's face took on a less formal expression. If Tommy hadn't have known better, he would have said it was sympathetic. "Says your brother apparently."

Tommy stopped picking at the chair and met Steven's stare, his face one of confusion and shock. "You're lying."

"I wish I were," he said with a shake of his head. "I was advised this morning that there is a warrant out for your arrest based upon a signed confession from Alan Myers stating that you were involved in a robbery which took place on the 14th August 1985 at the Port of Tyne."

Tommy stood up and moved in front of Steven, his stance provocative. "I wasn't involved in any fuckin' robbery and even if I was, there is no way my brother would rat me out."

Steven waved his hand in a submissive gesture. "Mate, I'm only telling you what I was told. The fact is I figured you deserved an advanced warning to do with what you wish."

Tommy paced the floor waving his hands in an exaggerated fashion. "All I've fuckin' done since coming out of prison is keep a low profile. I want to get to know my son, spend time with my sister – the sister I went inside to protect – and see my family who were kept from me for years. I've never asked for mercy and sought no one's sympathy. But you don't get a fuckin' break do you? The world just won't allow it."

He had gone from pacing to stalking, so angry he was struggling to breathe. Steven watched him, surprised to find him so emotional yet imagining it was more to do with the allegation against his brother than the one of his involvement at the port. Steven knew it had been him, he had friends outside the force who'd told him. Nothing was ever that secret, not in the world of crime and criminals. But he had no intention of pushing Tommy on it. Never mind he was a police officer, he knew better than to press Tommy Myers. He wanted to walk out of here with his face still intact. Tommy slowly relaxed his stance, moving over to stand by the window.

The rain overnight had been relentless, leaving the sky with a passing resemblance to a faded watercolour painting. The gutter running along the bottom of the window was overflowing, an action Tommy realised was reflective of the situation - overburden something and eventually it will burst or collapse. Is that what had happened here? Had Tommy put too much pressure on his brother causing him to break down? He knew he'd suffered from depression after Mam had died, but had honestly not given it another thought since getting out. He realised he should have asked him how he was or if he was still on medication.

Had he been covering up a deeper pain all this time and this was his way of dealing with it?

Steven's voice broke the silence. "Is Alan around?"

Tommy shook his head. "Nah, he doesn't live here," he replied quietly. "He has his own place in town. I haven't seen him since yesterday."

"Maybe it would be better to speak to him. I think there's more to it than what's been said, but in any event mate you need to make yourself scarce."

Tommy turned to look at Steven suspiciously, leaning back to rest on the window ledge. "Why are you helping me?"

Steven smiled as though remembering times long past. "After you kicked the shit out of me that day, I respected you. I would never have said it at the time but I felt shitty for saying what I did, it was bang out of order. When I lost my own Mam I really realised what it must have been like and that only made it worse."

He paused for a moment, trying to find appropriate words. "Listen, I know however the money you've been earning since you got out isn't legit, but honestly I don't care. What you did for your sister is well known. Christ, the whole of Northumberland knows you took the blame to save her from prison. Irrespective of what anyone does in their spare time, that makes you a good bloke in my eyes Tommy Myers and providing I don't actually see you committing a crime, then as far as I'm concerned ignorance is bliss. Besides, Jack Hudson needs knocking down a peg or two and you might just be the bloke to do that."

Tommy recognised the inference that Steven knew he had been the one at the docks that night and immediately gained a newfound respect for his old school friend. He had little love for the police, but realised there might be one or two good ones amongst them.

"I need to find him," Tommy said in reference to his brother. "I need to know what's going on."

Steven stood and placed his helmet back on. "In that case, I'll leave you to it. Just don't do anything stupid, all right?"

"I can't promise you that," Tommy replied.

Steven nodded his understanding and moved past him towards the stairs. Tommy called out to him as he was leaving.

"And Steven... thank you."

Steven turned and smiled before making his way downstairs and out the back door of the pub.

Tommy turned back towards the window and closed his eyes, listening to the sound of the cold, merciless rain as it started up again, pounding against the glass like steel rivets. He had a disquieting feeling that Steven had been more than just a messenger; he had been a potential harbinger, bringing with him the threat of a storm that could obliterate everything in its path.

He refused to believe Alan had betrayed him. But if it was true god help him, family or not.

If it wasn't true and somehow Tommy was being set up, then he would find whoever was responsible and tear down everything around them brick by brick. They would never replace what he took.

He would leave nothing for them to replace it with.

"The jail you planned for me is the one you're gonna rot in."

The Color Purple

Chapter Twenty-Three

Newcastle Upon Tyne,
Tyne and Wear

Alan stood on the quayside, staring out towards the Tyne Bridge. The rising sun bounced light off the water and onto the windows of the surrounding buildings. He found it almost hypnotic.

He'd left Balmbras last night and headed off to The Junction on Northumberland Street to meet a few friends. The night had been going great – a bit of dancing, some sexy-looking woman paying him attention, plenty of drinks and a lot of Charlie for good measure, both for selling and personal use.

Alan had always enjoyed a night out on the town. Granted people thought the town was bleak and had no future, especially given unemployment being on the rise, but where once there had always been some knacker looking to pick a fight because of the way you looked, Alan had begun to notice that there were less dress codes being imposed to stop you on the door. People were suddenly able to embrace their New Romantic image and Flock of Seagulls haircut. Maybe it was down to the fading spirit of the recent punk movement. Or maybe it was just because people were actually becoming more tolerant.

He'd been able to push his arrest and interrogation to the back of his mind, secure in the knowledge that they had nothing on him and Ronnie and, most importantly, nothing on his brother. After all they'd been through, the one thing they had and valued more than anything was loyalty. Tommy's sacrifice had been the antithesis of that devotion. All Alan had wanted to do was follow his little brother's footsteps and show him that he was just as devoted and loyal to him as he had been to Karen. But it wasn't meant to be. Patrick Campbell had seen to that.

He should have realised right from the get go that there was more to his off-the-book interrogation than just a test of his allegiance. All the time, Campbell had been setting him up and he'd been too stupid to see it. He couldn't blame the drink or drugs. It had been hubris, plain and simple. He thought he'd been the cleverest man in the room last night, when all the time it had been Campbell.

Alan had spotted him in The Junction, leaning nonchalantly up against the bar and staring over in his direction with a smirk on his face like he knew something Alan didn't. He had tried his best to ignore him, but it had been as though he was deliberately moving around the club in order to constantly remain in his eye line, a persistent itch he couldn't scratch or perhaps a prescient omen.

Having had enough, Alan had said his farewells to his mates and made his way outside, unusually taking notice of the crunching sound as he made his way across the broken glass. It was familiar and real, a sensation and realisation that he had suddenly become concerned he would not feel again.

Campbell had accosted him outside in the most unthreatening yet intimidating manner possible, moving in front of him to block his path but making certain not to touch him.

"Evening Alan," he had said in an insouciant tone. "Good night?"

"It was," Alan had replied nervously. "Can I help you, Officer?"

"Detective," he had corrected. "And no, I just thought you

would appreciate some forewarning regarding your brother."

Alan had looked puzzled. "Tommy? What about him?"

"He's to be arrested in the morning under suspicion of robbery," Campbell had replied with a smug smile.

Alan's skin had gone cold and tingled as gooseflesh had rippled across its surface in a physiological response to the fear he'd suddenly felt. Maybe that was why he hadn't gone home. Perhaps subconsciously, he'd known all along that this was coming.

"What do you mean?" had been the only response he'd been capable of producing.

"The robbery at the docks a few months ago. You should know, Alan. You gave us a signed confession to that end."

His legs had become so weak in that instant that he felt as though the very ground was collapsing beneath him. "What are you talking about?"

Campbell had produced a piece of paper from his pocket and waved it in his face. Alan had seen typing and spotted his signature at the bottom of the page. He knew it was a forgery; he hadn't signed anything except...

The memory flooded his brain as clearly as though it had just happened. Never mind the alcohol he'd consumed earlier that night or the night of his arrest, he saw his hand grabbing the pen, the swirls and flow of his signature appearing before his eyes in a fluid image. His mind raced, trying to process what he realised to be true. The whole thing, from his arrest to his release, had been designed for one, sole purpose - to set up his brother.

"I didn't sign that," Alan stated with as much assertiveness as he could muster, the vibrancy of the night around him making the whole situation seem surreal and disjointed. "Of course, you did," Campbell confirmed. "It says right there,

Alan Myers. Very poor form, rolling over on your brother like that. He'll be so disappointed."

Alan stepped up to Campbell, so close their noses were almost touching. "I'll fucking kill you for this."

With little chance to respond, Alan found himself spun around and bent over, his right arm twisted up his back beyond its natural flection. Campbell lent down close to his ear, flecking him with spit as he spoke. "You'll do fuck all is what you'll do sunshine. You'll go back to your nice little pub and sit with your fuckin' cunt of a brother, tell him you're a rat and that Jack Hudson wants him to know who really rules Newcastle. Not some poncy, little wannabe who thinks because he served a little time he's a gangster. Everyone thinks they're a gangster until a real one walks through the door. So why don't you be a good boy and fuck off home to your Daddy and pretend Mam and see how much respect they have for you now."

Campbell shoved Alan away with enough force that he fell to the floor, his face scraping along the concrete. A couple who had just been leaving The Junction looked down at him and then up at Campbell before heading back inside, not wanting to be part of whatever altercation was taking place.

Alan had lain still for what seemed like minutes, letting the emotion of the situation and the implications of Campbell's words wash over him. When he had finally picked himself up he was alone on the street, the only activity coloured lights flashing across the windows of the nightclub and the occasional taxi passing by. He had wandered the streets in a daze, rigor mortis having set in on his soul before finding himself standing at the river with the town he loved silhouetted in the background.

As the sun rose higher, the gentle undulating sound of the River Tyne was cathartic. It beckoned to Alan with the promise she could soothe all his worries. He tried to process how he could have ended up in this situation, coming to the conclusion that it was possibly fate or perhaps even destiny.

The proverbial law of social gravity; the higher you are when you start something, the more painful it'll be when you fall flat on your face.

The poignancy of his thoughts was almost measurable. He berated himself for not having been more alert around Campbell the day of his arrest and for having had so much to drink that day. He wondered if he had been more circumspect would he have realised what was going on. It wouldn't matter that he would tell Tommy it had been a set-up. Yes, what had really happened would come to light eventually but at that moment he would see his treachery reflected in Tommy's eyes.

The past became blurred like an old photograph and the future suddenly immutable whilst the present was a narrow, unemotional moment where he had all the choices in the world and no choices at all. He saw his Dad and Donna stood with Faye, Karen and Tommy, all of them looking down on him in judgment at his alleged actions. Their faces were all etched with the same expression – disappointment. Tommy had been tried and tested at the highest level just as Alan had… as Karen had. They had both endured and survived, refusing to be defeated yet when Alan's turn had arrived, he'd failed.

He couldn't bear the thought of what Tommy would think of him. Alan felt as though he wanted to vomit but had no mouth, the urge impossible to bring to a conclusion and causing it to just sit uncomfortably in his stomach. He had waited so long for him to be released from prison, to have the opportunity for them to be truly brothers and take on the world together. He had wanted nothing more, yet all of those memories and dreams would be lost like tears in a thunderstorm.

There was only one-way out that Alan could see. Tommy would understand. He would read the note he had made certain would be delivered and maybe even respect his decision to spare them the pain and ignominious consequences of his actions.

The Tyne called out a siren's song, enchanting him to sink into her cold embrace. He made his way slowly around the dock and up towards the most celebrated of the Tyne's seven bridges, making an effort to take in its every nuance, its every imperfection as though it were the last time he would see it. Its green hue seemed oddly comforting where before he had always found it garish.

He moved along the footpath, ignorant of the steadily building traffic as people made their way toward their daily responsibilities of crunching numbers, serving drinks or caring for patients. Each of them had a story, just as he did. But whereas theirs was continuing, his had reached its conclusion. An ending forced upon him by a courted official whose job it was to keep him safe. He laughed at the hypocrisy of his thoughts, knowing that he was a criminal, albeit a low-level one. But Patrick Campbell was scum and would eventually experience the karma he deserved. Maybe that was what Alan was doing – jump starting Campbell's destiny.

It was that thought that comforted him as he stepped up onto the metal railing and allowed himself to tip over the side. The sound of vehicles skidding to a halt sent Alan on his final journey to be with his mother, the woman he had missed for so long.

There was no chance to prepare myself, not like I'd had with Mam.

All I had to form the basis of my grief were two things - a hand-delivered letter from one of Alan's friends telling me he was so sorry and the news from a police officer stood at the door. I think I kind of knew when I saw him there... Alan had been gone for more than 24 hours, something he never did. There'd been a sense of foreboding hanging over me the entire day for a reason I couldn't fathom.

The best way to describe it is as if a huge boulder had fallen from the sky and had landed on all of those around you, destroying hopes, dreams and memories. I was blindsided, we all were, by the conceit that we hadn't seen it coming. I know it's a cliché, but we had no idea... I had no idea. Alan and I had always been close but never as close as I would have liked. So when I got out of prison and we started working together, I discovered a fresh sense of companionship I'd never had with him before. He'd had the contacts; I'd had the knowledge to make our scores work. I didn't take any offence at the fact he had made an assumption that just because I had been inside and was now to be labelled a criminal that my skill set now lay in the illegal. He was right. Charlie Woods had taught me that. Embrace who you are and you'll find a whole new world open up to you. Alan had simply given me an outlet for that realisation.

We'd been making more money than we'd ever imagined, not large amounts granted but more than we'd had before and certainly more than I'd ever had in my back pocket. I had ideas and dreams for how it was going to work – me, him and Ronnie, taking over the Tyne and making ourselves known as proper players.

Now all I had were unanswered questions, missing puzzle pieces, and a desperation to understand why he had taken his own life. During the day I became a private investigator, searching his flat for clues to his state of mind, speaking to his friends… no stone was left unturned. At night I was tormented by the what ifs, would haves, should haves and could haves.

People would visit to pay their condolences to us all, yet I would notice the shame tainting their words, the unspoken assumptions as they told you how sorry they were. Fucking sycophants, all of them. I never thought I could feel as hollow as I had when Mam had died, but here I was, an incisive sense of loneliness taking me captive with the passing of every moment. Part of me was glad Mam was gone so she couldn't experience this. I think she would have died of a broken heart at losing her first-born child. As much as her and Dad loved us all, Alan was their eldest child and would always hold a special place in their memories. That love for a first child simply spills over onto others.

I guess it's like tripping up and falling down a steep hill you've just climbed to the top of. Angry thoughts and sounds raged in my head, comprehending the capricious and cruel nature of the world. I didn't like to think it wasn't fair, after all if life was fair then all the bad things that happened to us would be because we deserved them. So I took comfort in the fact life was unfair, but it did little to assuage the guilt I felt that I could have done more to save him.

We had the funeral that was sad and the wake which was as it should be, celebrating his life with everyone telling their tales of Alan, every word illustrating how important he was to them. Dad had managed to say a few words at the church, but remained quiet for most of the afternoon back at the pub. I think it was just so much to contemplate. Donna understood and gave him space whilst letting him know she was there for him and for all of us. Any subconscious animosity I may have still had for her replacing Mam when I was a child disappeared that day. She was amazing and really kept us all going… I think Mam would have liked her a lot.

And then all that was left was memories and recriminations, speculation over and over again about why he did it, why didn't anyone notice he was suffering and could we have done something to prevent it. Of course, it was only a few weeks later that I realised no one could have done anything to prevent it, not really. Alan hadn't been suffering a sense of worthlessness that had eaten away at him, gestating inside him over a long period. It wasn't even that he wanted to hurt himself. It was because he had been conned, manipulated, tricked, duped... you could use whatever fucking word you wanted to describe it. He'd been made out to be a rat, someone who would betray his blood for a free pass.

I only found out because Steven had told me. Told me about the night Alan was arrested, about him being at the station. By telling me he was putting his own job and potentially his life in danger... I respected that. He knew I'd want to know. Fucking Northumbria Police... I wondered how they'd be remembered in years to come, as beneficent or corrupt?

I'd told Kaz straight away. I thought she was going to burst a blood vessel she was so angry. It was at that moment, lost in amongst the grief and injustice for our murdered brother that I saw it for the first time. And yes, I meant murdered. Alan may have died by his own hand but that prick may as well have fuckin' pushed him off the bridge.

But Kaz, man, she was going off on one. Not with wild accusations of what she was going to do to him, but with specific, detailed descriptions of how she could get revenge. I mean it was bullet point by bullet point fuckin' standard operating procedure shit. I always knew she was smart, a lot smarter than I or anyone else ever gave her credit for, but in that moment I'll admit I was a little scared. She was almost Machiavellian in her thinking. I was just going to fuck him up and drop him at the bottom of the Tyne. But Kaz, she had something altogether more poetic in mind.

It was in that moment that his suffering became our mutual focus.

His name was our only thought.

Patrick Campbell.

"Everybody I know is desperate, except for you."
Desperately Seeking Susan

Chapter Twenty-Four

Newcastle Upon Tyne,
Tyne and Wear

Since being released for armed robbery more than twenty years ago, Jack Hudson had taken a singular approach to business and life. Being overconfident and arrogant had been the failing that had got him arrested in the first place, that and having placed his trust in people he didn't really know. Since then he'd made certain of two things – he only had people on his crew he knew or had been vouched for. He paid his people well enough to know that if it all went tits up, others would take the fall for him. Out of loyalty, because they took his money… he didn't care. His only interest was that they knew it.

Currently he was wondering if Campbell had ever been paying attention.

"He fucking killed himself, you idiot! What did you think would happen when you set him up as a grass?"

Campbell swallowed hard a few times. "I don't know, but I didn't think he'd do that. I was just trying to scare him. I figured he'd leave Newcastle or his brother would knock him about or something like that. I didn't think he'd fucking top himself."

Hudson paced from one side of the office to the other.

"Well, now you've turned him into a martyr his brother'll be on edge. You'd better be sure your plan is air-fucking-tight. If any of this even looks like it's pointing in my direction I'll have you, Campbell. I mean, Christ, if Myers finds out we set his brother up he'll never fucking stop until we're both dead."

Campbell forced exhalation through his nose. "You don't need to worry about him. You could easily take him out."

Hudson stopped and stared, surprised at the police officer's ignorance. "You obviously don't understand the power of family. That kind of man is the kind who keeps getting up every time you knock them down. I told you, I saw him fight back in the day, the guy's a fucking nightmare. No one fucks with me because they know it would be their life. But Tommy Myers, he possesses that most irretraceable and inflexible of attributes – loyalty. Someone who serves a ten year sentence for a crime he didn't commit just to protect his sister isn't someone you want to fuck off. I'll be honest, I'm scared of no man and that man scares me."

Campbell found himself a little surprised at hearing his boss acknowledge weakness. But Hudson was lost in a maelstrom of anxiety at Alan's suicide. Campbell hadn't intended that to happen and had to admit he was slightly apprehensive of the consequences should it ever come out that it was down to him. He knew that if anyone discovered he was involved then it would only be a matter of time before they found out about his working relationship with Hudson. That would be the end of his career and, most likely, his life. But there was no way anyone could know what he did that night.

No way.

*"You had to be big shots didn't you. You had to show off.
When are you gonna learn that people will like you for who
you are, not for what you can give them. Well, in your race for
power and glory, you forgot one small detail."*

Weird Science

Chapter Twenty-Five

1986
Newcastle Upon Tyne,
Tyne and Wear

The warmer weather felt to Karen as though it was trying to bring with it a promise of better things to come.

As she made her way up the chare towards Broad Garth, she noted the drifts of snow once under the protection of darker skies were now vulnerable to the sunshine steadily breaking through with every passing day. The ground was littered with patches of grass as the snow melted, bringing a much-needed colour to the drab and dreary scenery of Newcastle. She found it difficult to believe her home would ever win a city of culture award. This was despite the fact that the city was steeped in so much history, the chare she was walking up a primary example. Once initially one of twenty that had become infamous for their unsanitary conditions, with typhus and cholera killing over 1,500 people in the 1800's, now they were simply examples of a medieval alleyway with historical interest rather than epidemiological significance.

Tommy had said he would meet her as she had requested, though he was still ignorant as to the purpose. She preferred it that way. The life she now led was a million miles away from the one she'd envisioned.

She had dreamt of being an accountant or perhaps a nurse. But life had seen fit to redirect her focus towards something altogether more illicit and yet oddly rewarding.

After many months of therapy and different antidepressants, Karen had found herself unable to shake the sense of worthlessness Eric Doyle had bequeathed her. There was nowhere she'd felt she belonged and nothing that maintained her enthusiasm. It was purely by chance one evening that she'd got chatting to a girl who worked most nights behind Central Station. In her mid-forties, she had a nice figure and wide-spaced brown eyes that sparkled every time she spoke. Her long thick hair had an auburn sheen to it, its placement around her shoulders giving her a passing resemblance to Jane Russell. Karen thought she had slightly too much makeup on which, if removed, would show that she was quite an attractive woman.

Pat, as she had introduced herself as, had told Karen things were changing dramatically for women like her. From the police cracking down on prostitution to many of the girls just not feeling safe any longer, they were in need of new guidelines to protect them.

"The oldest profession in the world and they still can't provide fucking legislation to keep us safe, only to demonise us," she had pronounced between mouthfuls of whisky.

Listening to Pat's stories of their vulnerability had made Karen realise the reality that they were essentially trafficked women, abandoned by their families and communities in the majority of cases. She remembered many of Pat's peers coming in to the pub regularly when she was growing up, often finding herself surprised and shocked in equal measure at their loose talk and free-spirited attitude towards sex. It had been the case that if you did right by them then they would do right by you. They never solicited for business in the Horse & Hammer and had always been respectful towards Karen's parents and her family. That was one of the reasons she found it so hard to understand why law enforcement and social services always saw fit to slight them.

They met regularly after that, striking up quite a friendship whereupon Karen learnt just how dangerous their profession actually was. Though they were trying to move away from the streetwalking and towards more of an escort service, Karen could appreciate that there were still inherent difficulties in assuring security for themselves. She knew they accepted their work wasn't without risk, often taking false reassurance that because they were now trying to provide a service in men's houses rather than down a back alleyway they were somehow safer. A few of her friends had begun to join the two of them as the weeks went by until it had resembled a therapy group.

It had been during one of those sessions that Karen had been asked if she would be interested in looking after them. She'd almost choked on her drink, thinking that they were obviously drunk and uncertain of what they were asking. As it turned out, they'd been deadly serious, explaining how their pimp was a misogynistic arsehole with little to no respect for women. She had thought about it, decided she would help them and paid him a visit.

Before Eric, Karen would never have put herself in a confrontational situation and certainly not with a man who could easily overpower her. Now, she had little concern about the consequences of her actions or of her own personal safety. It had only taken some sleeping tablets in his drink with the illusion that she was going to sleep with him, alongside some restraints across his body for when he awoke to persuade him that he was no longer responsible for the girls and that he should avoid contact with them altogether. A set of pliers to his testicles and she had felt confident he wouldn't bother them any further.

From then on, it had been more straightforward than Karen had thought. A property had bought with help from George, a series of meetings convened with all the girls who were interested along with reassurances for those who weren't that her door would always be open for them. Now, with the provision of protection for them at the house she was suddenly a madam for more than a dozen girls who sold sex to make themselves and her a fair amount of money.

As she waited outside the house in the West End of Newcastle for Tommy to arrive, she scanned it and made a note of a few cosmetic jobs that would need to be addressed before the end of the year. She was mentally trying to work out the cost when she saw her brother walking towards her.

"Hey Kaz." He looked about him, oblivious to the purpose for his being summoned. "So, you wanna tell me what we're doing here freezing to death? I just passed a brass monkey crying his eyes out."

Karen smiled. "We're here because there's something I want to share with you… something that I think will help us avenge Alan."

Tommy's expression became one of sadness at hearing his brother's name. He moved from foot to foot in an attempt to keep warm. "How? We never found out all the details."

Karen gestured him towards the door. "Come inside and I'll explain."

He looked around him as though checking his immediate surroundings before nodding and making his way inside. Tommy felt a surge of emotions he hadn't felt since prison when realising his life had taken an altogether unexpected direction.

This time though, it was accompanied by inexplicable belief that he could be in control of the outcome.

They both could.

Tommy was suitably impressed with what he saw. Though he had yet to learn the purpose of the building, he couldn't deny that it was clean, tidy and well-decorated. The ceilings were high with ornate pieces in each corner, the floors were polished wood and the colours muted and soothing.

It had a warm, inviting feel to it that, once he learnt what Karen was doing there, made complete sense.

"So," he asked as he slowly walked around the large foyer. "What are we doing here, Kaz?"

"We are going to talk about how we're going to get Patrick fuckin' Campbell. And we're going to do it using my girls."

"Your girls?" Tommy asked, confused.

"I lied to you that day when I visited you in prison. Well, not so much lied as willfully participated in a campaign of misinformation."

Tommy laughed. "Okay..." he said in a long drawl. "So, you don't work at C&A?"

"No, I do. That was true. But I also look after this place and the girls in it." She paused for dramatic effect. "And it's certainly more profitable than working in a department store."

She studied Tommy's face closely, amused as he started to slowly put the pieces together. She could almost see the cogs in his brain whirring as everything clicked into place.

"So, you're either a foster parent or this is a brothel," he stated empathically.

"Correct," she confirmed. "About the brothel I mean."

"Well, I never saw you as a surrogate parent... except Daniel of course," he confirmed as an afterthought.

"That's okay, no offense taken."

Tommy moved into the living room and collapsed into one of the pieces of handmade furniture, shuffling about until he was comfortable. "Nice," he stated whilst indicating towards the chair and the general room.

"Glad you like it," Karen said, taking the seat opposite and leaning forward. "I have twelve girls who work for me, from this house."

Tommy frowned.

"It's bigger on the inside," Karen replied. "They all have their own room, their own routines, we split the take fifty-fifty with whatever extras they get theirs to keep. I have an assistant who deals with the phone calls and bookings, organises transport if required. I prefer the clients come here but the girls can go to them if they prefer... more money of course, but extra risk."

Tommy nodded, still a little thrown by the fact his sister was the owner of a brothel. "How can you afford all this?"

"George paid for it all."

"Your boyfriend? The one I've yet to meet?"

"You will," Karen confirmed. "When the time is right."

"So, rich?"

"No, George," Karen joked. "He's not doing too bad," she confirmed.

"And he doesn't mind you... you know."

"I don't sleep with anyone you daft bastard," Karen stated with faux indigence. "I just look after them."

"And how do you do that?" Tommy queried.

"By ensuring they feel safe and promoting the fact, subtly of course, that this is a decent establishment and not some fuckin' knocking shop where anyone can come for a cheap shag. The girls here are clean and have really classed themselves up. Any

188

punters who come here are not only in for a good time but know my girls are good at what they do and professional, no pun intended. If you get the right clients, you don't get trouble. The blokes, and women, who come here know that they do right by us we'll do right by them discretion-wise. They also know if they fuck with me or my girls, the whole of Newcastle'll know what they do in their spare time, as will their wives."

"Where's Karen and what have you done with her?" he asked.

She laughed, something he hadn't heard her do in a long time. "I've changed a lot since you were inside. I had to grow up."

"Because of Daniel?" Tommy asked.

Karen nodded.

"Because of that night?" he followed up sadly.

She hesitated before nodding again. "I wasn't going to be weak or vulnerable after that night, screaming at the world that no one was there to help me."

Tommy shifted uncomfortably in the chair.

"I don't mean you, what you did for me can never be put into words Tommy. You saved me. More than I ever thought I could be. But it didn't change the fact that I felt betrayed that life allowed it to happen. Therapy helped a little, medication helped a little… Daniel helped a lot, but nothing really made me feel I was worth anything until I found these girls and found George. He made me see that I wasn't just some slut who'd been asking for it that night."

"And the girls?" Tommy asked.

"The girls? The girls gave me the chance to make certain the same thing didn't happen to them and that they could do what they did, turn a profit and be respected at the same time."

Tommy stood and began pacing around the room. He moved

to the window and stared at the growing number of pedestrians outside. He turned to face Karen but remained silent as though contemplating his next words, the ticking of the grandfather clock in the foyer the only sound as it evidenced the passing of time.

"My son's kept well away from this, isn't he?"

"What do you take me for?" Karen responded angrily. "Of course he is. That's why I have the job in town. I'm not here every night. One of the girls oversees everything for me because I don't want Daniel involved in any way. Only my manager knows about him, no one else. He might be your son, Tommy but I love him, like my own. I brought him up, wiped his bum, sang him to sleep and wiped his tears. This shitty life I've built for myself might not be classy, but there's no way I would expose him to any of it. I give you my word. And one day, when you and he are ready, he can be with you."

"I didn't mean to upset you, Kaz. I know you've done the best you could and your best was amazing. Sorry."

Her smile let him know she acknowledged his apology.

"What does this have to do with Alan?" he finally asked.

Karen moved to stand beside him. "One of my girls was assaulted and humiliated by a john a few months ago. Turns out he's a detective and a nasty one at that. Seems he has quite the reputation for being bent as the proverbial with a cruel streak to match. I was reliably informed that it was him who arrested Alan that night and forged the confession."

Tommy couldn't hide his surprise that she had found out something he'd struggled to uncover. Karen noticed his expression and hugged him condescendingly. "Don't worry, your image's still secure. I just know more people than you, that's all."

"So, what's his name?" Tommy asked, trying hard not to show frustration at not having found out first.

"Patrick Campbell," Karen replied.

"And what else do we know about him?"

"Not much outside of the fact he's a dodgy motherfucker. History of extortion, drug-dealing, violence… the standard, stereotypical fare."

Tommy momentarily looked like he had the weight of the world on his shoulders, his thoughts drifting back to Frankland and how every day had been one where you had to fight to keep your soul, integrity and life.

This was one of those moments. Revised and reproduced with a new coat of paint, but the same nevertheless.

"So, what's the plan?" he asked Karen as he sat back down.

Karen moved and stood in front of him. "One of the girls he abused has a sister, Rita. One of my first actually. No parents worth mentioning, both on the game. Campbell has always had girls from us and pays good money. He often humiliates them but they know the score and I always give them a chance to opt out. No one has to do anything here they don't want to, regardless of the money. Their dignity and safety comes first, but they can also see the bigger picture and know who the people are we need to have leverage over. Politicians, policemen, governors and bureaucrats, they all come to me because they know the quality. I have enough on all of them to ruin them professionally, Campbell included. But I want to hurt him permanently. I want him to suffer."

Tommy interrupted. "So, the sister…"

"Right, the sister. Rita knew Alan…"

Tommy frowned.

"Not like that. He knew her from the pub and she wants to help. She knows the risks, knows what we're up against and knows it's dangerous but I didn't ask her to. After what he did to Barbara, Rita wants him gone. Two birds, one stone."

"And Barbara is...?"

"Rita's sister," Karen clarified.

"Right," Tommy said, pausing for a moment. "Are you certain about this?" Tommy asked.

"Abso-fuckin-lutely. Alan died last year, Tommy and that fucker's had more than enough time to think he got away with it. Then wasn't the time... *now* is the time."

Tommy pursed his lips. "Okay, sis. What's the plan?"

Karen remained silent, her widening smile unsettling even the hardened Tommy Myers.

"Oh, he's very popular Ed. The sportos, the motorheads, geeks, sluts, bloods, wastoids, dweebies, dickheads - they all adore him. They think he's a righteous dude."

Ferris Bueller's Day Off

Chapter Twenty-Six

Newcastle Upon Tyne, Tyne and Wear

Rita checked herself over once more in the full-length mirror. She knew she was still an attractive woman, perhaps not to everyone's tastes – her breasts were full, her stomach wasn't completely flat and her skin only looked its best with a layer of make-up on it.

But she knew she was a true woman, none of this plastic surgery nonsense augmenting her body that seemed to be all the rage nowadays. Women were paying thousands of pounds to get huge knockers when men didn't really give a shit about that. It certainly made it easier to persuade them to part with their money if the girl was pretty and looked filthy, but Rita knew they were more interested in whether they actually were filthy when it mattered.

She noticed her posture, making an effort to stand up straight and, by doing so, pushing out her heavy breasts to the point that they looked like they were going to spill out of the basque she was wearing. Her instructions had been specific in regards to what to wear – high heels, suspenders and her hair down. Yet despite the lack of clothing she felt as though the weight of the world was on her shoulders.

She had virtually thrown herself at Karen when the opportunity to get Patrick Campbell had come up in conversation. Ever since her sister's abuse and humiliation, Rita had been looking for a way to get back at him, to the point she'd been considering just stabbing the bastard. But then Alan had killed himself and retribution against Campbell had elevated to another level, with Karen's plan both poetic and simple. It needed only the two things they already had at their disposal; her profession and his arrogance.

She realised the magnitude of what she was about to do. She knew of Campbell's reputation as a misogynistic bastard and was fairly certain it would only take a few choice words to offend the ego of a man like him. Everything hinged on her provoking him into doing what came naturally.

She wasn't afraid of getting hurt, only afraid of letting down Karen, Tommy, Alan and her sister. They were trying to bring down a police officer, something that demanded a healthy appreciation of the situation. Once she opened the door to him, there would literally be no closing it.

As if prophetic, the doorbell rang. She gave herself one last look in the mirror, satisfied that she was good enough for what needed to be done.

Rita made her way to the door and took a deep breath before putting on her best smile and pulling it open.

"There can be only one."

Highlander

Chapter Twenty-Seven

Newcastle Upon Tyne,
Tyne and Wear

Tommy finished his third neat Jack Daniels in one mouthful, savouring the burning sensation as it massaged his throat and warmed his stomach. He'd previously been on the McEwan's but had quickly switched drinks upon realising that, despite the price, it was essentially watery piss in a tall pint glass that would ensure he left as sober as he'd arrived. At least now he was on the JD he was getting somewhere. Tommy wasn't quite pissed, but he could just make out pissed at the next stop. Little wonder the punters sought their intoxicants from a hip flask rather than the bar.

He checked his watch for the fifth time in so many minutes, feeling more agitated as time ticked by. The Mayfair had its usual clientele out in full force this evening, the sea of dreadlocks, tie-dye and fragrant smoke unfurling before him. It made him feel old. If he hadn't known better, he would have thought he'd wandered in on student night. At least then he would be getting a free half with every pint for 80 pence, though doubted even that would get him lathered.

He gestured the barman for another shot before downing it and made his way from the main venue towards the side room that hosted The Drop. Whether from his torturously slow inebriation or the draped sheets hanging from the ceiling and walls, Tommy found himself feeling over-relaxed. He walked towards the balcony in the main ballroom and positioned himself so he could see the Stock Aitken and Waterman fans go through their moves on the dance floor, replicating Rick Astley's funky groove in order to impress the current object of their affections which happened to be whoever was stood in front of them at the time. Tommy felt old, realising that courting had gone from being something you took seriously to something transitory. Even his mental use of the word courting made him roll his eyes.

Music still had him confused. Alan had spent a lot of time trying to get him up to speed with the music world when he was released, playing him a three-hour Maxwell videotape of Live Aid, horrendous editing using the record/pause method included. He had even gone so far as buying him a Walkman so he could listen to tapes whilst out walking or on the bus. The first time he had used it he'd nearly blown his eardrums, hastily lowering the volume. There hadn't been much call for music inside, meaning Tommy's memories were still of Simon and Garfunkel, The Carpenters and Don Williams. Nowadays everything seemed similar, all electro beats and synthesizers. He would often wait for what seemed to him a cacophony of noise to become music before he actually understood it was. It certainly wasn't something you could seduce a woman to. Stick on a bit of Chicago and Peter Cetera's voice would compel most women to drop their clothing. The only reason Tommy could fathom you would stick on some of the music nowadays would be to drown out the screams of the person you were murdering.

He smiled to himself, sounding just like his father. Tommy Myers, the oldest thirty-odd year old in Newcastle. His lightened mood quickly swung back to the present situation, the cultural spectacle unfolding before him doing little to shift his anxiety about the plan Kaz had laid out for him earlier. He had to applaud her initiative and devious scheming, finding himself both impressed and surprised at how much his sister had changed during his time in prison. He had always known she was strong, but her steely resolve was something he had never appreciated before. Karen had certainly thought her plan through, telling them that she wasn't doing it out of some misguided loyalty; she was doing for Rita's sister, Alan and because Campbell was the kind of man where absolute power had corrupted him absolutely.

"I'll be doing a fucking social service getting rid of that bent bastard," had been her exact words.

That said, it was Rita taking all of the risk. It was a big gamble to take with someone's life, something Karen seemed blasé about.

Tommy knew his preferred solution would have most likely ended up with him being in prison again. He would have unleashed all his fury on that man and not stopped until he was dead. The emotions he was feeling about Alan were directed towards someone real and tangible, someone who he could find, touch and avenge himself upon. He recalled words from Herman Melville. *'He piled upon the whale's white hump the sum of all the general rage and hate felt by his whole race from Adam down; and then, as if his chest had been a mortar, he burst his hot heart's shell upon it.'*

Karen's plan and Rita's involvement would leave little leading back to them and simultaneously destroy Campbell's reputation and his life.

All it hinged on was Rita surviving the ordeal.

"I'm a reasonable guy. But, I've just experienced some very unreasonable things."

Big Trouble in Little China

Chapter Twenty-Eight

Newcastle Upon Tyne,
Tyne and Wear

Patrick Campbell settled into the chair and watched Rita making them drinks in the kitchen with salacious desire.

He had been more than impressed upon her answering the door. Granted she was older than he usually liked them, a lot older in fact, but she had a good body, supple breasts and long legs which more than made up for her age. He thought she looked familiar, but he put it down to having fucked her before. It wasn't like he made a note of their names.

Her flat was nice, nothing flash but tidy and welcoming. Soft lighting emanated from the conical, glass pendant lights that hung from the ceiling in the dining room whilst the spherical floor lamp in the corner cast light upwards towards the collectibles on the glass shelves. A few of Memphis Milano's geometric pattern pictures adorned the walls, the neon colours and abstract design a contrast to the gentle blue and white preppy style, Ralph Lauren sofa and chairs.

His gaze drifted back towards Rita who was making her way towards him with two glasses, the sway of her ample hips almost mesmerising. She looked like she could suck a golf ball through ten feet of hose. Rita handed him his drink and tilted her glass towards his in a salutatory gesture. He finished it in two large mouthfuls, wanting to move past the amiable shit and get her into the bedroom.

He asked her where the bathroom was, intent on doing a few lines of coke to maintain his stamina. She directed him towards the bedroom, stating it was an *en-suite*.

Closing the bedroom door as he entered, he fished the small, folded piece of paper from his pocket and knelt before the set of drawers by the bed. Campbell quickly set up a few short lines and cut them a little further with his credit card. Using the small metal tube he always carried with him, he snorted the cocaine and rubbed his nose vigorously, the drug causing his throat to sting and eyes to water momentarily. Wiping his nose on the back of his hand, he went to the toilet anyway before venturing back into the living room.

Rita was in the process of lifting the needle onto a record already placed on its turntable. The familiar hiss of vinyl filled the air before the dulcet tones of Alison Moyet's 'All Cried Out' filled the air. He looked Rita up and down, salivating at the thought of removing her suspenders and freeing her breasts from the basque.

He travelled the distance between them in two large strides, grabbing her by the back of the head and kissing her hard. His free hand drifted over her body, exploring every inch of her as though it was the first time he'd felt a woman. The feel of her exposed skin against his hand was electric, the smell of her perfume making him more eager to do what he'd come here to do.

His satisfaction was paramount. All other priorities rescinded.

* * *

Rita had to fight to stop the bile rising in the back of her throat from turning into a full-on scene from *The Exorcist*. His hands on her body made her skin crawl, but she kept telling herself she was doing this for her sister and for Alan. She had been with customers before who weren't her type, who stunk or had poor genital hygiene that was bad enough to make her gag. You just accepted when you were a prostitute you couldn't be particularly picky and had to remind yourself whilst they were grunting and sweating all over you that there was a fair pay packet at the end of it.

But Campbell sickened her in a different way. Maybe it was because of what she knew he'd done and that he'd shown no compunction over it. Perhaps it was because she knew what it was she had to do and was becoming more anxious with every passing minute.

What she did know was that she had to get her shit together and perform like she always did for a customer. Make him think his head was going to blow off with the best orgasm he'd ever had and the rest would take care if itself.

In this case that meant making certain she got him to remain on his mark and pray that the hidden video camera Tommy had set up in the bedroom didn't run out of tape

* * *

He threw Rita down onto the bed and ripped at her suspenders, tearing them in multiple places as he thrust his hands up between her legs. He knelt over her and began working on his shirt, taking a few attempts as his fingers fumbled down the placket.

Getting frustrated, he left the last few buttons and pulled it over his head before starting on his trousers. He didn't need to struggle with those, pulling them off and throwing them on the floor. He left his socks on as he so often did. Campbell thought of it less as a fetish and more that he just got turned on wearing them. Besides, he didn't want her fucking cold feet rubbing up against him.

Rita tried to push herself up from the bed, but Campbell forced her back down hard. Using his bodyweight to pin her, he felt himself rubbing up against her thighs and becoming more excited at how keen she was to have him inside her. He pushed her legs open with his knees and repositioned himself, sucking on her face and neck.

His hands moved back up her body and grabbed hard at her breasts, squeezing them so roughly she omitted a small yelp. Taking it as a sign of enthusiasm, he forced his hand between her legs and pulled off her knickers.

* * *

Rita tried to keep her face away from his intrusive tongue as much as possible without making it look as though she wasn't interested. She felt angry at the thought of him beating and humiliating her sister. When Rita had asked her why she'd let him do it, she'd told her it was because she refused to look weak in front of a man, especially one who felt powerful beating on a woman. She wanted him to think she liked it so she could maintain her own self-esteem.

"Working this life is bad enough, sis," she had told Rita. "We've got no one but each other. I'll be damned if some fucking man is gonna destroy the strength you helped me build."

But it hadn't only been the physical abuse that had angered Rita, it had been the humiliation afterwards as he'd thrown her sister out like a dog's chew toy – played with and now bored of. There are some things no working girl should have to endure. Granted you can't complain of having a bad day and come back home smelling of shit if you choose to work in a sewer, but you certainly don't have to drink the water whilst you're down there.

With Alan's death compounding the issue, alongside Campbell's reputation as one of the most corrupt police officers in the northeast, then it became obvious that he had to go. No one else was offering so they'd decided they would bring it all crashing down around him.

She just needed to get him to do what he did for the camera.

It would only take a few choice words.

* * *

Campbell licked her neck, his hands moving down beneath her buttocks in order to pull her closer into him. He was surprised at how willing she was at being used roughly. Most of the girls he was given were either reluctant or prudish, but this one was different.

He kissed her roughly, biting her lip. Rita moved her head to the side to whisper something in his ear.

"I thought you were supposed to be a man not a faggot."

Campbell pulled back, taken by surprise at her comments. His eyes narrowed as though a hidden part of his personality was waiting to be unleashed at the articulated threat to his manhood.

He slammed her head back down on the bed, screaming at her. "You want a fucking man? I'll give you a man."

He became more vigorous in his movements, slamming into Rita with inconsiderate force, losing himself in the euphoria of his approaching climax when he suddenly felt nails claw and drag down his cheeks. Rita struggled beneath him, suddenly resisting his actions.

"You fucking bitch," he screamed, grabbing at his bleeding face. He stopped thrusting and backhanded her across the cheek before grabbing hold of her chin to keep her head steady.

He forced himself into her hard before repeatedly punching her in the face. Not hard enough to cause damage but enough to leave bruises. His hands moved to her neck where he began to squeeze as his thrusts became less controlled. Rita began struggling beneath his grip, fighting to breathe with the minimal amount of oxygen flowing through her restricted windpipe.

Ignorant to her gasps for air, he moved his hands from her neck and grabbed her by the wrists, pinning them over her head. Rita felt his body stiffen and then relax as the moment washed over him.

Collapsing limply on top of her, Campbell let out a huge sigh. Despite his increasing feeling of exhaustion, he considered that a job well done.

* * *

Rita felt nothing but contempt.

Her face felt like it was burning, her eyes already swelling and her lip bleeding. She wiped her hand across her mouth and examined the blood, hoping that this had all been worth it.

"How was it for you?" he asked.

"The pleasure was all yours, I'm sure," she replied as she leaned over and began smacking him on the back of the head and across the face. She thought it would be good to scream at him and hurling obscenities for good measure. He slapped her hands away and jumped back off the bed, throwing punches at her with an incredulous look on his face.

Leaning over, he grabbed Rita by her hair and pulled her out of bed, doing his best to avoid her feet that were lashing out in all directions. He kicked her hard twice in the ribs before stepping back to survey the scene.

Rita had taken up a fetal position, her arms wrapped around her midsection as though protecting herself from more punishment. Campbell snorted derisively as he collected his clothes from the floor. He checked his face in the mirror and lightly ran his fingers over the scratches, wincing every time he went over a sensitive area. They weren't severe, but would leave scars.

"Fucking bitch," he said aloud before walking into the bathroom and getting dressed.

When he emerged, Rita was sat on the edge of the bed, still naked. His outline was intimidating as he lifted her head towards him.

"I don't know what that was all about, you daft skank but you were a good consolation prize, feisty too, so please thank your mistress for me."

He let go of Rita's head but she held it up, maintaining her stare. She wanted to knock the smug grin right off his face but knew that what they had done this evening would do more than stop him smiling... if it had worked.

"Get the fuck out of my flat," was her only response.

He gave a sarcastic bow towards her. "My fucking pleasure."

She watched him make his way through the living room and out of the door, slamming it shut behind him. Taking a few moments to compose herself, Rita tentatively stood up and moved towards the wardrobe, pulling open one of the slatted white doors. Reaching in, she retrieved the small, pencil-thin camera and pressed the off button on the side.

Tommy had installed it a few days earlier, connecting it to the VCR she already had in the wardrobe that was occasionally used to watch films in bed. He had told her it was a charged-coupled device using microchip technology, the particular model he had bought being all the rage apparently. Reminding him she was just a dumb prostitute, Tommy had laughed and said that it allowed low light and night recording, meaning they would have a better chance of a clear picture. He couldn't promise that the recording wouldn't be choppy and would most likely have poor sound, but had stated that, for their purposes, it would do just fine.

"Just don't let him go in your wardrobe," Tommy had reminded her in a semi-serious tone.

Rita clicked off the VCR and ejected the tape, noting it had been close to running out. Placing it back in the video recorder she rewound it and pressed play, blinking slightly as the bright, black and white image appeared on the television.

Flickering, panoramic images of her empty bedroom filled the screen, a subtle hiss of white noise filling the air. Tommy had been right when he'd said the sound would be crap. Rita held down the fast forward button, watching the image of her bedroom become obscured by lines of interference. She released it at the sight of Campbell moving into the room and closing the door, watching as he made his way to the bedside cabinet and set up what she recognised as lines of cocaine.

Rita couldn't help but smile at her stroke of luck. Not only had she caught him on film beating her up, but doing drugs as well. An unexpected but pleasant surprise that convinced her even more that what she had just put herself through had been worthwhile. This must be a slam-dunk for getting him kicked off the police force with an additional prison sentence in his near future. Rita could just see the headlines now.

An Officer not a Gentleman.

Oh, Cokey Copper Busted

She depressed the fast forward button again, stopping at the scenes of them having sex. Letting it play, Rita felt herself wince as she watched him roughly positioning her about the bed, absentmindedly touching the swollen areas of her face where he had hit her.

His beating her suddenly appeared on screen, promoting Rita to hit the stop button. She didn't need to see it from an abject perspective. First person had been more than enough.

Ejecting the videocassette again, she held it tightly as though it were something precious. She would call Karen and arrange for its collection. Rita didn't want it in her flat, not only because of what it showed but what it represented. It was their only leverage against a corrupt, government official and she didn't want the responsibility of keeping it safe.

Rita had done her part and the Royal Shakespeare company would be proud.

Rita had sacrificed a lot to get Campbell, going so far as to put her life in jeopardy. It worked. The videotape was accidently on purpose delivered to the Daily Mirror, News of the World, The Sun... all the reputable papers, all who ran a front page spread on the corrupt police officer who been caught with cocaine in his possession and filmed beating up an, as yet, unidentified female.

It would probably come out eventually that Rita was a prostitute. Would it make any difference? He'd still been filmed punching a woman that oddly doesn't go down well in the police force. Kaz helped relocate her for the time being in one of George's other properties in South Shields. Campbell had been sacked from the police force and was awaiting trial for possession of illegal drugs, but on the off chance he went looking for revenge, we all agreed it was for the best if she laid low with her sister for a while.

Of course, if I'd known then what I know now I would have killed the fucker. But as the song says 'Ain't That A Kick in the Head'. Was it enough for Alan? I guess it depends how you define justice.

Campbell went to ground and couldn't be found. I tried, fuck me I tried. But no one had any idea of his whereabouts, not even Steven. In the end, Kaz located him. Underestimated that woman from day one. There was me thinking I came out of prison the big man and my step sister was... well, anyway I think she always knew where he was, but kept it back specifically... waiting for that right moment to tell me. She once said she didn't believe in fate. How could she, otherwise she was always destined to be raped no matter what she did. I understood her view.

Me, I did believe in fate and knew that Patrick Campbell would get his one day.

And he did.

A few months later, my old mate Andy Ross was paroled from prison. I hadn't expected to see any of the boys for some time, but it turns out good behaviour in prison does count for something. He turned up at the pub one Thursday afternoon; same old story, nowhere to go and zero prospects. Dad said he could sleep there for a few nights until he got his dole and things sorted. The pub was becoming a communal gathering point for ex-cons, much to Dad's irritation. He wouldn't have said anything, but I could tell he would rather I wasn't there, attracting other criminals. I got that. If I had a business I wouldn't have wanted former murderers and armed robbers hanging out in my public house either. I promised myself I would find a little flat somewhere and be out of their hair. Besides, it would be nice to have somewhere Daniel could stay over... start to build that trust I needed from him.

I can't deny, mind, that seeing Andy was just like old times. We spent a good few nights drinking, laughing... I told him about Alan and the whole deal with Campbell. Andy stated he wished he could have been out to help us with the whole thing. I'm glad he wasn't to be honest. It was a personal matter and needed to be handled as such.

Still, it was good to see him, really good. Ronnie and I had built up a solid friendship, but seeing Andy again reminded me of how lost I'd felt in prison and how he and the rest of the guys had become a surrogate family.

As it turned out, Andy's being free presented an opportunity for him and for us all. One of those 'once in a lifetime' kind of things.

It was planned to perfection. Every facet of it had been reviewed, surveyed and perused over. Nothing had been left to chance. I was all cocky, thinking I was now a master criminal after only a few local jobs. How hard could it be? What could possibly go wrong? Piece of piss.

So of course, it all went tits up.

"Stop your grinnin' and drop your linen!"

Aliens

Chapter Twenty-Nine

Newcastle Upon Tyne,
Tyne and Wear

"I hope you're paying attention, gentlemen. There can be no room for showboating or doing your own thing on this. No one is to attempt to grow a brain."

Karen stood front and centre in the room, holding court over the three people occupying it. Tommy and Andy were sitting in a semicircle before a long, mahogany desk in George's office situated on Grey Street. From where Tommy sat he could see the 130-foot high column that was Grey's Monument from the window, the sky's fiery hue making it look like it was ablaze. There was an orange burn where the sun had once been and the clouds slowly drifted by, scattered and disappeared in the fall of dusk.

The Grade I listed monument had presided over Grey Street since 1838, erected to celebrate the passing of the Great Reform Act of 1832 in acclamation of former Prime Minister Charles Grey. The man had spent nearly half his life fighting for civil and religious liberties. Tommy remembered stories his Mam had told him about how the Reform Act had led to the abolition of slavery throughout the British Empire. As a child the tale hadn't really interested him. The one about his statue being struck by lightning causing his head to be found lying in the gutter had always intrigued him more. He admired the man's passion and devotion to his cause. They were principles Tommy prided himself on, seeing something through to the end. Showing you had the courage of your convictions illustrated the type of man you were.

One day I might even climb the spiral staircase to the top.

Tommy had been suitably impressed upon arriving at their destination. Making their way up the Tyne's north bank, Karen had escorted them towards a row of leaning merchant houses from the sixteenth-century. Stopping outside a five-storey Jacobean building, he had marvelled at the symmetrical array of windows, turrets, chimneys and gables. Inside was no less impressive as his sister moved him towards a staircase, past stunning oak carvings and chimney-pieces carved in marble and alabaster. Andy's gasping and hawing at the architecture had accompanied them all the way, causing Tommy to wonder if his friend was having a stroke.

Walking up the stairs, he had noticed a portrait of Elizabeth I, dressed as if for a masque. It was inscribed with the motto *'Non sine sole iris'*. *No rainbow without the sun.* He preferred the one he had learnt in Frankland - *'Video et taceo'*. *I see but say nothing.*

True in prison. True in life.

Karen had shown them into a plush, neutral décor office and had directed them to the chairs they now sat in. George had followed a few moments later, kissing Karen on the cheek before taking up a position by the window.

"I take it then we're not knocking over some bookies then?" Tommy said.

"On the contrary," Karen replied. "This is something that could potentially change your life. Change all our lives."

Tommy leaned forward his chair. "Okay, sis. I'm interested."

Karen sat down behind the large mahogany desk and settled back into the leather chair. She looked at Tommy intently, her eyes flicking over every facet of his person as though it was the first time she had seen him. She smiled before spinning the chair slightly to the left.

"George," she announced.

"Newcastle Banking Company," he stated. "Are you familiar with it?"

Tommy shook his head, still feeling a little puzzled at his sister's seemingly powerful position.

"It's basically a storage facility for safety deposit boxes. Local families have been using it for a few years now, ever since it moved to Grey Street after years of being dormant. House deeds, photos, alimonies, jewellery... all of those things people with far too much money consider precious and valuable."

Tommy looked around him in disbelief. "Forgive me, Kaz but this doesn't exactly smack to me of someone short of a few quid. I mean, look at all of this shit. You have enough money in here alone to topple a small dictatorship."

"This isn't mine," she interjected, gesturing around the room. "I only work here. Dark times are coming Tommy, financially and emotionally. The recession that hit America in '82 was just the beginning. If there isn't a stock market crash in the next year or two I'll be very surprised. Since Reagan the world's gone all neoliberal; low taxes, deregulation of the stock market. I mean, you have people like that fucking idiot Donald Trump being lauded as a poster boy for *laissez-faire* economics. The day someone like him decides to run for President we need to be praying for a zombie apocalypse I swear to Christ."

Tommy looked at Karen, in Andy's direction and then at George. "I'm sorry. I'm still not following why you have us here?"

"Because something needs to be done to knock the

social elite down a peg or two. I have a plan, but can't do it for a number of reasons. But you... criminals around here are getting nervous, Tommy. They know you've been inside, they know you're intelligent for a hard lad. You understand that violence isn't always the way. Look at Campbell and what we accomplished."

George gestured towards Karen. "Your sister speaks very highly of you. Not many men would have made such a sacrifice for anyone, never mind their family."

Tommy nodded his gratitude at the comment.

"And because your sister respects you," George continued. "We know you're the right man to do this. No ego, no desire to impress, just a motivation to get things done. You're a doer, Thomas."

"Don't call me Thomas," he snapped. "Just Tommy."

"Tommy," George repeated with an assuaging smile.

Andy nudged his friend. "I don't know about this, Magpie. I just got out for chrissake. This all seems a little too easy, don't you think?"

Tommy smiled at Andy's use of his prison nickname, causing his mind to drift back towards Charlie. He could almost hear his voice in his head, paraphrasing Sun Tzu.

"There are some roads which shouldn't be followed, Magpie. Then again, there are some commands which you shouldn't obey."

"Don't worry, mate. We'll be all right," he reassured his old friend. "So, you were saying...?"

He looked at Karen and smiled for her to continue. "The Newcastle Banking Company... a lot of the possessions in the boxes are things that have been passed on through family lineage, but they also contain things like land registry documents which are worth a lot of money if you know the right people."

"And I'm guessing you know the right people?" Tommy stated.

"We do," Karen said. "The process is relatively simple; swap the box out for a facsimile and take the contents of the original. These boxes have been there for years, so the chance of someone checking up on them is slim. Not impossible, but unlikely."

"It sounds like you both have it pretty well sussed," Tommy said, casting a judgmental glance at his sister. "Why would you need us?"

"I need someone who is capable of breaking into the bank and stealing them, but also someone I can trust."

"You know I'm not a bank robber, right?" Tommy asked.

Karen nodded. "Of course I do, dumb-arse. I also know how clever you are. I have no doubt you would be able to come up with a plan to break in, steal the boxes and get away clean."

Tommy turned and looked at Andy who had remained silent the entire time. "So, what do you think?"

Andy hesitated before he spoke. "I think I'm interested. I also think we need to decide whether or not to super-size this escapade to armed robbery."

"Nah-uh," Tommy intonated, shaking his head. "No guns. We do it in the middle of the night. Why would we need guns? It only runs the risk of turning a non-violent crime into a violent one."

"Okay," Andy conceded. "I'm thinking out loud. I just thought that travelling through Newcastle at night with thousands of pounds in shit and no guns seems a little foolhardy."

Tommy laughed. "It's Newcastle mate, not Detroit."

Andy returned a smile. "Fair enough."

Tommy thought for a moment. "Well, assuming we do it we would need blueprints, description of the building and the surrounding ones, description of the security system used and a Polaroid camera."

"A Polaroid camera?" George repeated.

Tommy waited a few beats. "For taking photos."

"Amusing," George said irritated.

Tommy stood and began pacing around the room. Andy leaned towards George and beckoned him to move closer.

"This is the first time we've been involved in anything like this, you know? I'm just out of prison with no desire to go back. We'll need time to think about it, never mind getting a crew together. This isn't a job only two can do."

Karen smiled. "You can have your time, but not too long, Tommy. But when you've decided, I need to know that you're all the way in or you come all the way out. Halfy-halfy won't cut it."

Tommy stopped his patrolling and faced Andy. "Charlie used to tell me that only by pushing our boundaries can we hope to break them."

"That sounds like ol' Riley," Andy said with a smile. "Come to think of it, I think I know a guy. Lives in Redcar and trains at the gym I used to go to. I'll give you the details."

Tommy nodded at his friend and turned towards his sister. "I'll let you know tomorrow."

"Fair enough," she acknowledged.

Tommy nodded towards Andy, indicating it was time for them to leave. As he moved past his sister, he stopped and gave her a hug. He was halfway through it before he realised it was the first time he'd held his sister since that night. Emotions he thought long buried bubbled to the surface, but he kept them subdued. There was no way he was going to let his sister's boyfriend see him unreserved.

"Take care, Kaz," he said as they parted. "We probably need to talk after this."

Karen nodded and held his hand. "We need to talk about a lot of things, Tommy. Your son being one of them."

"Why else do you think I'm considering this?" he replied, making his way with Andy towards the door.

It had been closed a few moments before either of them spoke.

"Do you think he'll do it?" George asked Karen, pouring himself a whisky from the bar in the corner of the office.

"He'll do it," she confirmed.

"How can you be so sure?"

"Because of something his mother said when she was dying." Her eyes took on a distant look as she spoke.

George cradled the glass in his hands. "And what was that?"

"She told him that at some point in your life you're going to want to give up on everything."

"That doesn't sound conclusive evidence to me," George said, sounding more condescending than he had intended.

Karen spun and faced him. And then she told him "'*Don't you dare.*'"

George put the glass down and moved to stand beside her. "I'm sorry, Karen. I didn't mean to drag up bad memories."

She pulled away from him and stood by the window. "It's not old memories that have me worried. It's the bad ones I know are going to be made from this moment onwards."

Her mind turned towards the preparations they needed to make if this was to work. Their plan was elaborate and risky but achievable. She couldn't deny she loved the sheer brazenness of it.

For the time being though, there was nothing to do but wait.

"The defense department regrets to inform you that your sons are dead because they were stupid."

Top Gun

Chapter Thirty

Redcar,
Cleveland

Much to Tommy's surprise, Redcar was mentioned in William the Conqueror's *Domesday Book*.

He was standing on the seafront reading a plaque on the wall acting as a barrier between the High Street and the ocean should the occasion arise where the sea became a little excitable.

Though he found the historical reference to the town's lineage interesting, his curiosity was piqued when he read that Larry Grayson had coined his phrase 'Shut That Door' whilst performing at the New Pavilion theatre that was now the Regent Cinema. Apparently the stage door had been open to the North Sea breeze, hence his desire to be out of the draft.

Tommy chuckled to himself and turned his collar up to the wind blowing in from the sea Larry had been so keen to complain about. The fifty-minute drive down from Newcastle had been uneventful. Andy had given him directions to the gym he had to visit and once parked up, Tommy had taken his time wandering up the seafront, past the many amusement arcades promoting *Outrun* which he could only assume was the latest game and stopping off at Pacittos to buy himself a lemon top. Tommy knew enough to know you didn't visit Redcar without buying yourself a lemon top.

He made his way past Leo's and up the seafront before turning onto Station Road, looking casually in the shop windows as he passed. His reflection appeared and disappeared as he moved between buildings, fading in and out of existence like a spectral figure. He stopped outside a shop selling framed artwork, taking particular notice of the pastel picture of the Sydney Harbour Bridge. The bridge was faded in the distance with the Redcar seafront at the forefront, referencing the town's contribution towards the building of the landmark, in this case provision of the steel to construct it with.

Tommy continued up the road and turned onto Queen Street, crossing over almost immediately. The alleyway entrance to his destination reminded him of the gym in his parents' pub; you only found it if you knew it was there. Someone could easily walk past the opening and not realise there was a business at the other end, never mind a gym.

He walked towards the painted black door leading into Iron Asylum. The garage next to it proclaimed they had been *'Creating Monsters in the gym since 1983'* besides an oversized caricature of what could either be The Hulk or just a really big bastard. Already the gym looked like somewhere Tommy would have loved back in the day and others would dare to tread.

He stepped inside and was immediate assaulted by the sound of Bon Jovi's 'You Give Love a Bad Name' playing one louder than you would normally find a comfortable listening volume.

A few men were scattered about the floor, some performing dumbbell flyes on the weight benches, others curling barbells. One bloke built like Arnold Schwarzenegger was on the Smith Machine pressing what looked like four times Tommy's body weight. He hadn't realised how much he missed a good old-fashioned gym until this moment. No posing, no posturing, just men wanting to better themselves and prove that if you put your mind to it, you could accomplish anything.

He glanced ahead and saw a man leaning against the counter in conversation with a customer. Tommy looked around him at the motivating insights daubed in white paint on the black walls.

'Squat or Die!'

'There is no place for the weak here!'

'Train insane or remain the same!'

His personal favourite was already 'You are being watched, so please put ya fuckin' weights away F.A.O selfish cunts.'

"Now then my mate," the man behind the counter said. "What can I do for you?"

"I'm looking for Mick," Tommy announced.

"I'm Mick."

Tommy looked him up and down. "I was told to ask for Big Mick."

"As in young Mick?"

"As in Big Mick," Tommy replied, indicating height with his hands.

"Do you think he means young Mick," the customer at the counter chimed in.

"Do you mean my son Mick? He's the bodybuilder." Mick extended his arms outwards to indicate his son's width.

Tommy looked confused. "For fuck's sake, I was just told to ask for Big Mick."

"That'll be me then... old Mick. The other Mick, my son, is often called Big Mick because of his size, where a lot of the older customers call me Big Mick 'cause I'm older. If that's the case, you've been speaking to someone who knows me from old. Come round the back." He indicated for Tommy to follow him into an adjoining area that housed a bar, racks of t-shirts for sale and a couple of treadmills.

"Buster, will you watch the counter for a bit?" Mick shouted towards the man he had been talking to.

"No worries," came the reply.

Tommy was ushered towards an office at the rear of the bar. He dodged the two bulldogs lying on the floor who both raised sleepy heads to make note of his presence before closing their eyes again, finding him uninteresting enough to warrant getting up.

Mick sat down on a seat beside a television screen displaying various black and white images from around the gym. "Good lad that Buster. One of the hardest lads I know. You know those fuckers who you knock down and they just keep getting up? He's one of those. Anyway, what can I do for you?"

Tommy leaned back against the counter on the opposite side of the room, confident that the sounds of Bananarama keeping Robert De Niro waiting whilst they talked Italian would drown out their conversation.

"Andy Ross said you might be able to help me," Tommy stated.

"Andy?" Mick said. "I thought he was still inside?"

"Nope, got out last month," Tommy confirmed.

Mick smiled. "We go back a long way, him and I."

Tommy could see he was reminiscing about events from their past. Given what he knew of Andy, he imagined they weren't recollections of legal occasions.

"Yeah, well he speaks highly of you and said you were the man who knows everything about everybody."

"Did he now?"

Tommy nodded. "You're a real life fuckin' Yoda the way he says it."

Mick gave a booming laugh that reminded Tommy of Brian Blessed. "I've been called worse. Well, if you know Andy you must be all right. Banged up together?"

"Yeah… Frankland."

"Ah, the garden spot of Durham. Not bad I guess as prisons go."

"I guess," Tommy conceded.

"So, my mate. What do you need from me?" Mick asked.

"I need the name of a schemer. Someone who's good at sussing out blueprints, planning for eventualities… that kind of thing."

"Organising a complicated birthday party are we?"

Tommy smiled. "Something like that."

Mick thought for a moment. "I do know a guy, trains in here. If you leave your number I'll pass on a message to him. Can't promise aught but it's the best I can do."

"Fair enough," Tommy said. He made his way out of the office and towards the weights floor. Mick followed close behind.

"So, what's business been like?" Tommy asked, scanning the room.

"Ah, fair to middling. Tends to get busier during the summer for obvious reasons, but we have our core regulars."

"Looks like you have some professional big fellas too," Tommy said, nodding towards the man who had been on the Smith Machine earlier and was now front lateral raising two twenty-kilo dumbbells.

"Yeah, we have a few. They're in the photo frame over there." He pointed towards a large picture on the wall that held shots of various bodybuilders posing during competitions. "Dave Bell, Jess Hart, my Ami…"

"*Your* Ami?" Tommy quizzed, turning to look at Mick.

"My girlfriend. She's won all of these." He gestured to the statues on the shelves behind them.

Tommy perused the awards, making approving noises as he went. The gold and silver sculptures covered a wide variety of bodybuilding championship events – local, regional, N.A.B.B.A.

"Impressive."

"Yeah, she is," Mick agreed with a smile that disappeared as quickly as it had appeared. "This job? It's not local, is it?"

Tommy shook his head. "No, a little further up north."

"Good," Mick said. "I've no problem with what people do for a living. And if Steve wants to work with you, that's up to him. I just don't want anything coming back here if it all goes tits up."

"I understand," Tommy agreed. "Don't worry, you have my word."

Mick studied him carefully. "I don't know you from shit, but oddly I believe you."

He held a clenched fist out towards Tommy. "Take care, matey. I'll tell you the same thing I tell the lads who come in here. Be a minority. Don't just settle for being the majority."

Tommy bumped his knuckles against Mick's. "I'll bear that in mind. And I'll tell Andy you send your regards."

"Please do," Mick said.

At that moment, a young woman with dyed blue hair and a physique most men would envy came down the stairs beside them and moved to stand next to Mick.

"This is Ami," Mick announced, putting his arm around her protectively.

Tommy nodded acknowledgement of her presence. "I hear you're the next big thing." He indicated in the direction of the picture frame.

"That's the plan," she said quietly.

"Well, good luck. Looks like you're in the right place to get there."

Ami smiled. "Best gym in Redcar," she announced.

"Fuck that," Mick said. "Best gym in the world!"

Tommy laughed and waved goodbye before making his way out of the gym and back into the alleyway.

It was odd how somewhere like that could make you feel like you could do anything. The people training in there believed they could do more with themselves – *be* more than themselves.

An old Oscar Wilde quote came to mind as he made his way back towards the cold Redcar seafront.

"We are all in the gutter, but some of us are looking at the stars."

Tommy was never going to be in the gutter. His stars however, were a darker shade of criminal.

"Somebody once wrote, "Hell is the impossibility of reason."
That's what this place feels like. Hell."

Platoon

Chapter Thirty-One

Newcastle Upon Tyne,
Tyne and Wear

Tommy sat in darkness, contemplating his future.

A storm was brewing, figuratively and literally. A stiff northeasterly wind had risen up, buffering the pub so hard the windows rattled softly in their frames. The lights from cars passing on the street below flared across his room, causing misshapen forms to strobe across the walls before bleeding away into nothingness as quickly as they had appeared; wraiths beckoning for him to join them in their silent lament.

The room was filled with a depth of stillness Tommy hadn't experienced since Frankland – those moments during the witching hour when an eerie disquiet fell across the prison as everyone slept. It was then that Tommy had often felt the rage of those incarcerated along with him, as if it had become a tangible presence in those twilight moments. Now, like then, he could feel it once more only this time it was the conflict building within him like pressure on a dam, demanding to be free.

His sister had provided him and Andy with what appeared to be a well thought-out plan. She had always been the smart one, but until now he hadn't realised just how clever she truly was.

The brothel had given him an idea that she was able to see the bigger picture, with her plan for Campbell clarifying she could also be inventive and vindictive. But until now he'd had no idea she was also a calculating, opportunistic businesswoman albeit with a criminal angle. She wasn't the sister he had grown up with, but then again he wasn't the same either. They had both endured so much. Maybe it had been inevitable that they would end up down this path. Broken souls longing to be mended, seeking solace in whatever form they could find.

Tommy had only ever dreamed of being a boxer. That was it. Circumstance had forced him to consider becoming a criminal. But life breaks in mysterious ways and fate can be a cruel mistress. Charlie had taught him that being a criminal didn't mean being cruel or despotic. You could maintain your moral integrity despite your chosen career path. It was that ideology Tommy had always fought to maintain. He had never forgotten his promise to himself after his Mam had died. Care for those who mean the most and never be cowardly or cruel.

He had tried to create some semblance of a normal life for himself, but what was normal? A house and nice car containing the requisite 2.5? Being in prison changed everyone, some for the better and some for the worse. Others, like Tommy, had come out somewhere in between. Caught between the realisation that you were a criminal and had the tools to be a good one, but didn't necessarily have enthusiasm for the job.

Once he had accepted he was destined to be a small-time Scarface, he had decided to keep it small - local jobs, nothing too dangerous, nothing too risky. Campbell had been an exception driven by justice. Or had it been revenge? Either way, it had been his first step into a game that didn't tolerate losing. He had never had ambitions to be carrying out big jobs with big risks attached, but he also knew that if you wanted the ultimate, you had to be willing to pay the ultimate price.

This job would be huge, enough for him to take Daniel away

from the North of England and go somewhere he could leave all of the shit behind and create new dreams.

With Andy and Ronnie on board alongside his contact from Mick, Tommy was confident they could do this.

But, sitting in the obsidian cloak of darkness, Tommy also knew whatever he decided now would define him for the rest of his life. In prison, you did what you had to in order to survive. Out here, you had a choice as to how you were going to define survival.

"Money won is twice as sweet as money earned."

The Color of Money

Chapter Thirty-Two

Newcastle Upon Tyne,
Tyne and Wear

A map of Newcastle was spread out on the table with an enlarged map of Grey Street and the surrounding areas on top of it. Polaroid photographs were dotted about showing the security cameras in the building from various angles.

"So, the Newcastle Banking Company is here, nearest police station is here on Pilgrim Street, about half a mile away and the entrance to the old coal tunnels is here on Ouse Street. Now the section of the tunnel that leads to the Tyne was demolished in 1878, however it's still accessible all the way to St Mary's Place, just off College Street. If we can get there, we're just off the A167 and then out."

Tommy looked at his companions individually, waiting for comments whilst using the opportunity to try and discern anything from their expressions. Ronnie looked almost excited, Andy was studying the map intently and Steve, who had come highly recommended by Mick, looked suspicious.

"Questions?" Tommy asked.

"How far is it from the bank to College Street?" Steve asked.

"About 700 yards," Tommy replied.

"How much traffic are we expecting at that time in the morning?" Andy spoke without looking up from the map.

"Four in the morning?" Tommy shook his head. "Hardly any, if at all."

"How are we getting there?" Steve pointed to College Street in the map.

"Quad bikes. Ronnie knows a guy… they're difficult to trace and small enough to traverse the tunnels."

Steve nodded agreement. "And we're using the tunnels, why?"

"No surveillance, less chance of being seen."

"How are we carrying the boxes?"

"Trailers on the back," Tommy said. Light and manoeuvrable."

"So, the plan is…?" Steve asked.

Tommy took a deep breath. "So, the plan is we take one of the bikes in a van to the back of the bank. I'll recce the tunnel from Ouse Street all the way to College Street and meet you there. We get in, remove the boxes and load up the trailers, drive the van to the tunnel entrance, burn it and take off up the tunnels on the bikes. Once we're out at Ouse Street we split up and meet up as agreed."

"How is all of this crap getting fenced?" Ronnie asked.

"Kaz'll know someone."

"You know, this could actually work," Andy said, finally looking up from the map.

"I fuckin' hope so," Tommy said with a chuckle.

"Who's financing this whole enterprise?" Steve asked.

"I'm guessing George," Tommy said. "He provided the blue-prints, the schematics for the security system and the funding."

Steve remained impassive. "You trust him?"

Tommy replied without missing a beat. "I trust her."

"Fair enough," came Steve's guarded reply.

"So," Ronnie said. "We're really gonna do this?"

Tommy nodded. "We are. This will be big… lots of money to be made. Once we cross this line, we're no longer second-rate nobodies knocking over cargo containers. The police will be all over this like fuckin' herpes. There'll be no going back and we have to do this fast. According to Kaz, the company is getting ready to move to Leeds in the next fortnight so if anyone wants out, now's your chance. I'll completely understand."

Tommy glanced around at his friends individually and took the silence as a sign they were in agreement.

"Okay then, we go a week today. I want everyone studying the plans and the escape route. I don't want any surprises… none of us do."

Everyone murmured in agreement before breaking off and talking amongst themselves. Tommy sat down on the chair behind him and took stock of what they were about to do. He couldn't shake the feeling that there was something he was missing. He just couldn't put his finger on it.

He just hoped he managed to work it out before they were knee deep in stolen deposit boxes and hip deep in shit.

"Humans are such easy prey."

From Beyond

Chapter Thirty-Three

Newcastle Upon Tyne,
Tyne and Wear

Tommy imagined most people walked the streets of Newcastle without ever knowing what lay just a few feet beneath them.

The Victoria Tunnel was a Grade II-listed structure that had originally run under the city from the Town Moor all the way to the Tyne. Originally built as a wagon way to transport coal from Spital Tongues Colliery to the river, it had been active between 1842 and 1860 before being converted into an air raid shelter in 1939. Cleverly, each entrance incorporated a right-hand bend to protect those within from explosions.

As he idled towards the exit on College Street, the bright headlamp of the quad bike lighting his way, he tried to imagine what it must have been like back then. Wooden benches would have lined the walls alongside bunk beds with chemical toilets available at various points along the way. It would have been damp, full of people afraid of dying down in the darkness whilst bombs fell above them, though he had heard his Mam tell him that the motto back then was "Better damp than dead". Families and neighbours would have been sitting in groups, exchanging gossip and singing songs whilst they waited for the 'All Clear' to sound.

Its consideration as a protective installation had continued all the way to the Cold War, when it had been earmarked as a nuclear fallout shelter should the situation escalate between Russia and the rest of the world. Tommy wondered how many people knew how close they'd come to using it in 1962 during the 13-day standoff between Khrushchev and Kennedy.

Andy had called Tommy half an hour ago informing him they were parked up and waiting for him. He had to admit he was impressed with the mobile phones Karen had provided them. Technophone had developed a 7-inch tall phone which was certainly an improvement on the portable bricks Nokia and Motorola were peddling. She had preprogrammed in her number so Tommy could let her know when the job had been done.

Tommy revved up the incline representing the end of his twenty-minute journey in darkness and exited the tunnel. He stopped at the top and quickly scanned the area, satisfied that it was deserted before pulling out onto St. Mary's Place.

A minute later and he was behind the Newcastle Banking Company and reversing the quad bike besides the black van. In the back of the attached trailer he had half a dozen safety deposit boxes that were exact replicas of the ones they were going to be stealing. Another twelve were in the back of the van. Supplied by George, the plan was that they would swap out the fake boxes for the real ones so that no immediate suspicions would be raised when the company opened in the morning. As all the fake boxes were sealed shut, meaning it would take some time for anyone to realise what had occurred.

The lads were already hunched down around the back entrance to the building, talking softly as Tommy approached. Dressed in black jumpsuits and balaclavas, Tommy had difficulty working out who was who. The sky was clear but there was no moon. Even in the vague light he could barely see them. It was only when one of them stood up and spoke that he recognised him as Ronnie.

"We were beginning to wonder if you'd bottled it, mate."

"Not a chance," Tommy replied grimly.

The other two stood, allowing Tommy to work out from the body building physique that the one to his left was Steve. By process of elimination, the one on his right must be his old prison friend.

"It's beginning to feel a lot like old times," Andy said a little too cheerfully despite the mask muffling his voice.

"I don't recall us robbing anything in Frankland," Tommy replied curtly.

"Pardon me all over the fuckin' place," Andy countered glibly. "Who pissed in your cornflakes?"

Tommy took a deep breath. "Sorry, mate. I'm just a little tense, you know?"

Andy's eyes betrayed the smile Tommy couldn't see. "No worries. Just by the numbers and we'll be fine."

Tommy took one last look around their location. The only signs of life were the occasional moth fluttering around the streetlights and a dog nuzzling around some overturned rubbish bins in an alleyway on the opposite side of the street. The men around him held a wary silence like those attending a funeral or in this case, about to commit a crime.

Tommy turned and nodded towards Steve. "You're up, mate."

He approached the door and removed a black fabric pouch from his pocket. They had surveyed the building intensely since their meeting with George and Karen, taking Polaroids from every conceivable angle and studying the blueprints until they could have practically drawn them.

The building had only one external camera, a Sony XC-1 colour Videocam, which was positioned above the door where they currently stood. Tommy could see Steve had already disabled it, the recognisable flashing red light notably absent.

Inside, he had been told there were two further cameras, both equipped with Digital Alarm Communication that meant any alarm messages went out as a cellular transmission, allowing the police stations to receive the information faster than the previous analogue signals. In short, if they tripped an alarm they would have just four minutes to get out and away before they were arrested.

Steve had assured him he could handle the cameras, which meant all Andy, Ronnie and himself had to do was contend with getting into the room containing the deposits boxes and loading up the trailers.

They all watched in fascination as Steve worked on the wires running along the side of the door, sliding what looked like a metal plate between two contacts at the top. He continued manipulating his lock pick, slowly rotating it around whilst inserting a hooked length of metal in simultaneously. After what seemed like a long three minutes they heard him say "Got it," and watched as he pushed the door open.

Tommy nodded for them to enter. "Flashlights out and follow Steve's lead. We need to take out those cameras before we go anywhere."

Everyone uttered agreement as they filed into the building, taking up positions along the wall and out of the camera's line of sight as Tommy pulled the door shut. He could feel the tension in the air; no chance of turning back now.

Individual beams of light cut through the darkness, reminding Tommy of the lightsabers wielded in Star Wars. He realised he was making the thrumming noise in his head as they moved from side to side.

Tommy took a deep breath, sucking in warm air through the fabric of his mask. They needed to keep the momentum up. It was fear and the anticipation of action that kept criminals focused. Lose your sense of fear and you ran the risk of getting complacent. Tommy had no intention of getting cocky. A future with his son was at stake, not to mention the lives of the men beside him who had put their faith in his sister and a man they hardly knew. Tommy couldn't deny there was something he still found a little off about George. It was his sister that he trusted and always would. His mind briefly drifted to Alan and how much he would have loved to have been part of this.

Twisting his neck from side to side until he felt a satisfying crack, Tommy pushed the image of his brother from his mind and signalled towards Steve to go ahead. Andy and Ronnie maintained their positions against the wall, their eyes darting nervously from side to side. Tommy moved beside them and clapped them on the back reassuringly.

Steve slid along the wall, taking up position beneath the first camera. He reached into his inside pocket and removed some wire cutters, standing on his tiptoes to clip the cable at the very back. He signalled for them to move up and join him, nervously scanning the darkened building for any signs their presence had been detected.

"Where's the other one?" Tommy asked.

"I'm not sure," Steve said. "The only one watching the vault was that one." He pointed to the now defunct camera above them. "I'm guessing the other one is in the main part of the bank."

Tommy nodded his understanding and walked towards the vault area. The room containing the safety deposit boxes was secured behind iron bars with a gate in the centre. Steve was already kneeling in front of it, feeding thick wire on a spool he had removed from his duffel bag into the keyhole. He unrolled enough of it to allow him to take up a position back beside his friends and clipped the end of it with the wire cutters. He shoved the remainder of it back in his bag and pulled out a lighter.

"You might want to turn away. This could be a little bright," he warned.

Tommy shaded his eyes instead, curious to see what he was about to do. Steve flicked the flint and touched the brightest part of the flame to the end of the ribbon. Sparks flew up the length of the strip before consolidating themselves in a huge flare of white-hot light that burned for a few seconds. The ones who hadn't covered their eyes blinked away at the phosphenes dancing in front of their faces.

"Christ, what was that?" Ronnie asked.

"Magnesium ribbon," Steve replied.

Ronnie moved forward and blew at the white powder that had collected around the now melted lock. "Now that was very cool."

Steve stepped forward beside Ronnie. "And…" He pushed the gate gently with one hand, bowing as it easily swung open. "Voilà!"

"Very nice," Tommy said, clapping as he moved into the vault. The others followed close behind.

Being a public access area, it was all polished brass and silver and cream composite flooring; beautiful but of little substance as far as security went. Three walls curved before them, looking like the cross section of a spaceship. Each section contained safety deposit boxes numbered in 500 denominations. Tommy held the flashlight beneath his chin and pulled out a list Karen had given him that indicated the boxes they needed to be taking. He scanned the piece of paper and looked around the walls, quickly clarifying in which section the boxes they needed were being held.

Satisfied he had a rough idea, Tommy motioned for them to gather around him.

"Right, here's what we're going to do. Andy- you go out and

start unloading the trailer, bring the boxes in here and stack them on the floor. Ronnie and Steve - you look over this list and select twelve of the boxes to remove. We only need to remove them, not open them. That'll burn too much time. Take them out; replace them with a replica and then load them onto the trailers. Once they're full, we'll drive to the tunnel and then we're down and out."

Removing the boxes alone meant drilling locks. 2 drills; 18 boxes equaled about 45 minutes. He checked his watch – 0345. That would take them to about 0430. The streets would still be quiet enough for them to escape unseen.

"And you?" Ronnie asked.

"I'll be checking to make certain we're on our own and see if I can find that other camera. Don't want any surprises."

Ronnie looked as though he was about to say something, but he simply turned his attention towards the list of boxes they were looking for. Steve was busy removing the drills and an extension from the bag. He searched the room for a socket, locating one just outside the vault room. Plugging it in, he returned to the bag and sorted though a selection of bits before settling on two and securing them into the drills with the chuck.

Tommy could already hear the low whine as one of them burrowed into the first deposit box. He used the opportunity to begin searching the floor of the building, looking for anything that might resemble a security room. He located it almost immediately just along from where they had made their entrance. Inside were three monitors, displaying various angles of the building. Two of the screens showed static. The other displayed the main floor of the building. Tommy flicked the switches on the VCRs and ejected all three tapes. It didn't hurt to be cautious. Balaclavas or not, it wouldn't do to be all over the Nine O; Clock news.

He made his way back into the vault area and dropped the

videotapes into the duffel bag. Two boxes had already been removed and were stacked on the floor with the two lads already working on the third and fourth. Everything was going smoothly.

Now all he had to do was wait.

"You're a smart kid... figure it out."

The Hitcher

Chapter Thirty-Four

Newcastle Upon Tyne,
Tyne and Wear

"So, they're in?" Jack Hudson said, cradling the telephone between his shoulder and ear as he polished his glasses.

"They are," George confirmed. "It'll probably take them about forty five minutes to remove the boxes."

"And you're certain it'll be done?"

There was a pause at the other end of the line. "Yes."

"Hopefully, not too soon though, eh?" Hudson said in an excited tone. "We at least want them to think they have a fighting chance."

"What about Myers?" George asked.

Hudson put his glasses back on and poured himself a drink. "That little motherfucker is mine. Thinks he can jump rungs on the ladder and make it to the top quickly? Not in my town."

"I'll keep you updated," George instructed Hudson.

"See that you do," was his reply before replacing the handset.

He reclined back into the leather chair by the window. The

dawn was trying to break through the black sky, its burning hue slowly scorching away the night's embrace.

George had been the easier of the two to turn against Tommy. At least the other one had waited until his family were threatened before folding like a deck chair. Jack had simply thrown money at George and he had immediately given up his girlfriend's brother. Likely ex-girlfriend now.

No fucking loyalty, that was the trouble with the world nowadays. It was one thing he knew Tommy respected above all else. When they'd no longer needed him, George and Tommy's so-called friend had cast him out like a leper. Their moral code was no more than a bad joke, cast aside when no longer required.

Jack almost felt sorry for Tommy.

Almost.

Tommy Myers had been an insect buzzing around his person for far too long, making him itch and scratch. And like most insects, the most effective way of dealing with them was to have them squashed.

Jack Hudson finished his drink and found himself wondering if this new dawn would finally bring with it the promise of closure.

"I'm not going to lose him. Where is he?"

Legal Eagles

Chapter Thirty-Five

Newcastle Upon Tyne,
Tyne and Wear

Tommy paced the marble floor of the Newcastle Banking Company. He allowed himself a smile, quietly confident that everything was going as expected. Hell, better than expected.

They only had a few more boxes to remove and they could be out. He checked his watch.

Ten minutes ahead of schedule.

Another unexpected bonus.

Tommy didn't want to get too complacent but if this was big-time crime, he could see himself getting used to it.

Andy dusted himself off as he spoke. "Right, last two boxes and we're done. Everything else is in the trailers."

Tommy patted him on the shoulder. "Nice work, mate. Start collecting the gear and tidying up would you?"

Andy nodded and began collecting any rubbish that had been created, taking the drill from Ronnie who had already finished removing his box and was slotting the replica into position,

"Right, lets sweep this mess up," Tommy said, indicating

towards the metal shavings coating the floor around the vault.

Andy returned to the bag and removed a dustpan and brush, getting to work immediately sweeping the debris into a pile. Ronnie stood beside Tommy whilst Steve jumped into the truck and started the engine.

"Not too bad, Frankland. Not bad at all."

Tommy smiled at his friend's use of his full nickname. "I was just thinking that. Once Cinders there has finished his chores, we can be off. Lock this door behind us and no one will ever know we were here... until it's too late."

Ronnie remained silent and moved to the side, watching Andy finish brushing the shavings into a bin bag and wrapping it up before placing it in the duffle bag along with the dustpan and brush. He stood and placed his hands on his hips, admiring his work.

"Look at that. No one will be any the wiser."

"Yeah, yeah," Tommy acknowledged. "You did a grand job. Can we go now please? Burglars and all that."

Andy laughed and picked up the bag as he jogged towards the van. Tommy heard him say something to Steve but couldn't make out what it was. Whatever it was resulted in a muffled laugh.

"Looks like it's time for us to go," Tommy announced.

'You're right," Ronnie said. "And I'm sorry."

Tommy spun around. "Sorry, for what...?"

The gun was aimed directly at Tommy's stomach. Ronnie's hand was shaking slightly, but not enough that Tommy thought he could make a grab for it.

"I had no choice. He told me if I didn't do it then my family would be next." Ronnie sounded genuinely apologetic.

Tommy felt his heart rate rising, the body's physiological 'fight or flight' response flooding his bloodstream with adrenaline. Tommy had already felt amped up because of the robbery. Now his brain felt like it was going to explode. He swallowed the adrenaline jolt and took a few deep breaths, enough to clear his head and allow him to assess the situation. It wouldn't do to be stupid. Thinking was needed here, not action. Action would get him killed.

His old trainer's voice echoed around his head. *"Let your ego take the hit. There is no better lesson than trying not to pay attention to your ego. That's how people lose fights."*

He made certain his body language was disarming as he stared his old friend in the eyes. "You're betraying me, Ronnie. Is that it?"

Tommy waited a few beats as he thought, scanning the room as though looking for something. It was just teetering on the edge of his mind, tickling at his brain but he couldn't quite get to it. What was he missing? A cold shiver ran down his back as all the pieces suddenly clicked into place.

"Hudson." He said it matter-of-factly as he turned towards Ronnie.

"He's a fucking powerful man, Frank. You've been pissing him off ever since you got out. With this Ren fella trying to take over his businesses, I think you're just the proverbial straw, mate."

"I trusted you. We were supposed to be a home team."

Ronnie shook his head. "No, you don't understand. It's my fucking family we're talking about here. What was I supposed to do?"

Tommy moved forward slightly and smiled sadly. "Come and talk to me about it."

"Right, And how was that supposed to go? 'Oh, by the way,

Jack Hudson has blackmailed me into setting you up so he won't kill my family. Is that okay?' Don't be fucking stupid!"

Tommy moved forward again. "Yeah, that's right you could have. After everything we've been through…"

"Listen, I never meant for any of this to happen."

Tommy frowned in disbelief. "Whatever. Just tell me one thing…"

Ronnie cut him off, knowing what he was about to say. "She's not involved, As far as I know, she knows nothing about this. I only know George is in on it."

Tommy let out an audible sigh of relief. That was all that mattered. Despite the surreal scenario playing out before him, knowing Karen hadn't betrayed him made everything else seem less important. He felt ashamed to have even thought it, but then again he hadn't expected one of his closest friends to stab him in the back. But if she didn't know about George and Hudson, then she was in danger. His son was in danger.

"Ronnie, listen to me," he said desperately. "If Karen doesn't know, then she could be in danger. My son, Ron… for fuck's sake, you know she has my son."

Ronnie appeared to physically slump, as though a great weight had just been placed upon his shoulders. "I'm so sorry, mate. I don't want anything to happen to your kid, but my family, Tommy… you have to understand."

Tommy's face took on a look Ronnie had never seen before. His eyes seemed to darken to the point of becoming black whilst his smile took on a thin, cruel appearance.

"You know you're going to have to kill me, right? Ronnie, are you listening to me? You're going to have to kill me, because if you don't, when I get out of here, and I will get out of here, you know I'll find you and I'll kill you."

Ronnie had subconsciously taken a few steps backwards.

He was rarely afraid, but standing there in front of a man he thought he'd known, he suddenly realised he didn't know him at all.

He pointed the gun at Tommy's face, his finger shaking on the trigger. Beads of sweat ran down Ronnie's forehead, forcing him to wipe his brow with the back of his hand.

"Go on," Tommy goaded him. "You know you need to do it."

Ronnie moved the gun so close to Tommy's head that it was almost touching. Blinking rapidly, he made a noise akin to a whimper as his internal struggle manifested itself audibly.

"GO ON!" Tommy shouted, so loud that Steve and Andy got out of the van. They moved behind Ronnie, but kept a discrete distance when they realised what was unfolding.

"Jesus Christ, Ronnie," Andy cried. "What the fuck are you doing?"

"You stay out of this," he said without turning round. He knew if he looked away from Tommy for even a second, he was a dead man.

The gun was shaking uncontrollably. Ronnie's face had taken on a resigned look, as though the consequences of not killing him suddenly began to take hold. Jack Hudson would want him dead. Tommy Myers would want him dead. Everything had gone south in the space of five fucking minutes.

Shaking his head at his internal regret Ronnie moved backwards quickly, forcing Andy and Steve to do the same. With the gun still pointing at Tommy, he grabbed hold of the door.

"I'm so sorry, Tommy. I really am."

Tommy's face momentarily softened again, his voice full of sadness. "Me too, matey. Me too."

"They'll be coming for you... you might want this."

He threw the gun towards Tommy and quickly slammed the bank door shut. Tommy heard him instruct Steve to lock it again, made out a refusal and some debate as to leaving him in there before the familiar clicking of items in the lock signified he was sealed in. He heard arguing and raised voices, Andy challenging him, Steve asking what the fuck was going on. Ronnie told them to shut up and get in the van or they would all be nicked. He heard Andy refuse followed by what appeared to be a scuffle, someone being thrown into the side of the van perhaps. Either way, he recognised the doors being shut and the van driving away.

He immediately wondered if Andy and Steve had been in on it and whether the performance just then had been just that – an act. But they had seemed too surprised upon seeing Ronnie with the gun so he just didn't buy it. Or maybe he was just stupid.

It was something he would debate at some length later – once he was out of this clusterfuck.

*"It feels good because God has power. If one does what God
does enough times, one will become as God is.
God's a champ. He always stays ahead. He got 140 Phillipinos
in one plane crash last year. Remember that earthquake in
Italy last spring?"*

Manhunter

Chapter Thirty-Six

Newcastle Upon Tyne,
Tyne and Wear

Tommy paced the length of the room, trying to focus his mind.

He needed to get out of the building. It was still early enough that the streets would be pretty much deserted and he knew the quad bike was still outside as he had seen it still parked up before the door had closed and hadn't heard the engine being started.

Tommy picked up the gun and turned it around in his hands. He knew fuck all about guns and had never even fired one. All he knew was that they were like a camera – point and shoot. He looked over what he knew to be the safety. It was off. Ronnie had been serious about killing him.

A cold shiver ran down his spine at the realisation he had been so close to dying. He had been convinced Ronnie must be bluffing. To frighten a man who had served in Belfast during The Troubles took some doing. Hudson must have really convinced him his family was in danger. Tommy found himself feeling almost sorry for Ronnie rather than angry toward him.

Flicking the safety on so he didn't accidentally blow his balls off, Tommy placed the gun in the waistband of his trousers and

moved out into the large elongated area that was the business floor. Large windows bookended both ends of the room on opposite sides with customer service counters set at equidistant points along the floor to his right.

He moved quickly to the main door, curious to see if there was an easy way out. It came as little surprise to see that the door was made of solid oak, at least three feet thick and covered with a myriad of bolts and locks.

Probably bricked up and welded shut from the outside too, Tommy thought sarcastically.

Tommy walked slowly to the centre of the room whilst he considered his options, which he realised pretty much consisted of fuck all. He was making his way back into the vault area when he remembered.

The phone!

He had completely forgotten about the mobile phone. Quickly pulling it from his pocket, he keyed the button Karen had told him her number was stored under. Minutes seemed to pass before she answered though in reality it was only two rings.

"Hello."

"Kaz, it's me," Tommy said.

"Tommy, I wasn't expecting your call yet. Is everything…"

'Shut up and listen. I need you to get Daniel and leave town. Don't tell me where you're going, just take what you need and go."

"Tommy, what's going on? Is everything okay?"

He took a deep breath that felt almost cleansing. "It's all gone tits up, Kaz and now I'm locked in the very building I was robbing. There's irony for you."

252

"What? I don't understand. How did that happen?" The pitch of her voice was rising with panic.

"Ronnie... he set me up. Hudson threatened his family, told him they'd be killed if he didn't do what he asked, which was apparently to leave me to take the fall."

"What can I do to help?"

"Exactly as I asked. Take Daniel and leave Newcastle. Don't tell anyone where you're going, not Dad, Donna... do not tell George. I mean it, Kaz. No one."

"Okay, okay. I'll start now. What are you gonna do?"

Tommy considered his answer. "Whatever I can," came his stoic reply.

He lowered the phone and cocked his head to one side, listening intently to clarify what he thought he had heard.

"Motherfucker," he whispered under his breath.

Karen was shouting his name as he raised the phone back up. "Tommy? What's going on?"

"Karen, listen. The police are coming. Ronnie must have called them... part of his instructions I imagine. Or maybe I tripped something without knowing. Either way, I have to go. And so do you. Get out, Kaz. Promise me you're going right now."

"I am, I am," she assured him. "I'm going to wake Danny now and we'll go. Tommy... we were supposed to protect each other. That was the deal. Fucked that right up, didn't we?"

He smiled a genuine smile. "You'll still have time for that, sis. For now, get away from here and we'll call it quits."

He hung up, cutting her off in mid-sentence. Tommy didn't want her to waste any more time on the phone

He had a more immediate problem. The sirens were getting closer and he still had no way out.

Other than one.

Noise wasn't really an issue any more.

He pulled the gun from his waistband and moved towards the door they had originally entered through, tightening his grip around it. Though he knew little, he knew enough about guns that it would recoil and he needed a firm grip.

Taking an open legged stance to balance himself, Tommy raised the gun and pointed it towards the door. Locking his elbows and flexing his lower arm muscles, he steadied himself and tightened his grip. His palms felt sweaty, his breathing rapidly increasing with every passing second. The sound of the police sirens getting closer only enhanced the tension of the situation.

He squeezed the trigger four times, blinking with every shot. The wood splintered on and around the lock of the door, the echo of the gunfire bouncing around the vault before disappearing into the atmosphere.

Lowering the gun, Tommy moved forward and examined the door before kicking it open. It swung freely and banged against the wall before slowly closing again. The smell of cordite from the weapon's discharge filled the air, burning Tommy's nose and making him want to sneeze.

An overwhelming sense of relief washed over him as he saw the quad bike parked up against the wall. With the loaded trailer still attached.

Ronnie had obviously forgotten to empty it in his hurry to get away.

Daft bastard.

Tommy couldn't deny the contents might come in handy. Something he would consider another time.

With the sounds of the police cars getting close, Tommy considered the gun. It was one thing to be arrested for burglary.

It was another to be in possession of a dangerous weapon.

He quickly wiped his sleeve around the grip and barrel to remove his fingerprints and threw it onto the lower part of the roof behind him.

Jumping on the bike, Tommy kicked the engine in and reversed back slightly before pulling away so quickly the rear wheels spun for a few seconds. He shot up towards Hood Street and turned onto Pilgrim Street, the trailer bouncing gently behind him. If he could get to the tunnel entrance at St. Mary's Place then he would be hidden all the way to Ouse Street. Once out he could stash the trailer, ditch the bike somewhere on the Quayside and make his way towards Gateshead. He needed time to collect his thoughts and work out what his next move would be.

His foot was like a lead boot on the accelerator. He could still hear the sirens in the distance, far away but not far enough. He kept telling himself to slow down, not draw attention to himself but his foot seemed nailed to the pedal.

He was about to turn off onto Market Street when he saw the light from a car expanding in front of him as it travelled up the parallel road. He quickly spun the bike around and accelerated into the grounds of Cornerstone Church, turning off the engine and allowing the bike's inertia to carry him forward a few feet until it stopped at the side of the building, out of line of sight. He climbed off and peered around the corner of the church.

He saw a police car turning off Carliol Street and slowly pass by his hiding location. His heart was knocking hard enough to shake his arms, forcing him to hold onto something to counteract the dizziness he felt.

If they spotted him, he would be trapped. They were between him and his exit onto the main road towards the tunnels.

Tommy wasn't going back to prison. He would die first.

He felt his heart rate slow as the car continued on up Market Street and in the opposite direction to where he needed to be. Climbing back on the bike, Tommy took a moment to compose himself. He couldn't remember the last time he had been so afraid. Quietly thanking whatever gods were watching over him, he turned the ignition and slowly backed the bike onto the road before accelerating away at high speed.

It was a few hundred yards before he felt comfortable enough to ease his foot off the pedal, allowing the bike to slow as he moved off John Dobson Street and onto the B1309 that would lead him around in a semi-circle to College Street.

Tommy's jaw was clenched in anticipation of what would be greeting him as he pulled onto St. Mary's Place. He had almost been expecting to see a row of police cars waiting.

The opening to the St. Mary's Place tunnel appeared in the distance, welcoming him in like the monstrous maw of a huge beast.

He flicked on the headlight, blinking as its incandescence lit up the darkness like an explosion. A few rats scuttled into the shadows as he sped down the incline and onto the home stretch of his journey. The rattle of the trailer echoed around him, causing the tunnel to feel just that little bit smaller.

As the darkness behind him appeared to swallow him whole, he had a sudden epiphany. It was never going to stop. For everything, there were consequences. Tommy realised he had never considered it in those stark terms before. They might be unforeseen or unaccountable for, but there would always be a price to pay both for the crimes he had committed and the ones yet to come.

The bank job had been his chance to really make his mark. Right about now they should have been sitting somewhere with a few beers talking about it, joking that the closest thing they'd had to a problem was the location of a socket for the extension cord.

No violence, no drama.

Fucking George.

He had known all along there was something off about him. Trusting his sister shouldn't have distracted him from what he knew in his gut. George's misguided loyalties and Ronnie's personal reasons had made the job memorable for completely different reasons.

He had finally come to accept that all of his roads stemmed from that one moment in time.

It was a polestar around which his existence would forever turn.

I made it back to the pub that night without incident.

I had intended to dump the bike and head off towards Tyneside, but decided to double back on myself and go back home instead. I figured I had a good few hours where all concerned would assume I was locked up in either the bank or a police cell. Either way, they would think I was incapacitated and that meant time to get my head together and grab some sleep.

Not that I got any. All I could think about was that motherfucker Hudson and how he had fucked my life up at every turn. It was like he was my own, personal Lex Luthor, constantly scheming and obfuscating. His knowledge was my Kryptonite.

I needed to take him down. How I had no idea, but something had to be done. He had too much power, never mind the fact that he was responsible for three of the most traumatic experiences in my life so far.

The trouble was that I didn't know what was coming. Funny that. You spend all that time in prison, thinking it has made you savvy and aware of everything going on around you. Inside I had known every move, every scam and no one dared come near me after word got around about Caplin. Did I kill him? You're fucking right I did. Stabbed him in the gut with a shiv and snapped off the end so he couldn't pull it out. Left him bleeding to death sitting on a toilet. Everyone had pretty much known it was me, but as there was no proof that was that. That's how it was inside. You stood your ground and said to others "No, you move."

What I hadn't expected, aside from the being shot thing which we'll be coming to in a moment, was that I would get to see Patrick Campbell one last time.

Isn't life a bitch.

"You say that so often, I wonder what your basis for comparison is?"

Labyrinth

Chapter Thirty-Seven

Newcastle Upon Tyne,
Tyne and Wear

10 Park Road.

That had been the address on the piece of paper Tommy had found slipped under his door in Karen's handwriting. She must have dropped it off after he'd fallen asleep.

Bloody woman. He had told her to leave, but she'd had to do it on her own terms. She'd always been the same.

Once he'd read the note and absorbed the information, he had understood why she had taken such a risk.

No personal message or well wishes. The note had simply said 'Patrick Campbell. 10 Park Road.'

She had found him. Tommy had no idea how she'd managed it when he'd been unable to, even with Stephen's help. One day he would get her to explain her penchant for knowing all she did.

His sister; madam and devious mastermind with a particular bent for the creative.

He had often wondered if anything good could have come out of that night. For so long he had thought it unlikely, but perhaps enduring what she had unearthed part of her that she hadn't even known existed.

Tommy had taken the road less travelled towards being somebody, but realised now that his aspirations had made him indistinct from every other wannabe criminal in the North East of England and probably the world. There was no trophy he could put back. No magic words that would change what happened that night or what he had done subsequently.

For the first time in his life, Tommy Myers realised he was truly out of options. Therefore, he had nothing to left to lose. He would do this for his brother and for Karen.

Karen.

Tommy still felt there was more to her than she was letting on, but now wasn't the time to worry about that.

He had an appointment with an old friend.

* * *

Patrick Campbell's two bedroom flat was located in a building on the outskirts of the city centre. Tommy had to admit, the view of Newcastle from the eighth floor where he currently stood looking out of the window was impressive.

Decorative shutters, scalloped fascia boards and fanciful rooflines gave the block of flats a futuristic air, reminding him of something out of Logan's Run.

He had waited for someone to enter via the door at the side and tailgated in behind them, using his most charming smile and self-effacing manner to explain he was visiting a friend. The attractive, middle-aged lady had simply smiled and been on her way, leaving him to make his way towards the flight of stairs. Noting the security cameras on his way up, he'd made certain to keep his face turned away and his baseball cap pulled low. It wouldn't do to have his face splashed all over *The Northern Echo* for what he was about to do.

Studying the panoramic view as though it were the last time

he would see it, Tommy turned away and moved towards his destination.

Flat 10.

As he got closer, he could heard Sade's 'The Sweetest Taboo' coming from inside. He put his ear to the door and heard a man and woman laughing in between the breaks of the songstresses' meaningful lyrics.

"There's a quiet storm coming indeed," Tommy said to himself quietly. "Right. About. Now."

He glanced around the lobby, but was satisfied he was alone. Bracing himself, he took a deep breath and kicked the door hard. It only took two solid blows for the wood around the lock to splinter, causing the door to swing open.

The woman in the bed on the opposite side of the room screamed, instinctively throwing the duvet over her naked body. Campbell, shocked at the unexpected arrival of Tommy, hesitated for a few moments before recognising that the man who had forcibly entered his flat wasn't making a social call.

"Patrick Campbell," Tommy announced. "You're a hard man to find."

He noted the cocaine lining the surface of the bedside table before pointing to the woman who had backed herself up against the headboard, a look of fear on her face.

"Don't worry, love. I'm not interested in you, just this piece of shit. Get dressed and leave."

She jumped off the bed, suddenly not concerned about her nakedness and picked up her clothes scattered around the floor. Pulling on her knickers and skirt, she was already on her way out the door whilst still putting on her bra.

"You need to find yourself a better quality of fuckbuddy," Tommy shouted after her, closing the door and securing it with the bolt at the top. He turned and looked at Campbell, shrugging his shoulders nonchalantly.

"I'm sure someone'll fix your lock. Not that you'll need it anymore after today."

Campbell stared at Tommy, burning hatred in his eyes. He was sitting on the edge of the bed, naked but seemingly unconcerned about the fact.

"Tommy Myers, well, well, well. I thought you'd forgotten about me. Knowing your feelings about loyalty and all that bullshit, I'd expected you to turn up a lot sooner."

Tommy locked onto the first part of his statement. "Forgotten about you? Not a chance. Like I said, I'll admit I had no idea where you lived but a little bird told me and well, here I am."

Campbell appeared to be considering his next words carefully. "It wasn't personal, you know. I was told that was what needed to be done, so I did my job."

"Your job?" Tommy said, taking two large steps towards Campbell. "Your job was to protect people, not set them up. He died thinking he'd betrayed me. That thought keeps me awake at night."

"None of it keeps me awake at night," Campbell said in a gleeful tone. "I just wanted you to know it was business. Besides, I'd say you got your own back, wouldn't you? The slag... she was your idea?"

Tommy shook his head. "Nope, not mine. I was in on it and thought as ideas go, it was a fucking belter, but aside from that... worked though, didn't it?"

Campbell studied him as though he were a new species. "That it did. Lost my job, charged with possession of drugs... you did well, bravo."

Tommy ignored his slow clapping. "So, who told you to do it?"

"What do you mean?"

"Set up Alan. Who ordered it?"

"Do I look fucking stupid to you?" Campbell asked.

"Is that rhetorical?" Tommy asked casually.

"Amusing."

"Let me guess. You won't tell me because of the old 'He's more scary than you' cliché. Doesn't that ever get old? I mean, why work for someone who's that dangerous?"

"Because it's worth it," Campbell said defiantly. "You know nothing about power or the respect that brings. Being a copper I learnt only one thing – nothing you do makes any difference. Everything I saw on the beat only made me feel helpless. I knew the law and the system, but no matter how many arrests I made, how many criminals I stopped, the apathy of this country towards crime and criminals is perverse. I found someone who wanted to make things better, who had his own way of doing things. Take control of all the crime and the criminals are no longer a problem, just a commodity. Then all you have to do is keep them in check. Once I was high enough, the organisation reached out to me, offered me a position. Keep the less savoury thugs in check, skim a little here, misplace a little coke there and all's well. I mean, what's not to like. Look around you. Look at all my shit. I'd say it was worth it."

"Worth it?" Tommy said passionately. "You killed my brother."

"I fucking told you, that wasn't my idea. They didn't want him, they wanted you. Still do as far as I know. You're a marked man, Tommy Myers. And this certainly isn't going to help your defense."

Tommy remained impassive. He recognised the truth in Campbell's words but would be damned if he was going to let him see that.

"I'll ask you again, who wanted me set up?"

"Go fuck yourself, Myers. You'll have to beat it out of me, but tick-tock… you don't have much time."

Tommy moved forward so he was standing over Campbell. "I can't be arsed. I'm just going to kill you instead."

Tommy had time to register the scared look on Campbell's face before he smashed his forearm into his nose, the resulting explosion of blood and snot splattering the white bed sheets like a Jackson Pollock painting.

Campbell's vision blurred as tears filled his eyes. The shooting pain he felt caused him to feel sick.

Tommy grabbed him by the neck and pulled him to his feet, lashing out with a head-butt to his already shattered nose.

Campbell slumped in Tommy's hands, so he let him fall to the floor. Whimpering in a manner akin to a small kitten, he began to crawl towards the living room area. His body smeared blood pouring from his nose across the floor in his wake.

Tommy stood astride him and placed a booted foot on his back, pushing him hard to the floor. "We're not done yet, Detective Inspector Campbell. I'll give you my permission to die in a minute, but not quite yet."

He stepped aside and flipped Campbell over with his foot, this time placing a boot on his neck.

"You're a… dead man… you know that right?" Campbell spat the words out between fits of blood-coloured coughing.

"I've been a dead man so many times, I'm fucking Lazarus," Tommy said. "So fuck you and fuck that."

Tommy moved his foot from Campbell's throat and positioned it over his left knee. He smiled at his brother's killer before stamping down hard. Campbell's knee gave a satisfying crunch as it shattered into half a dozen pieces.

Campbell screamed and moved his hands down to grab hold of his now destroyed leg.

Tommy moved around the other side and did the same to his other knee, relishing in the vision of his leg folding in backwards.

Campbell's screams were unearthly, causing Tommy to remember that he was in a block of flats where the walls were unlikely to be soundproof. He didn't have a lot of time.

"People like you, you're all the same. You think just because you have all that power that you can get away with whatever you want. That no one will stop you. Well, guess what fuckface. Consider yourself stopped."

Tommy moved to Campbell's head and looked down at his trembling face. "This is for my brother, you sonofabitch."

He raised his foot and smashed it down, heel first onto Campbell's face. His cheeks cracked almost simultaneously, blood pouring out of what was once his nose but now resembled an open orifice. A gurgling sound as he choked on his own blood filled the room, his whimpering now more like a groan of desperation from his collapsing face.

Tommy brought his foot down again and again, each time harder than the last. With every motion, he saw his brother's face. He imagined how scared he must have been, stood on the bridge looking down towards the water. The sense of hopelessness Alan must have felt was like a burning ember in Tommy's mind.

Campbell's face had begun to resemble a bloodied husk, the skin and muscle shorn away from his skull by the rough tread of his boot.

Stopping more through exhaustion than desire, Tommy staggered back, panting and gasping for air. He looked down at the now unrecognisable visage of Patrick Campbell and let out a huge sigh.

Dave had taught him to fight like a man, not beat someone

when they're down. He had never killed anyone in cold blood before, only in self-defense. He wasn't entirely certain how he felt about it.

Guilty?

Afraid?

What he did know was that he needed to be away from here. He had made far too much noise and expected someone would be investigating very soon. Besides, Campbell had been right about one thing. He was still wanted for questioning in regards to the robbery at the port.

Wiping the base of his boots with a kitchen towel and checking his face in the mirror to ensure he didn't look like Ash from *The Evil Dead*, Tommy walked out of the flat and back down the stairs into inexplicable blazing sunshine.

He felt like it was there to burn away his past indiscretions, absolving him of his sins and allowing his soul closure.

As he made his way back towards the centre of Newcastle, Tommy could see the warmth wasn't going to last. The mottled sky in the distance seemed like a portent of something fearful, grey like the ashes in a crematorium and bordered by a black as dark as coal.

It said to Tommy that after what he had just done, there could be no happy ending for whatever came next.

"It happens sometimes. Friends come in and out of our lives, like busboys in a restaurant."

Stand by Me

Chapter Thirty-Eight

Newcastle Upon Tyne, Tyne and Wear

Karen ushered Daniel gently ahead of her towards the train idling at the platform.

She had done as Tommy asked, collecting a handful of things for them both before leaving the flat without telling anyone. She felt guilty about not letting the girls know where she was going, though in truth she didn't really know herself.

She would contact them later and try to explain. They all knew the situation when you were running a less than legitimate business. What was the saying? Have nothing in your life that you can't walk away from in thirty seconds flat.

Aside from her family and Daniel, she had nothing. Not even George.

He had been a means to an end. She'd had suspicions that he had been working for Hudson for some time, but had never been able to confirm them.

The banking company job had been in the planning for a while, its overall intention to make them both a lot of money. She wasn't certain what his interpretation of their relationship had been, but for Karen it had purely been for convenience and business. He had helped fund her other ventures; the house for the girls, a few shops as a front for stolen goods, but the brains behind every decision had been her.

If the odd fuck to keep him on side had been what it took, she had been prepared to make that sacrifice. Sex was now her tool to wield, not something that was dependent on the whims of others. Eric Doyle had shown her that in the most perverse way imaginable, true power wasn't in what you thought you could take but in what you could offer. And men were so easily swayed when it came to sex. Flash a bit of thigh, eat your ice cream a certain way and you could have them eating out of your hand.

Dicks instead of brains. Listen to the wrong part of their anatomy every time.

But the job going sideways hadn't been part of the plan. Despite her suspicions, she had honestly thought that George would want to go through with it as it had had the potential to be a huge earner for them all. It would be a shame for her to have to kill him, though she knew if her brother got to him first he would save her the trouble.

Her thoughts drifted towards Alan, opening a portal to her guilt. There was never supposed to be casualties, certainly not members of her family. They might have never particularly connected as children when her Mam had married Thomas, but there had been affection for her stepbrother and she had always respected how much he meant to Tommy. The odd telephone call here, the occasional tip off was all that had been required for him to be onboard with another job.

The main objective had always been to fuck up Jack Hudson's supply chain and businesses. Eric had been his man, therefore Hudson had been inadvertently responsible for Tommy's incarceration and her rape. Jack could have cut that fucker loose any time he wanted to, given that he was already guilty of raping two other women. But he had kept him on his payroll, out of some misguided loyalty. That allegiance had cost Karen her soul and Tommy his freedom, neither of which could be easily forgiven nor forgotten.

Finding his previous victims hadn't been easy. Karen had only been successful in locating one of them. But a few choice words in her local one night and word got around that the man who had assaulted her had died. Once she came forward so did the other one and her brother was released from prison early but eight years too late.

Campbell had simply been an extension of Hudson's sociopathic ideal to keep people close to him whom he thought were valuable yet actually were a liability. His involvement in Hudson's plan to take Tommy out of the picture had been an unforeseen consequence. Karen had always known Campbell worked for Hudson, beating up potential witnesses, threatening other up-and-comers, but she hadn't considered that he would target her own family in order to get to Tommy.

Her hubris had resulted in Alan's death.

She had thought herself so clever, slowly taking over the prostitution business in Newcastle, right from under his nose. Undercutting his organisation at every opportunity and ensuring that he suffered the occasional robbery courtesy of Tommy and his crew. Meeting George and persuading him to consider robbing the Newcastle Banking Company had been the pinnacle of her achievements so far. But again, she had allowed greed and the promise of power to cloud her better judgment.

All that mattered now was Daniel and keeping him safe. She knew Tommy could look after himself. Getting away from Newcastle was her first priority, the second was setting herself up somewhere else. Maybe a little further south. Middlesbrough or Billingham.

She needed time to reevaluate her plan. The brothel would

continue. It was a nice little earner and now that Campbell was out of the picture, Rita and her sister would be safe. Karen hoped they would want to go back home. If so, Karen would ask Rita to mind the business for a while.

As they boarded the train, she directed Daniel towards the set of booked seats at the rear of the quiet coach. He climbed onto the seat nearest the window and sat his Teddy Ruxpin down on the table, humming to himself as he stared out the window and marvelled at the trains pulling out of Newcastle Station.

She gently stroked his head, prompting him to look up at her and smile. He was such a gentle boy with a kind heart. She was determined to keep him as far away as possible from the world she and her brother occupied. Tommy would agree. As much as he loved his son and had been trying so hard during his visits to connect with him, Karen knew he would want him to believe the world was a safe place.

Not filled with darkness and sharp angles that could pierce your soul at a moment's notice.

Whatever came of the robbery, Tommy would have secured his name as a player. Criminals talked. Ronnie's deceit would be uncovered upon which point he would learn that the level of loyalty criminals can have amongst those they consider family is unprecedented.

Hudson would be next. All Tommy had to do was stay out of his way and avoid getting himself killed.

As for her, she needed to work on her legacy. A name was no longer enough. It needed to be associated with a person.

Hiding in plain sight was no longer an option.

"The only evidence I see of the antichrist here is everyone's desire to see him at work."

The Name of the Rose

Chapter Thirty-Nine

Newcastle Upon Tyne,
Tyne and Wear

Tommy weaved his way between people in the street like a seasoned ice skater.

He had just left Dean Street and was making his way over the Tyne Bridge. Images of Alan flashed through his mind, cold and afraid standing on the railing and staring down into the abyss. He couldn't lie. He needed to be away from here for a while. He loved Newcastle, but his motivation to be somewhere else was not only driven by need due to his murder of Campbell, but by a compulsion to be somewhere less tainted with dark memories.

The rain overnight had left a fecund smell on the air, swollen soil and wet grass mixed with exhaust fumes from the myriad of cars flying by him in a blur of colour. Overhead, the sky was a tapestry of gloom, woven with varying shades of grey and black. Ominous portents of what was to come perhaps. Tommy had no intention of waiting to find out.

He turned onto Pipewellgate and began his journey towards the Gateshead Metro. From there he would catch a bus to Thirsk and then another to London, most likely arriving early tomorrow morning. Once there, he would evaluate his circumstances and decide his next step.

He had just crossed over the road and taken a shortcut down an alley off High Level Road when something struck him across the back of his head, knocking him to the ground. A flurry of blows struck him about the side of his face and on the back of his neck. Tommy threw his hands up behind his head to try and protect himself from the punches, managing to block a few whilst others managed to get through.

Tommy had always thought it was hyperbole when people said you saw stars after a solid blow to the head, but in this case he could actually see bright lights swirling around his head like tiny, blurred Tweety Pies.

From his position face down on the concrete, he could hear numerous voices behind him. One spoke loud enough to be heard above the others.

"You're a dozy cunt, you know that?"

Jack Hudson was standing over Tommy with a shotgun resting against his right shoulder like he was some sort of hunter.

Suddenly, the unnatural colour of the Newcastle sky seemed destined to keep its promise of the malevolent dread it had been threatening him with earlier. Had he been facing the other way, there is no chance he would have been caught off-guard like a punk. Fuckin' Jack Hudson. What a coward. What else should he expect from the man who had kept a rapist and corrupt police officer in his pocket.

"You Myers', you're all the same," Hudson said, crouching down beside Tommy and placing the shotgun across his knees. "Always whining about the hand you've been dealt. Karen, Alan... moaning all the time about having been pissed on from a great height. You need to learn to get over things, move on. None of you are too bright either. All this time and you still haven't figured it out. Don't you know who Campbell was workin' for? He may have metaphorically fired the gun that killed your brother, but who'd ya think loaded it in the first place?"

Tommy lay still on the floor, trying to comprehend what he had just heard. Hudson was saying he had put Campbell up to framing Alan? If that was true, then Tommy had been played for a fool.

If he had been paying more attention to what was going on around him instead of trying to become some sort of low-level crime boss, he might have been able to protect his brother. Campbell framed Alan as a grass to spite Tommy.

He lifted his head and counted four men flanking Hudson. All heavyset, all with disdain in their eyes. Or maybe it was embarrassment at his predicament. Either way, in his dazed state Tommy knew he couldn't take them all.

On a good day, he would have knocked them all out and smiled as they lay twitching in their own bodily fluids. But today wasn't a good day. It was fair to say that Tommy Myers was about to have the worst day of his life.

"You've no right to be up here with the big boys," Hudson said, signalling for two of his men to pull Tommy to his feet. "Who the fuck do you think you are? Michael Corleone? Just because you did some time, you think that makes you somebody?"

Hudson grabbed Tommy by his collar with one hand and pulled him close, venom in his voice and hatred in his eyes. "You're a fuckin' nobody and you know the thing about nobodies? Nobody misses them."

Hudson considered smashing Tommy in the face with the weapon, shattering his nose. That would have been satisfying enough. But it left open the possibility that he would come for him at a later date. Hudson knew that if you left someone like Tommy Myers alive after what he had just learnt, you would wake up with more than a horse head in your bed. Men like him would just keep getting up, no matter how hard you put them down. He had been like that in the ring. A force of nature, an unstoppable juggernaut that just kept coming. He had to put him down in the knowledge he wasn't going to be getting back up again.

Hudson pushed him backwards and raised the shotgun. The flash was blinding as the shot hit Tommy squarely in the chest. He flayed in an almost comical fashion, the force of the blast carrying him backwards a few feet.

Hudson's men looked around them anxiously, aware that the noise would have attracted unwanted attention. One of them approached his boss and whispered in his ear that they should get going and turned to signal for one of the others to collect the car.

Hudson walked up to Tommy's prone body and leaned over him, the look of satisfaction on his face so overt it could have easily been mistaken for smugness.

Blood had begun to pool across his chest and down his side, providing Hudson with all the evidence he needed that there would be no last minute Michael Myers rising from the dead scenario about to occur.

The sounds of police sirens in the distance motivated Hudson to move towards the car that had pulled up behind him. He knew there would be questions. Whenever anything untoward or illicit occurred in Newcastle, his door was one of the first the police called at. It had almost become an expected practice. He wasn't worried. They would find nothing to connect him to what had just happened.

The car sped away off towards the City Centre, its blurred image flashing past Tommy's line of sight as he lay on his side, the motion of it spinning around in his mind. Everything around him became a spiral of darkness into which Tommy Myers tumbled around and down and away.

He could just make out 'The Lion Sleeps Tonight' as the dark grip of eternity wrapped itself around his cold body.

'I can't fix it if I don't know what's broken.'
Heartbreak Ridge

Epilogue

Newcastle Upon Tyne,
Tyne and Wear

The rhythmic rise and fall of the ventilator was almost alluring.

Karen stood at the foot of Tommy's intensive care bed, looking at the myriad of tubes and wires seemingly plugged into his very person and all leading back to a bank of monitors. Respiratory rate, PEEP levels, heart-rate and oxygen saturation, everything Tommy had been was now reduced to numbers on a television screen. A nurse was tending to his tracheostomy, carefully cleaning around the stoma site whilst ensuring that all the subsequent tubing was clean and functional.

Karen had once thought of becoming a nurse. She had felt a pull towards becoming something bigger than herself. Where the actions of one individual could truly make a difference. The path she had chosen still held the same potential, only less socially acceptable.

Her Mam had come and sat with Daniel the moment Karen had learnt what had happened to Tommy. She had sworn Donna to secrecy in regards to their living location, insisting she couldn't even tell Thomas. They were far enough outside Newcastle to not be easily found, but close enough that it was only a half hour train ride back into the city.

Upon arrival at the Freeman, the doctor had told her the only reason Tommy was still alive was due to his timely transporting to hospital. The shotgun blast had ruptured the right side of his heart, damaged his intestines and liver and caused trauma to his spleen. Aside from the physical injuries he had sustained, he was also at risk of infection due to the contents of some of the aforementioned organs spilling their contents inside his body. The next 72 hours were crucial, during which time the doctors would not only be able to assess his psychological recovery chances but any long-term damage his injuries may have caused.

Karen knew who was responsible.

Ronnie, George and Jack Hudson.

Each of them had played a part in this. Ronnie had left Tommy during the robbery under the instructions of Hudson. As far as she was concerned, that made them both complicit in what had happened, irrespective of who had pulled the trigger.

As for George, he had been a means to an end. She had liked him, perhaps even cared for him. But not enough to forgive this.

They had all crossed a line and would now pay the price. She would see to it.

Karen moved beside Tommy and held his hand before kissing him on the forehead. He would be in danger once Hudson learnt that he was still alive. She knew someone who could help keep him safe whilst he was in here. They would deal with what to do after he recovered when the time arrived.

If he recovered.

Karen silently swore to herself that she would make it right. Everything that had started that night in the pub so long ago would come full circle.

She had already made certain her message was clear in that respect.

Jack Hudson should have been reading it right now.

* * *

Jack sat alone in his living room, curious as to how she could have learnt his home address. It was known only to those in his inner circle, a cohort that consisted of very few.

He wouldn't go so far as to say he was scared, but he had to admit he was apprehensive. In his blind vengeance towards Tommy Myers, he had never once considered the sister. He had thought her weak.

Yet the evidence in his hand showed she was far from broken, but capable of so much more. And he believed her. No one would go to the trouble of threatening someone like him unless there was something behind it.

He read the note again, impressed with its brazenness and worried at its implications.

Jack,

By the time you read this note I will no longer be in the city. Don't bother trying to find me. You won't.

It will probably come as no surprise to you to learn that I hold you responsible for what happened to me that night. However, what will probably come as a huge surprise is that I chose to shed any bitterness I might have felt and decided to walk a different path.

All your recent troubles are down to me. I gave Alan the information about the docks and all the other little misfortunes you suffered. He had no idea it was me of course. I did it through various other individuals who passed on the information. My only regret is that I used Alan and not someone else as perhaps it could have saved his life. That is my guilt to carry and rightly so.

Campbell got what he deserved for what happened to my brother... you're next. Not today, not tomorrow, but one day in the future when you least expect it. I know you won't be too worried, but you should be.

I forgave Eric for what he did a long time ago. He was a desperate, lonely man whose only method of reaching women was to take what he wanted by force.

But forgiveness isn't the same as forgetting. I know he worked for you. I know you knew what he had done in the past. You could have prevented it happening to me. You could have prevented Tommy going to prison.

So now you are the one who shall be held accountable. There will be no weakness. No hesitation. No exceptions.

I will be coming for you, Jack Hudson. There will be no mercy and nowhere on earth that you can hide from me.

Everyone knows me as Karen.

You can call me Ren.

Hudson sneered at the audacity of the note. This Ren character who had been slowly destroying his businesses had been under his nose all along. Tommy Myer's little sister. Who would have guessed?

He realised it was true after all. Whatever didn't kill you...

He crumbled up the note and let it drop to the floor. A woman had been responsible for all of his problems. A fucking woman!

Ren's arrogance might end up being her fatal weakness.

As the shadows deepened around him in the fading sunlight, Jack thought it was a hope worth nurturing.

Afterword

by David McCaffrey

This story was entirely Stephen's. I might have embellished, augmented, enhanced and elaborated in places, but the main thread, narrative and story arc were 100% his.

A true gentleman, I have only seen kindness, enthusiasm, support and most importantly for a writer, understanding from him. This book was very important to Stephen, but he gave me the space I needed to write it and never once interfered. His comments were only ever relevant and pertinent to the story. We had many phone conversations, all of which were interesting and usually had me in stitches and a few face-to-face meetings where I never saw a reputation, only a man who was nothing but friendly and encouraging. I consider it an honour to have had the opportunity to write this story. *His* story.

However, I also found it a challenge. Writing a story based upon someone else's ideas carries with it a great deal of responsibility. I hope I did it, and him, justice.

Many of the locations, street names and reflections from the 80's are accurate though there are some areas where I took an artistic liberty in order for them to fit the story as authors do.

Any mistakes are my own.

Acknowledgments

As always, the only reason you are reading anything I have written is because of my mentor, bestselling author and friend, Steve Alten. I will forever owe you one!

Murielle Maupoint who gave me my shot in the first place. Thank you for believing in me.

Siobhan Marshall-Jones, my amazing proof reader who is one in a million and is the reason what you are reading actually makes any sense.

My fantastic team of beta readers; Noelle, Sarah, Bex, Gill, Richard, Zoe, Suzie, Maxamillions, Emma, Sylvia, Helen, Eden, Donna, Lesley, Nia, Jane and Gordon, who read it in record time and pointed out all my mistakes. A special mention goes to Robert Enright, whose input was invaluable. Thank you!

My girls in Infection Prevention and Control at James Cook University Hospital.

My Mum who puts up with me – you're the best.

Thank you to Sarah Hilary… just because.

Andy, Paul and Kev – my friends and inspiration for a few anecdotes that found their way into the story!

Thanks to my Lou Lou, Shell, Gigi, Emma, Llainy and Jane at the Crime Book Club. They do all the hard work for the site and simply tolerate my presence because of a friendship. Ladies, you are awesome!

My beautiful Kelly who is my sun, moon and stars. You gave me some great ideas that helped it all make sense! Your belief in me keeps me going during moments of doubt. Thank you turtle!

Jakey and the Gruffalo who make every day unique and amazing. My two sons, you are my inspiration.

Special mention must go to Simone, my web designer who still refuses to take payment for all she does.

Steve Wraith and Stu Wheatman – your support and guidance are without measure. Little did I know that one event in Newcastle (thanks to Jackie Collins) would lead to this!

The biggest thank you must go to the man himself, Stephen Sayers. You gave me a story very personal to you and allowed me to weave a narrative through it. Thank you for trusting me with it, thank you for believing in me and thank you for your friendship. This is only the beginning!

And finally you, the readers. Your support and encouragement is without measure. Thank you and know this author... *these authors*, only exist because of you.

David

Author's Note

This story is fictional, but deals with some very real issues. One of the most horrific is rape.

A great deal of time was spent in discussion with a lady who, for obvious reasons, wishes to remain anonymous and was a victim of rape when she was young. She spoke candidly, without vitriol or hatred towards her attacker. Her insights were vital to ensure that at no point during the description of the rape in the story was it sensationalised. Heartbreaking to listen to and humbling to be in the presence of, she demonstrated repeatedly her bravery and strength. Her recollections of what was going through her mind at the time of her attack were amongst some of the most heartbreaking words I have ever heard spoken.

It was a true honour to be in her presence.

No one should ever be subjected to anything against their wishes. We know it happens.

For anyone who has been the victim of rape, regardless of gender, please know there is help and support.

R.E.A.C.H (Rape Examination Advice Counselling Help) – 0191 2219222

Graceland Northumberland Rape Crisis – 0191 222 0272

Tyneside Rape Crisis Centre – 0191 2329858

Newcastle WOMENS Health – 0191 477 7898

Someone Cares – 0844 811 5522 ext. 28255

Women's Health Advice Centre, Northumberland –
01670 853 977

Women's Health, South Tyneside – 0191 454 6959

Male Rape Happens, Survivors Help Line – 0845 122 1201

MESMAC, Gay & Bisexual Men – 0191 233 1333

Panah, Black/Asian Women Advice & Information on
Domestic Violence – 0191 284 6998

Newcastle Lesbian Line – 0191 261 2277

Victim Support Newcastle – 0191 2813791

Victim Support Sunderland – 0191 5672896

Meadowfield Centre, Durham – 0845 606 0365 ext.
6684843

Helen Britton House, Teesside – 01642 516 888

Rape Crisis England and Wales –
rcewinfo@rapecrisis.org.uk

About the authors

Stephen Sayers is one of the most feared men in the country with a reputation that proceeds him. He is also a proud citizen of Newcastle whose family have been known on the streets of Tyneside for decades. A father and bestselling author of *The Sayers – Tried and Tested at the Highest Level*, Stephen is respected by all those who know him. *By Any Means Necessary* is Stephen's first fictional crime thriller.

David McCaffrey is the author of *Hellbound*, *In Extremis* and *Nameless*. He lives in Redcar and has a Kelly, a Liam, a Jake and an Obi.